Acknowledgements

I am grateful to members of Manchester Women's Writers' group for their critiques of many of the chapters and to Nick Seymour who edited the manuscript for me.

Cover photograph credit: Terry Healy
(Unfortunately, it's not the class of yacht mentioned in the text – but commissioning a special photograph would have been a bit expensive).

John mentions going to the Blue Café for a meal in December 1997. It had been my personal favourite and I would, as John says, check out the specials board and I was never disappointed by what Lisa the chef provided. Unfortunately, it closed earlier in 1997 — but I wanted to acknowledge the great meals I had in there! The other venues mentioned were as described

Also by Helen Dale

Summer Dreams

An authentic transgender tale set in 2003 against the introduction of the Gender Recognition Act. Inspired by a genuine incident involving the author

Operation Busted Flush

Faced with attacks on their community by the White House Administration, a group of transgender veterans decide to take action

A Tale of Two Lives:
A Funny Thing Happened on the Way to the Palace

Autobiography

Transgender Tales
Adventures & Misadventures on the Journey
from Transvestite to Transsexual

an anthology of a diary I kept when I first moved to Manchester plus some short stories and other humorous anecdotes.

Understanding Gender Variance -

A Practical Guide: including Intersex, Trans, Non-Binary & Gender Fluid Individuals
based on the author's award-winning transgender awareness workshops.

Part One. 1997

Chapter 1. Nigel – Friday 28th November 1997

Come on, come on," I yelled as the old biddy in the ancient Austin Metro dawdled along. "For God's sake woman, get through those lights before they change."

She didn't.

Although she was only feet from the line, she stopped when they changed to amber. I hit the brakes hard. Thankfully my BMW M3 stopped before I hit her. I slammed my hand on the steering wheel. What does she think she's doing? Why can't she keep off the roads while those of us with jobs to go to drive to work? She could do her shopping any time without getting in our way.

The lights change and she pulled forward, then stalled.

Bloody Hell. Why do they still allow old people to drive?

I had an important meeting to get to. My agency's major client had appointed a new Marketing Director and we were due to present our ideas for a new product launch to her.

At last. The Metro pulls away. It almost reached the speed limit. If the road was wide enough, I'd have passed her — but it wasn't.

Then she stopped again. This time at a Zebra Crossing. Jesus wept. What is she doing?

No, No, No! She wasn't letting that bus out, was she? Yes, she was. I tried to attract her attention but, naturally, she wasn't looking in the mirror otherwise she'd have seen me gesticulating.

Eventually, she pulled in and I could get past. I looked over at her and shook my head then turned my attention back to the road.

Just who was Mary Sanchez? I tried to get some background before meeting her but drew a blank. All I'd discovered was that she was British but has been over in the states for some years working for one of SeaCon's competitors.

George, Marketing Manager at SeaCon, hadn't been able to help either. Funnily enough, I hadn't been able to get through to him since our golfing trip to Le Touquet. That was unusual.

Chapter 1 – Nigel November 1997

I parked the BMW in my reserved space. I hadn't done too badly for myself. Nigel Hall Associates wasn't one of the big boys of the advertising world but it gave me a decent living — well it did as long as I could hold on to clients like SeaCon.

Having dropped my case in my office, I wandered down to the studio to check that everything was ready for the presentation. Bill and Jerry, the creative team, had it all under control. They were just about to take the work along to the boardroom to prepare for Mrs Sanchez.

On the way back to my desk, I confirmed that Nicky, my secretary, had organised the catering for lunch.

"Yes, Nigel. They'll deliver at 12.30. And reception will call you as soon as Mrs Sanchez arrives. Now stop worrying. I'll get you a coffee, shall I?"

None of the other staff would dare to speak to me so casually but we did have a special arrangement which my wife was, thankfully, unaware of.

I sat down, lit a cigarette, took a sip of the coffee, leant back and reviewed the position.

On the debit side was Mrs Sanchez' lack of urgency to come and see us; the fact new people like to stamp their own style and she has been appointed over George. Against was her recent return from several years in the States so she didn't have any relationships with any other UK agencies. Plus, the imminent launch of the new OceanMaster range. On balance, I felt we were safe — all other things being equal.

My reflections were disturbed by Nicky telling me Mrs Sanchez has arrived. I put on my jacket and took the stairs to reception to welcome her.

That's when I realised all other things were not equal.

Chapter 2. John – Friday 28th November 1997

By the way, what was going on at the Pelican Lodge Hotel in Southampton last weekend, John? I saw someone drive up in your car and was going to come over and say 'hi' when a brunette in a long blue dress got out."

This comment stopped me in my tracks.

Tony and I were enjoying a very pleasant pre-Christmas lunch and relaxing over brandies. Our conversation ranged over the usual topics — business, sport, including the prospects for the 1998 Formula One Grand Prix season — and plans for the forthcoming holiday.

"At first, I thought you might have lent your car to someone but, as she passed where I was parked on the way to the entrance, she looked remarkably like you and she was wearing shoes like those you had for Comic Relief Day in March. It wasn't another charity event, was it?"

Earlier in the year, some bright spark had come up with an idea for fund raising for Comic Relief. If the women in each department contributed more than the men, the men had to dress in drag. If the men gave more than the ladies, the ladies had to dress as schoolgirls or French maids. The guys in the marketing department had raised seventy-five pounds, but the girls had outbid us by donating eighty. To be fair, however, the girls had also dressed up.

Because I take size eights, none of the girls could lend me a pair of shoes that would fit and I'd sent Chris, my secretary, out to buy me a pair. She had returned with three inch stilettoes with diamante trim.

Tony had come down that Friday to clear some last-minute details for a show. When he'd laughed at me tottering on the high heels and dressed in a tight mini skirt, I challenged him to try to walk in them. He entered into the spirit of the occasion and tried himself with no more success than me; he also made a generous donation to the fund.

Tony passed me a package. "Anyway, I thought whoever it was might like these," he said with emphasis on the 'whoever'.

There is, of course, nothing unusual about suppliers giving Christmas gifts to their clients, and DeskTech are Raven's biggest client, but something in Tony's tone made me suspect he was concerned about my reaction.

I unwrapped the package. Inside was a jeweller's box. Opening it I found a necklace, bracelet and matching earrings with sapphires and zircons set in a silver metal.

"I thought they'd go well with the dress and the shoes."

I looked at Tony not knowing what to say. It was a fabulous present, but looked too expensive for a normal supplier's gift to a client. Did he want something from me? Was this a sweetener? Or could it even be blackmail?

"Are you suggesting it was me you saw?" I challenged, trying to look bemused.

"I don't know if it was or wasn't — it was definitely your car and it certainly looked like you. But what you get up to is your business."

I lit a cigarette as I looked into Tony's eyes. "What are you after?" I asked.

"Nothing, John," he replied. "We've got a really good relationship going, we've done excellent work for you as you've been the first to acknowledge, our prices have been acceptable — so there's no real reason for you to stop using us. But I'm not complacent. We may make mistakes, or you'll have an approach from a competitor which may be more attractive than ours. I'd like to think you'd give us the opportunity to revise any proposals we submit to match those from other sources if necessary."

"And if I don't?" I asked.

"I'm not threatening you with anything," he said. "How can I? IF I said anything, you could simply deny it was you — and I'd certainly lose your business. On the other hand, I might be a useful alibi for you. We usually stay in the same hotels when we are setting up shows but occasionally you've stayed elsewhere for no apparent reason. Now I'm wondering if you were attending other charity events on those evenings."

In all fairness, Tony wasn't asking for much. But did he think he had something over me? Did he think I'd be concerned about his assumptions? Would he believe the explanation I would offer?

I passed the box back to Tony.

"Keep it," I told him. "Even if I had been me you'd seen at the hotel and I had been interested in your proposal, which I'm not because it wasn't me, I'm not into backhanders and this looks far too expensive for a Christmas box."

"As it happens, it was a lot less expensive than it looks. We get them at cost. In fact, the complete set only cost us the same as the malt whisky we gave you last year.

He pushed the box back to my side of the table.

"Take them, John. No one else knows who they are for. We've given other sets to Jane at Gemini Cosmetics and Sylvia at Abacus Retailing."

I picked up my coffee and took a sip while I considered my response. It was obvious Tony suspected, but couldn't prove, I was a cross-dresser. He had

4

couched his remarks in terms of 'charity events' to give me way out if it had been me. I looked him straight in the eye. Then I took a photograph out of my wallet. I slid it across the table to Tony.

"It's a fascinating discussion — but my cousin Carol used my car last weekend. She dropped her brother and me off at Chichester so I could help sail his yacht round to Christchurch. She's the one next to me in the photograph. We were born within a few days of each other, our mothers are twin sisters and our fathers are identical twin brothers. So, it's not surprising we've often been taken for twins as you can see — but I'm not sure though she'd be pleased at being taken for me in drag! I played along with you because I wanted to see if you were going to try to put the squeeze on me. If you had, I would not only have fired Ravens, I'd have done my best to see you didn't get another job in the industry."

Tony nearly choked on his coffee and started to splutter an apology.

"Forget it, it was an understandable mistake. I appreciate Ravens do give us an excellent service and I don't underestimate your own contribution. If the situation arises where another supplier offers us a better deal, I reckon Ravens have earned the right to respond — and I don't see why I shouldn't put in a good word for you if we ever do decide to go with an alternative exhibition company. I don't need pressurising to do either.

"As for these," I continued, picking up the box. "you are absolutely right they would go very well with Carol's blue dress — not to mention the shoes I gave her after Comic Relief Day — but I insist on paying for them. Just let me know how much they were and I'll give you a cheque."

Chapter 3. Nigel – Friday 28th November 1997

Mary Sanchez was Mary Jones until she'd apparently remarried. Oliver Jones, her first husband, was my partner until we split up.

I knew she blamed me for his death but the truth was he tried to set up on his own and had lost everything whilst my business grew.

I went to Oliver's funeral but, after a torrent of abuse from Mary, had left. She swore then she'd get her revenge. That had been ten years ago.

"Hello Nigel. Surprised?" she asked as we faced each other. I tried to read her emotionless face. Did she still harbour a grudge or had she come to realise I wasn't solely to blame for Oliver's death?

Chapter 3 – Nigel November 1997

"Mary, of course it's a surprise and a very pleasant one! You really look terrific — the States obviously agreed with you," I replied.

It was true. Gone was the slightly frumpy, shy, overweight, plain individual with dull brown hair I'd known ten years ago – the Mary Sanchez facing me was slim, fashionably dressed with a haircut that looked as though it needed minimal effort each morning but was clearly the result of a very experienced hand wielding the scissors – the colour was much lighter, not quite blond but with highlights – radiating health and the overall effect oozing confidence.

"Come on up to the boardroom," I invited.

"I think we should go to your office first," she said. This didn't sound good.

"Take a seat, would you like coffee?" I asked as we entered my office.

"No thank you, I'm not staying that long."

My heart sank — I knew what was coming.

"I'm not going to use your agency for the OceanMaster launch and I'm sure you know why."

"You surely don't still blame me for Oliver's death. OK so I was rough on him, but it wasn't my fault he couldn't make it on his own," I said. My mind was racing as I tried to think of something to change her mind.

"That's a load of rubbish — of course you were to blame. You didn't just get rid of him, you destroyed his confidence and told everyone you'd split up because he wasn't good enough. The real reason was he wasn't prepared to ignore the bribes you'd been paying to clients to keep their work. Bribes which I know you are still paying because that's what's cost George Collins his job. And that's why I'm dispensing with your agency's services with effect from now."

So that was why George had been incommunicado? Shit. Could she actually prove I'd given him money? If so, it was worse than I feared. If not, there might still be a way out of this mess. Maybe she was assuming that I'd slipped George the odd 'brown envelope' as she knew I'd done that when working with OJ. Maybe I could bluff my way out of this. I didn't know how she'd got to her present position but when she was married to OJ she'd been a timid mouse.

"This is pure vindictiveness. As for bribery, you'd have a hell of a job proving it and if you repeat any such accusations in public, I'll sue you," I said angrily. "We have a contract with SeaCon and it not only entitles us to three months' notice, it's for an initial period of a year so we've got six months to go. If you use another agency, we are entitled to commission on any advertising placed during that period. If you try to break the contract, I'll tie you up in so many injunctions you'll be lucky to launch OceanMaster in 3 years let alone 3 months. You've also got several thousand pounds worth of work in progress which you'll still have to pay for — and where will that leave you with your MD?"

Mary held up her hand with just the thumb extended.

"Number one, you'll be lucky to have an agency for long if word gets around about bribery — your clients will be forced to desert or have their bosses wondering if they're also on the take." I could feel the knife sliding into my back.

She straightened the forefinger.

"Two, without the agency, you won't be able to afford to sue. You've always spent money as quickly as you've earned it and a credit check shows you, personally, are up to your eyes in debt." I thought about my overdraft and credit cards and swallowed.

She smiled as she straightened the middle finger.

"Three, it's not down to me to prove bribery — you have to prove the accusations are false and, in any case, I've got records of the bribes you made when Oliver was your partner." I could feel the knife twisting.

I could see she was enjoying making me suffer as she calmly extended her ring finger.

"Four. Under the terms of our contract, all conceptual work is speculative and we only need to pay for any which is used."

"Five — you breached any contract by bribing George Collins and by failing to pass on discounts to which SeaCon were entitled and which the publications allowed."

With that, she picked up her handbag, opened it, took out an envelope and threw it on my desk. "That's the official confirmation of the termination of your contract. It was the first letter I signed at SeaCon and I doubt if any other will give me as much pleasure."

She stood up and left the room.

As I slumped into my chair Nicky came into my office.

"What the hell has happened?" she asked me.

"It's a long story," I told her, "but we may have lost the SeaCon account. Keep that news to yourself until I've spoken to Bill and Jerry. Tell them to come and see me after lunch, I need time to think. In the meantime, get me Peter at SeaCon immediately."

Peter Judge was the principal shareholder as well as Managing Director and we'd always got along well — probably because of our shared interest in offshore racing. Maybe I could persuade him Mary Sanchez was acting out of personal spite and the best interests of SeaCon lay in keeping the business with us at least until the OceanMaster launch had been completed. I knew how vital that project was to SeaCon who'd been going through a difficult time themselves with the recession biting deeply into the boating market.

Nicky told me Peter was out at present but was expected back later.

I asked Nicky to get me some sandwiches. When she brought them in to me, however, my appetite had gone.

"Shiiit," said Jerry as I broke the news to him and Bill that afternoon. "How the hell can the bitch do that — what in Christ's name did you do to the woman to make her so vindictive?"

"Where do we go from here?" asked Bill. "What has Peter Judge said? Have you spoken to him?"

"How the fuck do I know?" I replied. "Hopefully I can convince Peter Mary Sanchez reasons for firing us are personal and he needs to put the company's interests first. If not, there will have to be cutbacks — but how deep I don't know."

Nicky knocked on the door then looked in. "Mr Matthews from the bank on line 1," she announced.

Just what I didn't need at that moment.

"Hello Howard, what can I do for you?"

"I've heard you've lost the SeaCon business. Is that right?"

Mary bloody Sanchez had obviously wasted no time at all in turning the knife.

"They've taken on a new Marketing Director who's reviewing the account, which is common practice as you know, but I'm confident we'll hold on to it," I replied. "As I mentioned when we last met, we've got a lot of work on for them at present and I can't see them changing horses in mid-stream with the OceanMaster launch imminent."

"Yes, well, you'll appreciate your overdraft facility was granted with that work in mind so if there is any doubt about it, we'll need to review your position. When can you come in with some up-to-date figures on your other work?"

"It'll take a few days to evaluate the position — how about sometime next week?"

"OK, but in the meantime, I'm afraid we'll have to reduce your limit to eighty thousand — which means you are currently five thousand over it. When can you let us have a credit?"

"We are paying in around fifteen thousand today, but we'd agreed a limit of a hundred and twenty-five thousand — and we've payments we need to make immediately including salaries and Christmas bonuses at the end of the week."

"So, what do you need as an absolute minimum Nigel?"

Matthews was reluctant to allow us the ninety thousand I suggested but eventually agreed to do so until I could give him our cash flow projections. He told me to come and see him on the Friday and asked if ten o'clock suited me.

It didn't suit me at all. I knew without the SeaCon work the bank would be reluctant to give us even an eighty limit. But there was no way I could let them know I was rattled.

"Let me check my diary. Yes, that's fine; I'll see you on Friday at ten."

The ninety thousand overdraft would just about cover the immediate expenses if I halved the Christmas bonuses. The staff weren't going to like it — but nor did I.

When Bill and Jerry had left my office, I asked Nicky to try again to get me Peter Judge as quickly as possible. I'd sort Mary Sanchez out.

Peter was inclined to delegate work and then leave his subordinates to get on with their jobs. Which is why it had been relatively easy to retain the account while George Collins had been Marketing Manager.

Chapter 3 – Nigel November 1997

George was always short of cash but appreciated the high life. Like Peter and me, he enjoyed yachting. Using Clippa to entertain them justified the cost being charged against the company — even if it wasn't tax deductible.

Yachting also provided the perfect opportunity for overnight stops at various places along the northern coast of France, the Channel Islands and even Amsterdam. George could be relied on to take advantage of everything I laid on for him — from meals to girls and gambling.

Visiting casinos gave me a perfect opportunity to slip him cash which couldn't be traced. He would buy a few chips himself, but I would then toss extra ones his way during the course of an evening. He would invariably lose some of them but always kept the rest which he cashed in.

Peter, however, was as straight as they come. He would let me entertain him, because that was expected of a supplier. But he had shown no interest in accepting any other offers I had hinted at during our early meetings.

I tried to concentrate on other work while waiting for Nicky to contact Peter, but it was quite impossible. Where was he? Was he deliberately avoiding my call?

Just after five, Nicky stuck her head round the door "Peter's still tied up in a meeting, but his secretary managed to pass him your message and he says he could see you at the Albion Lodge at 7.30 this evening if that's convenient."

I told her to confirm 7.30 would be fine.

Having finished her call, Nicky came in, closing the door behind her. She walked over to my drinks cabinet and poured a generous helping of Islay Malt which she brought over to me.

"You look as though you need this," she said as she handed it to me.

I took the glass from her with my left hand and slipped my right up between her legs.

"That's not all I need, darling," I told her, feeling her legs open as my hand slid higher.

Nicky is 23, tall and slim, with long blonde hair and blue eyes. She makes no effort to conceal her figure and was wearing a skirt which ended several inches above her knees. She usually wears tights around the office as her short skirts would expose her stocking tops and suspenders when she sits down.

Occasionally, however, when we have a bit of overtime to do, she changes after the other staff have gone. Today she hasn't waited.

Her hand was massaging my shoulder as I stroked the inside of her thighs.

I rubbed her crotch and could feel it was already damp. I slipped my fingers inside the loose legs of her French knickers — almost certainly a pair I'd given her after my last trip to Paris.

"Do you want me to come with you this evening?" she asked.

"I'd like you to come with me every evening — but I don't know what sort of mood I'm going to be in later."

"Don't worry. I'll help you to celebrate or drown your sorrows depending on the outcome."

"Has everyone else gone yet?" I asked.

"I'll go and check."

She returned a few minutes later. "Bill has just gone and he was the last."

"Come here then, at least I can enjoy something today."

Chapter 4. John – Friday 5th December 1997

I left work early on Friday and drove to Manchester where I checked into a motel near the city centre. After registering, I parked the car outside my room, took my suitcases from the boot and went inside.

I unpacked my case and laid out the clothes I would be wearing that evening.

Then I took out the bracelet, earrings and necklace Tony had given me and held them next to the long blue dress I'd hung on the rail. He was quite right, they were perfect! I would be the Belle of the Ball at tomorrow evening's Transchester Christmas Disco — the second such event for me this year; two weeks ago, at the Pelican Lodge had been Southampton's party.

Tonight, I'd go out around Canal Street in a black top with a sequined pattern I'd bought in C&A, a knee length bias-cut black skirt from M&S and a pair of black court shoes with two-inch block heels from Lilley & Skinner's Tall and Small department.

11

Chapter 4 – John December 1997

As always when in Manchester, I'd start with dinner in the Blue Café on Sackville Street. I'd check the "specials" board and decide whether to have whatever Lisa the chef had produced for the evening or something from the main menu. Whatever I chose, I knew it would be excellent. Then it would be round the corner to Paddy's Goose where I was bound to meet other girls in 'Tranny Corner'. As Paddy's was opposite the coach station it was likely long-distance travellers, changing coaches in Manchester, would have been tempted by the apparently stereotypical Irish hostelry across the road. They were in for a surprise when the girls started to arrive.

No doubt we'd stay there for an hour or so before moving on, some would head for New York, New York or the New Union — personally, I preferred the atmosphere in Dotz piano bar.

At the end of the evening most of us would gather again in Napoleons; a cross-dresser's heaven with mirrors all around the upstairs dance floor. There would probably be the usual number of tranny-chasers eyeing us up but, if you weren't interested, and I wasn't, they'd usually leave you alone. If they didn't, the bouncers would deal with them and I'd seen one come down the stairs without touching any of the treads on one occasion. The owner sees us as bait for the tranny-chasers; which is why we were allowed free admission while everyone else had to pay. It was the dream for visiting trannies to be convincing enough to be stopped by Ernie on the door and asked to pay.

On business trips I would, if possible, plan overnight stops near a gay scene such as Brighton, Blackpool or Birmingham where I would have somewhere to go. All too often this wasn't possible so I might just go out for a meal or to the cinema. Manchester, however, had the best scene.

While my bath was running, I applied a face pack then made myself a coffee and took it into the bathroom. I eased myself into the perfumed bubbles, lit a cigarette and lay back and relaxed anticipating two evenings of fun and, perhaps, a day of shopping en-femme at the Arndale Centre.

I thought again about Tony's offer to cover for me while we were away.

I'd been on the point of accepting it earlier when I had suddenly realised he could have been recording our conversation. I was 99% certain he hadn't been and it would hardly be in his interest to cause me problems; but, if he had, I'd now covered myself with a plausible explanation and I'd insisted on paying for the jewellery. I'd had the photograph of Carol and me in my wallet for some time just in case there was such an occasion as Monday's when someone linked my female persona to my car. I'd had to take care on Comic Relief Day to give the impression of struggling with the high heels to avoid looking too experienced wearing them.

I wasn't ashamed of being a cross-dresser but nor did I admit it to all and sundry. I didn't want to risk losing my job so, while lots of people knew me as John and an increasing number knew me as Angela, only one person now in my life was aware of both sides of me.

Luxuriating in the scent of the bubble bath and feeling the face pack hardening, I thought back to my first experience of cross dressing almost exactly sixteen years earlier.

Part Two. Christmas 1981 to Summer 1985

Chapter 5. John — Christmas 1981

As my parents were in Hong Kong with the Army, I was spending the Christmas holidays with my Aunt Judith, Uncle David and cousin Carol. They lived in an old cottage on the edge of Upper Charsworth, a village about 6 miles north of Norwich. Uncle David was a Flight Lieutenant in the Royal Air Force based at Coltishall, flying Jaguars.

Carol was playing Cinderella in the local village pantomime, or she had been until 45 minutes ago when she had fallen off her horse and injured her ankle. There was nothing broken, but she could hardly stand — let alone perform on stage. The doctor, whose surgery was, conveniently, next door had reluctantly told her she must rest it as much as possible.

The sprain would heal within 3 or 4 days but the first performance of the panto was a little over 4 hours away and, to make matters worse, Carol's understudy was down with measles.

Dr Gibbs reluctance to prescribe total rest; and his quick response to the accident, was because he was also chairman of the drama society and director of the planned production. It was supposed to run for 3 days with a matinée on Saturday and now looked doomed.

"It's a disaster for us" he moaned. "What on earth persuaded you to go riding today of all days?" he asked Carol. "No, that's not fair, I know you were given Topsy as a Christmas present after doing so well in your exams," he continued. "The trouble is we don't have anyone who can take your place. With Tania down with measles, none of the other girls know your lines and, even if they did, there simply wouldn't be time to alter your costumes by 7.30."

"John knows my lines and we're the same size," Carol replied quietly.

I wasn't exactly overjoyed to hear her implying I could take her place but it was quite true. I had helped her to practice over the last few days and she was always borrowing my jeans, T-shirts and jackets — not to mention the boots she'd been wearing when she'd fallen off Topsy. I had also been helping with the scenery and had attended all of the rehearsals and knew the moves almost as well as she did.

"It's a pantomime after all and part of the tradition is for men to take the female leads and vice versa," she went on. "Liz is playing Prince Charming so why shouldn't John play Cinderella"

"Thanks a lot, Carol," I replied. "What makes you think I'd be prepared to dress as a girl?"

"Scared of what the others will say, are you?" she challenged.

"Not at all. I'll be going back to school in a couple of weeks so I couldn't care less," I replied, realising I had fallen for her ploy. Daring me is the quickest way to get me to do something!

"I suppose it could work," said Dr Gibbs. "But would you be prepared to do it?" he asked me. "As you know, we've put a lot of effort into the production and the profits are going to charity. If we have to cancel, we'll have to refund nearly five hundred pounds in advance ticket sales."

I hesitated.

"Chicken!" called Carol.

"Be quiet, brat. You caused this problem, not me," I replied.

Aunt Judith had met Uncle David at the stables where she helped clean out the stalls and look after the horses in exchange for riding lessons. A few days later David had popped into the café in town where my mother worked part time for pocket money. When he'd said "Hello again," mum realised he was mistaking her for Judith and explained she had an identical twin. David had laughed and said that he, too, was one of twins and that he and his brother often caused the same confusion. One thing led to another and after double dates, and playing games substituting for each other; they eventually became two couples and married at a double wedding.

Carol and I were born within days of each other — Carol being just a week older than I. With our parentage, it was not surprising we looked very much alike and were often taken for twins ourselves and were best of friends.

I pointed out, though, just because Carol could get into my things, it didn't mean I would be able to wear hers.

Aunt Judith sighed and said there was only one way to find out. She went to fetch the costumes. This consisted of the rags worn by Cinderella in the first part of the story and a ball gown. The rags would be no problem — they were made from a dress several times too large to deliberately suggest it had been handed down to Cinders from one of the ugly sisters. I went to my bedroom where Aunt Judith had left the ball gown and the shoes.

I stripped to my underpants and pulled the dress on. Aunt Judith knocked on my door and asked if she could come in. She realised the dress was a bit tight and rather than risk splitting any of the seams, fetched a pantie girdle of her own which she suggested I should put on first to trim an inch or so off my waist.

With this in place, the dress was still a close fit, but would be all right — except for the bust. This was solved by giving me one of Carol's bras to wear and stuffing it with cotton wool. The shoes were also a tight fit, but I could just about manage to walk around in them.

As the story involves Cinderella downtrodden in rags being transformed into a beauty, it had already been intended to use a wig for the ball — and as my own hair was as long as Carol's in any case, it was fine for the first act.

It seemed to be a forgone conclusion trying on the costumes meant I had agreed to take Carol's place. Typical of the forces, I thought. You get volunteered for anything.

As it happens, I had my own reasons for being prepared to take on the role. I fancied Liz, who was playing Prince Charming, but she had a regular boyfriend who was a Senior Aircraftman based at the station. This way, I'd get to perform with her during the panto — and that included dancing together, hugging and a kiss at the end. Even if our roles were reversed, I'd have some consolation for having to take Carol's place.

The panto went ahead almost as planned with me in the starring role for all four performances. The audiences took the need for the substitution in good heart and, although I felt very self-conscious waiting to go on stage the first time and I got a bit of ribbing from some of Carol's friends, it was all regarded as a bit of a laugh. By the end of the last performance, I'd become quite adept at walking in the heels and the initial shocks I'd had seeing myself in the mirror had been replaced by a strange normality.

Liz had also been amused by my taking Carol's part and held me close as we'd danced and hugged. "I prefer acting with you," she whispered during one performance. The final kiss of the final performance certainly lingered longer than strictly necessary — but I wasn't complaining!

The day after Boxing Day, Liz came round to discuss what she and Carol were planning to wear for the New Year's Eve fancy dress party. I thought they'd sorted this out before Christmas but it seemed Liz had come up with a new idea.

I was sitting in the lounge reading when Liz arrived. When Carol let her in, Liz stuck her head into the lounge and called out "Hi Cinders" to me then, giggling, quickly disappeared upstairs with Carol.

I heard them laughing and joking for a while, then their voices became inaudible so I went back to reading "Goldfinger." I planned to go to the New Year's Eve party as James Bond and had rented a white dinner jacket for the occasion. I'd also bought a pistol cigarette lighter which looked a bit like a Beretta which I would keep in a shoulder holster — ready for when any ladies needed a light.

As far as I was aware, Carol and Liz were going to the party as Cinders and Prince Charming — and had permission to use the costumes from the panto. I was looking forward to the party rather more than I had been now I'd had the chance to break the ice with Liz.

Fortunately, Liz's boyfriend would not be at the Officers' Mess party because he was 'other ranks'. He was also several years older than Liz and her parents were trying to persuade her to stop seeing him. It wasn't they were snobbish about Tim's rank, but Squadron Leader Fraser was in charge of the section in which Tim worked and he was aware of some disturbing, but, as yet, unsubstantiated rumours about SAC Williams.

Carol and Liz came back downstairs and joined me in the lounge.

"Have you got your costume yet for the party?" asked Liz.

"No, I'm collecting it tomorrow," I told her.

"Going as James Bond, I hear," she continued. "Hardly a fancy dress — is it? I mean a DJ in the mess. Surely you could have come up with something better than that. I'm surprised you aren't going as Biggles."

I should have known I was being set up, but I was just pleased Liz was taking any interest at all in what I would be wearing. Previously she had ignored my presence.

"I suppose you've got a better idea, have you?" I asked — thinking if she became involved, then I'd be well in with her for the party.

"As it happens, yes, we do have an idea."

"Oh yes? What?"

"That the three of us go as Cinders and Prince Charming. Carol's going to wear the rags and I'll be your Prince Charming for the evening. That's if you'd like to escort me — otherwise, Prince Charming can hardly dance with another man, can he?"

It was hardly a logical excuse — but I wasn't about to spoil the chance of escorting Liz.

"Come on, be a sport!" Carol added. "We could then have an excuse for making a collection to add to the proceeds from the panto — or we can use the excuse of the collection for you dressing as Cinders again."

"It also means Tim can't object to me having danced with you — he really can be very jealous, especially as he resents my parents' attitude to him," Liz remarked.

It was my likely to be my only chance to get closer to Liz and I knew if I blew this opportunity, she would go back to ignoring me.

"OK, providing Carol's parents don't have any objections, I'll do it," I agreed.

"Great! I can see we are going to have some fun," laughed Liz coming over to me and kissing me on the lips. She stepped away again before I had a chance to respond.

When told we were hoping to make a collection at the party, Aunt Judith and Uncle David said they had no objections to our plan.

On New Year's Eve, Carol doctored my running bath water with some perfumed bubble bath and, as it would take too long for the water to heat up again for everyone else to have their baths, I had no option but to soak in it.

I then went to my room and dressed in Aunt Judith's girdle, Carol's bra stuffed once again with cotton wool, a pair of tights and the ball gown with its built-in layered petticoat. Once I had dressed in the costume, Carol helped me with my wig and did my make-up. When she had finished, she picked up her perfume and, before I could stop her, had sprayed me with scent to match the bubble bath. I then looked into the mirror. If people had taken us for twins before, they would be totally convinced now, I could hardly believe it myself.

Uncle David called up the stairs to tell us Liz and her parents had arrived and ask how much longer we would be.

"Nearly ready, Dad," replied Carol.

We went downstairs to the lounge. Uncle David was dressed in one of the ugly sister's costumes — as was Liz's father, Robert, while Aunt Judith had been transformed into the fairy godmother and Liz's mother was dressed as a page.

"I thought we ought to complete the set," explained Uncle David.

"No coach and horses, I'm afraid," remarked Liz's father, Robert, opening the door for Gwen, his wife who was driving their Volvo. "Perhaps you would like to come with us, John," he invited. "Save you trying to scramble into the back of your aunt's shoebox."

Aunt Judith was also driving because Uncle David said he couldn't drive in a long dress and high heels, so they were taking her Fiesta rather than his Rover.

The snow which had been threatening that afternoon had given way to rain but the bitterly cold wind had lost none of its strength as it swept down off the North Sea and over the flat Norfolk countryside.

It was only a couple of miles from the house, which was off the station, to the Officer's Mess. As we drove along, Liz's hand settled on top of mine and squeezed.

"You gave a splendid performance in the panto," commented Robert turning round towards us. He clearly noticed Liz's hand holding mine as he smiled, but didn't make any remark.

"They certainly make a lovely couple," laughed Gwen, glancing at us in the rear-view mirror.

"Mum! You'll embarrass him," complained Liz.

The party had already started by the time we arrived but we were still able to find a table. Robert went to the bar where he bought Champagne and served each of us.

"Come on, Cinders — plenty of time for drinking later." Liz reached for my hand and led me onto the dance floor.

I had a marvellous evening. Liz didn't hold back at all as we danced together and not only responded to the occasional kiss I gave her but tended to take the dominant role. All too soon, however, it was time for Auld Lang Syne. We hadn't counted the money we'd raised through our collection — but it looked impressive with quite a few fivers in amongst the pound notes and silver.

As we left the Mess, I asked Liz if she would like to go to the cinema with me the following evening.

"I'd love to," she said. "But do you mind if we go into Norwich rather than the station cinema?"

As I lay in bed that night, I regretted for the first time I would be returning to boarding school in just a few days. I knew Liz was a bit on the wild side and even if her parents persuaded her to give up Tim, she would be going out with other boys when I wasn't around. And, let's face it; it was quite unreasonable to expect anything different.

Chapter 6. Carol — October 1982

'll get it," I called to mum when the doorbell rang. "It's probably Liz." We hadn't seen each other for months as John and I had spent the long summer holidays with his parents in Hong Kong and she hadn't been around for the May half term.

For a moment, I didn't recognise the person standing in the porch. Instead of the usually bouncy, fashionably dressed individual who wouldn't step outside her bedroom without perfectly styled hair and immaculate make-up, she had a baggy jumper on over crumpled jeans and trainers. Her hair was lank and couldn't have been washed for days. She wore no make-up at all. Her eyes were dull and she glanced from my face down to the floor, unable to look straight at me.

"Hi Carol."

"Liz?"

I just stood there for a moment.

"Can I come in?" she mumbled. "I need to talk."

"Of course, Liz, come on in." I stood to one side so she could pass. "Let's go up to my room."

Chapter 6 – Carol October 1982

She climbed the stairs ahead of me, one weary step at a time — instead of bounding up them excitedly as she would normally do, chattering non-stop. What on earth had happened to her since Easter?

I closed the door behind us as Liz turned to me.

"Oh Carol, I'm in such a bloody mess. You've got to help me; I've got no-one else to turn to. Please say you'll help. Promise."

She gripped my hands in hers and squeezed them tightly. She started sobbing so I pulled her to me for a hug.

"Of course I'll help, if I can — but what is it?"

We sat down on my bed and I put my arm around her shoulder.

"I've been such a bloody fool." She wiped tears away from her eyes and turned to me. "You've got to promise not to tell anyone what I'm going to tell you. Nobody. It's got to be our secret. Promise me."

I hesitated. I had a horrible feeling that she was going to tell me something that I really couldn't keep secret.

Before I could answer, she blurted out "Oh Carol. I'm pregnant. Mum and Dad are going to kill me. I've got to get rid of it."

"How? Who? Is it Tim's?" I asked automatically.

"I don't know. It's a mess. And I'm scared."

"You don't know if it's Tim's? Surely it's not John's?"

"No, of course not. John and I never did anything. He was sweet. Too sweet for me really — I needed someone with a bit more go. Well, that's what I thought."

"Then who? Not that it really matters. You'd better tell me what's been going on."

Liz took a deep breath and nodded.

"OK. Well, you know John and I had a couple of dates at Christmas and during the spring half-hols?"

"Yes."

Chapter 6 – Carol October 1982

"Well Tim found out about it and blew his top. He told me he didn't want a stupid officer's brat as a girlfriend and he was going to find a woman who could give him what he wanted."

She looked down, bit her lower lip and paused before continuing.

"You know what it's like being the child of an officer — we're expected to set an example and be perfect. I hated that; which is why I went out with Tim in the first place. I knew dad was his boss and it would piss him off. I just wanted to show him he couldn't order me around like the men under him. And, it felt great knowing that I could attract someone who was older than me and knew his way around."

She took out a packet of cigarettes.

"Mind if I smoke?"

I wasn't too happy about it but thought it might help her.

"Yes, but open a window and blow the smoke outside please."

She stood up, opened a window then lit up.

"Where was I? Oh yeah. Anyway, I told Tim that I wasn't a kid and I'd do anything for him. So, he took me out in his car and I let him have sex with me. I know it was stupid but I really wanted to hold on to him. It was actually a crap experience. He didn't care if I enjoyed it or not."

She took another pull on the cigarette and blew the smoke outside.

"After we'd had sex, he lit a joint and made me try it. It didn't do anything for me but I didn't want him to think I was too scared or strait-laced. A few weeks later, he took me to a party off the base. Well, I thought it was an ordinary party but it proved to be for swingers. He said I didn't need to join in but it was clear what he would think if I didn't."

She flicked the remains of her cigarette out of the window. I'd have to pick up the butt later.

"Anyway, he kept giving me drinks then, when I was pissed, persuaded me to do a strip tease. He encouraged other guys to fondle my tits and had me wanking him off while they did. At the time, I enjoyed the attention. I was the best-looking woman there, most of the others were in their thirties and forties and flabby. I could have had any of the guys I wanted."

22

"You didn't."

She looked down to the floor. I didn't need to hear her answer.

"Yes, I was totally out of my head on booze and coke so I let them do what they wanted. I feel sick thinking about it now but, at the time, I didn't care. I wanted to show Tim that I wasn't a kid any longer and could give him anything he wanted."

"So, is that when you fell pregnant?"

She lit another cigarette, lowered her voice and looked at the floor again, seemingly unwilling to meet my eyes.

"No. It was later. Tim got access to one of the old dispersal huts on the other side of the airfield — we'd go there and party. It was on our own at first but he started to invite some of his friends; we'd get pissed and stoned then they'd all have me. It was often two or three at a time."

My eyes must have been popping out of their sockets.

"Yeah, well, I think Tim was charging them to have sex with me but I didn't fucking care. I was queen of the castle, they all wanted me. Like I said, it felt great at the time."

She took another drag on her cigarette.

"Dad tried to warn me off Tim but I took no notice. Mind you Dad had no idea what was going on — though mum and he did nag me when my school work started to suffer. They kept asking why I couldn't go out with John instead of Tim and that got on my nerves and made me even more determined to hold onto Tim. Dad went on about how he would never amount to anything and would probably stay as a Senior Aircraftsman until he left the air force. Crazy thing is I knew they were right; I knew I was being stupid but the more they got on at me the more I did."

"Didn't you go on the pill or make them use condoms?"

"I didn't dare go to the MO to get the pill; I didn't trust him not to tell Dad. I did get to a clinic in Norwich in the end but, by then, it was too late."

"So, how far gone are you?"

"Twenty-six weeks."

"Really? I'm surprised you're not showing yet. Is that why you're wearing baggy tops?"

She nodded. "Yeah, but I can't hide it any longer and Tim has noticed. He wants me to get rid of it."

"But you can't if you're that far gone."

"There must be someone who can do it — there's another thing. I may have the clap. Tim told me last week that one of the guys I went with recently is now having treatment; he was laughing his head off as though it's a joke. The bastard."

"Shit, Liz. You are in a mess, aren't you? You really need to get to a clinic and you absolutely need to tell your mum and dad. I'm sure they'll support you — it's got to be better than risking an illegal abortion."

"I can't. I just can't. I'd rather die."

"I know things look bad now but you can sort it out. You have to."

She stood up.

"You promised to help me. And you promised not to tell anyone else. I trusted you. I thought you were my friend but you're like all the rest. I thought you'd understand — but you don't. Well sod you. You'll ALL be sorry."

With that she pulled the bedroom door open; slammed it behind her, crashed down the stairs and stormed out of the front door — rattling the glass as she slammed that shut behind her too.

As I stood at the top of the stairs, Mum came out of the lounge and looked up in shock.

"What was that about?" she asked as I went down.

"I'm not sure if I can tell you. Liz asked me not to tell anyone."

"That wasn't just a spat between friends, darling. Something very serious is going on and you have to tell me."

I didn't have a choice. I wasn't sure what Liz planned to do but her parting comments worried me. When I explained what Liz had told me, Mum and Dad agreed that we had to let Liz's parents know.

Chapter 6 – Carol October 1982

We pulled up outside the Fraser's house on the Officers' Married Quarter patch, walked up to the front door and rang the bell. Squadron Leader Fraser opened the door.

"Hello, David, Judith, Carol, to what do we owe this pleasure? Come in. Liz is out I'm afraid, Carol."

"Thanks Robert. I'm afraid we are here about Liz. She's been to see Carol this afternoon and we are worried about her," said Dad.

"Well, come on through into the lounge. Gwen, we have visitors."

Gwen joined us from the kitchen.

"This is a pleasant surprise. Would anyone like a drink? I've just made a fresh pot of coffee."

Mum and dad glanced at each other and mum said "I think that would be a very good idea. I'll give you a hand."

Once the coffees had been passed around, Robert said "So what's this about Liz and why are you worried?"

I told them what Liz had said. I felt very guilty sharing what Liz had wanted kept secret but knew I had no choice. I didn't mention that she had gone out with Tim Williams to annoy her father.

Robert and Gwen were horrified by the news.

"Oh my God. Do you really think she plans to do something, Carol?" asked Gwen.

"I don't know. She was really upset, so I think it's a real possibility."

"Well, thank you for telling us. It can't have been easy for you," said Liz's father.

"We'd noticed that she'd changed and was moody but put that down to her just being a teenager. I never imagined it might involve drugs or sex. I mean you don't think your own daughter could do such things," said Gwen, her face drained of blood. "I'll never forgive myself if something has happened to her."

"Right," said Robert, taking command of the situation. "First, let's organise a search of likely locations. You say they've used one of the old dispersal huts so we'll start with them," he picked up the telephone.

We could only hear his side of the conversation but he instructed the Duty Officer to organise a search for Liz and Tim Williams and to find Williams' car registration number.

"Is there anywhere else that Liz might have gone?" he asked me after putting the received back on its rest.

"I can't think of anywhere. Apart from the cricket pavilion, some of the kids used to use that to meet in. Or she might have gone to the NAAFI."

"Ok we'll search those as well."

The phone rang.

"Squadron Leader Fraser. Yes. Fine, yes, I've got that. Thank you."

He replaced the receiver then picked it up again, checked the address book and dialled.

"Graham, it's Robert Fraser. I need a favour. My daughter has gone missing and due to the circumstances, I'm seriously concerned about her. One possibility is that she's with one of our Senior Aircraftsmen, Timothy Williams. She's only 17. Can you put out a call to watch for his vehicle? It's a Ford Sierra registration... Thanks Graham, yes, we must have another round soon."

He put the phone down and turned to us.

"Graham is the local police division inspector, we play golf together," he said in explanation.

"David, we'll go and check the cricket pavilion and NAAFI. You ladies stay here by the phone in case there's any news. Hopefully she'll turn up of her own accord."

"She wasn't in either the NAAFI or the cricket pavilion," Dad said when he returned. "Robert has gone to the guardroom to see how the search is progressing."

Mum held Gwen's hand. "I'm sure it will turn out OK. Liz is probably just wandering around somewhere."

I couldn't just sit there. "Does anyone want another drink?" I asked. I'd just handed them round when the phone rang.

Gwen jumped up and answered it. She turned to us.

Chapter 6 – Carol October 1982

"That was Robert, they've searched all of the dispersal huts and found evidence of one having been used but no sign of Liz yet. They are now searching the area around the airfield."

We continued to wait, trying to make conversation from time to time but mainly sitting with our own thoughts.

Why hadn't I been a better friend to Liz?

I couldn't have seen her during term time as I was away at boarding school and she was here but I could have tried to phone her more. I could make all the excuses I wanted about being busy with school activities and the fact that every time I had tried to call her since Easter, she'd been out. I'd written a couple of letters and had nothing back in return but, still, I should have done more. How could I forgive myself if she'd done something to herself? Could I have helped her more today? Could I have offered to help her find someone to get rid of her baby? Was it my fault she was now missing?

Just before midnight, Liz's dad returned. Her mum looked at his distraught face and screamed.

"No, please God, no!"

He took his wife in his arms. "I'm sorry Gwen but they found her in a ditch near the end of the runway. They've taken her to the mortuary at Norwich General."

Tears flowed down my face as I lifted a hand to my mouth. Mum took me in her arms and hugged me. "Come on darling, we'd better leave them."

I couldn't sleep that night and just tossed and turned wondering what else I could have done.

Over the next few days, it came out that Liz had died from an overdose of drugs and alcohol — though there was no indication whether this was deliberate or accidental. Tim Williams was arrested and faces prison for dealing drugs. He tried to get a more lenient sentence by informing the police about his suppliers.

If there was any benefit to be taken from Liz's death, a couple of the kids at Liz's school who'd started to dabble in drugs have seen what they can do and have stopped.

It has also helped me to make up my mind about my career. I'm going to help stop the disgusting trade which killed Liz and to put those involved in it behind bars for a very long time.

Chapter 7. John — October 1982

If there is one thing growing up in a service family involves, it's losing friends as you move around. Perhaps this is why Liz's death didn't hit me quite as hard as it might.

I saw her during the Spring half term holidays and we went out to Norwich a couple of times as Tim was away on a course. By Easter she was changing, becoming more withdrawn and moodier. I initially thought this was because her parents were trying to push her towards me and she resented this, even if she liked me.

Even so, it had been a shock to hear from Carol that she was dead and, whilst the changes in her destroyed any attraction she had for me, I was saddened at the waste of a life which could have had so much promise.

Back at school after half term, I immersed myself in my A level studies. I enjoyed writing and art and had already decided I wanted to go into the creative side of advertising as a career.

I was aware from reading Campaign, the industry's trade paper, there were more vacancies for designers than for writers so it had seemed to make sense to concentrate on the graphic design side and offer writing skills as a bonus. As designs can span language barriers I also continued with French as well as my Art and English courses to widen my options after Art College.

Chapter 8. John — Summer 1984

As I arrived at the sailing club near Heathrow airport, I saw Anne Lucas, one of the other Laser sailors, preparing her boat. Anne spotted me and waved. I left my kitbag by my own dinghy and walked over to her. I fancied her but she always seemed to be surrounded by admirers and we'd barely exchanged half a dozen words.

"Hi, fancy a bit of tuning practice together?" she invited.

"Sure, it might give me the chance to see why you usually beat me," I replied. Maybe this was my chance to make an impression on her.

Chapter 8 – John Summer 1984

In fact, we were fairly evenly matched. In light winds, her weight advantage enabled her to pull away, but in stronger breezes my extra strength meant I could normally win. In today's conditions, however, we should be just about evenly matched and it would be sail control, boat handling and tactics which would be decisive in handling our craft. Our single-handed Lasers were virtually identical; hers had a red hull while mine was white with chevrons of three different shades of blue. The only other noticeable difference being the sail number.

I helped her to lift the mast into the hull of her boat, rigged my own and we wheeled them down to the launch point, I then told her I would be a couple of minutes changing.

It was a beautiful sunny day with around two-eighths coverage of cumulus clouds high in the brilliant blue sky. The temperature was in the mid-seventies and there was a gentle force three breeze blowing. All I needed to do was change into my shorts, sailing boots and buoyancy aid and I was ready to go.

For the next couple of hours, we sailed close together to keep in as identical winds as we could without interfering with each other so we could experiment with balance and adjustments of sail to find the optimum for these particular conditions.

Once we had finished sailing, and had derigged and stowed the Lasers, we went to get changed then meet for a drink. It took me no time at all to shower and dress so I was already at the bar on the upper level of the clubhouse when she came in and looked around.

She was stunning in her shorts, T-shirt and trainers. Her face, arms and legs were tanned and her shoulder length mid-brown hair had been bleached by the sun. She wore very little make-up, just a pink lipstick and nail varnish. My heart fluttered as she smiled when she saw me and came over.

I asked her what she would like to drink, then went to the bar to get the diet coke she had requested.

After handing her the drink, I told Anne I hadn't seen her in the Sunday morning races recently and asked her if she'd been away on holiday. She said she had been to St Jean de Monts in France for a fortnight with her parents.

"That explains the tan," I commented. "Were you at the Eurocamp site?"

"Yes, do you know it?"

"We were there a couple of years ago."

"So, what are you doing this summer?" Anne asked.

"I'm working evening and night shifts covering reception at the Travellers Rest hotel near the airport trying to raise some cash for college."

"Same here, waitressing in the restaurant at the Post House. What are you taking at college?"

I almost missed her question as I looked at her lips wondering if I'd ever get a chance to kiss them.

"Sorry. Graphic Design and Media Studies at Southampton, I've just finished my first year. What about you?"

"Modern languages at Leicester. I've also just finished my first year."

"Quelles langues?"

"Français, Deutch y Espagnol, tu comprends?"

"Oui, bien sur."

We continued to speak in French and I have to confess I showed off my idiomatic knowledge to try to impress her.

"Your French is excellent, especially your accent, John. I'm surprised you aren't taking languages."

"I want to go into advertising," I told her.

"Good money, I hear, for the top people — but a relatively short career for creatives."

We practised together the following three days while I was on night shift. On the Thursday, as we were leaving, Anne asked if I was OK for the next afternoon.

"Fine, but how about taking dad's Dart catamaran out for a change?" I suggested.

"Fantastic, what time?"

"Same as today suit you?"

"Great! I'll look forward to it."

Chapter 8 – John Summer 1984

Her eager response gave me a glow in my stomach. Maybe I stood a chance with her after all. I put on my crash helmet, dropped my little Suzuki motorbike off the stand and kick-started it; gave her a wave and rode home.

Over dinner, I checked that dad had no objection to me using the Dart the next afternoon, then left for work at about 11.00. This was when my little bike came into its own with buses being few and far between at this time of night.

The next day, I arrived at the club at about 3.30 and started to rig the catamaran.

After we'd changed, Anne and I walked over to the Dart and trailed it down to the launch point. Anne was wearing a one-piece swimsuit which showed off her fabulous figure. Once we had rigged the sails, I handed Anne the trapeze harness and helped her to put it on over her buoyancy jacket.

"Excuse me," I said as I reached between Anne's legs to reach the hook plate. She didn't seem to mind and smiled as I clipped the shoulder and waist straps into place. I decided to push my luck a little further.

"The straps need to be snug but comfortable," I told her as I slipped my hands inside the shoulder straps where they passed over her breasts and checked the tension.

"How does that feel?" I asked, looking her straight in the eyes.

"Fine," she replied, returning my look.

Anne took to the Dart as though she'd been sailing one for years; she hadn't mentioned that she'd had previous experience of trapezing on a Fireball. The wind had picked up a little from the previous day and we were screaming along with the wind whistling through the rigging.

"This is fantastic!" she called.

We had almost reached the southern bank and it was time to tack.

"Lee Oh!" I warned as I pushed the tiller away from me and we scrambled across the netting between the two hulls. The sails were soon adjusted to our new course as we set off again, reaching back the way we'd come.

As we approached the far side again, I saw a gust was about to hit us and deliberately sheeted in the mainsail as hard as I could. The windward hull lifted as the increased breeze hit, Anne leant out as far as she could to balance us.

I decided to take a chance that could go one of two ways. I just hoped it wouldn't make her think I was a total idiot.

I pretended to lean in to clear a snag on the mainsheet. The top of the mast fell towards the water. Anne suddenly realised what was happening and unhitched herself from the trapeze wire as we capsized. She then sat on the hull that was about seven feet above me as I slipped into the water.

"That will teach you," she laughed, as I pulled myself around the stern and clambered onto the lower hull.

She passed me the jib sheet then clambered down to join me. I told her to hold onto the sheet while I held her around the waist and we stood at the bow and leant out to pull the Dart upright again. As it came up, we climbed back on board.

"You only did as an excuse to hold me, didn't you?" she challenged. I was relieved to see a twinkle in her eyes rather than anger or, even worse, disappointment.

"Can you blame me?" I asked.

"Twit!" she yelled with a grin as she sheeted in the jib once more. As the Dart picked up speed, she moved back along the hull until she was standing right next to me.

I eased the main until the hull settled back onto the water and our speed dropped away. Anne sat next to me, her left leg touching my right.

"This is fabulous," she said, looking me in the eyes. I was holding the tiller in one hand and the mainsheet in the other. I locked the main off in the block and transferred the sheet to the hand holding the tiller and put my arm around her waist. She was holding the jib in her right hand and rested her left on my thigh.

I turned to her and kissed her. Her soft lips responded.

"Would you like to go out some evening?" I asked.

"I thought you'd never ask," she replied.

"What about tomorrow? It's my night off."

"Great, what did you have in mind?"

"Whatever you'd like. Dancing, cinema, bowling, a meal?"

Chapter 8 – John Summer 1984

"I love ten pin bowling. Mind you, I also love dancing and the cinema. What's showing at the moment?"

"I've no idea," I confessed.

"Let's settle on bowling then. Perhaps we can have a MacDonald's or something as well?"

"Fine — what time shall I pick you up?"

"Is eight o'clock OK?"

"Of course. I'll try to borrow mum's Mini."

I arrived at Anne's, a large, Victorian, detached house with a broad driveway leading to a double garage, just before eight. I left mum's Mini on the road and walked up the drive past a Triumph Dolomite and a Ford Cortina, both about two years old. Anne's father answered the door and let me in. The first thing I noticed was his dog collar.

He led me into the lounge and asked if I would like a drink while I waited for Anne to finish getting ready.

"Just a coke, please."

As he handed me a glass, Anne came into the room. My immediate reaction was 'wow'. I'd only ever seen Anne up at the club in sailing gear or shorts and a T shirt with her hair tied back in a ponytail. As lovely as she looked then, she was even more beautiful tonight in a dress and with her hair framing her face. I couldn't believe she was going out with me.

"What, ready on time, darling?" her father exclaimed. "That's an all-time record."

"I'll have a coke too please, Dad," she said as she came over to me. "Unless you want to get straight off, John?" I wanted to take her hand in mine but wondered how her father might react. Would it seem forward? Then I felt her take my hand in hers. I squeezed it and felt her respond.

"No, there's no panic. I booked a lane for us at 9."

"I hear you're quite a sailor — Lasers isn't it?" asked Anne's father.

"Yes, Mr Lucas. Anne and I have been training together this week but we took my father's Dart catamaran out yesterday."

"So I gather. I also hear you're planning to study graphic design and work in advertising." Anne had clearly been discussing me with her parents. Surely that was a good sign.

"Yes sir. I'm working at the Traveller's Rest hotel to raise money — but tonight's my rest day."

"Well, have fun both of you."

"You made a good impression on dad," said Anne as we drove off. She rested her hand on my thigh.

"I was scared I was going to say something inappropriate," I replied. "You didn't tell me he was a minister."

"He's chaplain at Greenways Prep School, where he teaches science as well as religious knowledge. Does that worry you?"

"Of course not," I assured her. "It's a nice place you've got," I added, changing the subject.

"Yes, mum inherited it from her Aunt Gladys about 2 years ago — together with a bit of cash. If it wasn't for that, we couldn't afford to live there."

"But you are still working to raise your own money for college?"

"Of course. The grant will pay for tuition, the money my Great Aunt Gladys left me will cover my basic living expenses but I still want to earn my own spending money."

"I get you. What's it like having a chaplain for a father?"

She paused.

"He's OK, but can be over protective. I mean, he always insists on seeing any boys I go out with and wants to know where I'm going. Can you believe it? I'm not a child any longer, for God's sake."

She looked across at me.

"Don't get me wrong, I love Mum and Dad and wouldn't do anything to hurt them. It just gets a bit stifling sometimes."

"I know what you mean. My dad's an officer in the army and I've always been expected to set a good example. Not that I'd want to do anything differently."

"Exactly. Anyway, as I said, seems you passed dad's inspection."

"But do I pass yours?"

"I'm out with you, aren't I?" She squeezed my thigh and I quickly looked at her and returned her smile.

"True."

"So, how good are you at bowling?"

"I usually manage to get around 120," I said. "Hardly championship winning class."

"Not bad though."

It was only about fifteen minutes from Anne's house to the bowling alley so we were there soon after eight forty and had to wait for our lane to become available.

While we waited, we collected some shoes and had a drink in the coffee bar.

"You really look stunning," I told her as I put my arm around her shoulder. She nestled into my arm, rested her hand on my leg and turned her face towards me so I could kiss her.

"I'm surprised you don't already have a boyfriend," I said.

"I could say the same about you and a girlfriend," she replied. "I was seeing someone before I went to France — but I haven't heard from him since I got back."

"He's an idiot then. What will you do if he asks you for another date?"

"I'll probably tell him I'm going out with someone else. Assuming, that is, you want to see me again."

"Of course I do."

"Good. So, it's bye-bye Harry."

Just then the loudspeaker called our names, so we finished our cokes and walked hand in hand to our lane. I set up the automatic scoring system and chose a couple of balls to use.

Chapter 8 – John Summer 1984

Anne got off to an excellent start with eight pins down on her first ball and clearing the remaining two with her second. I also scored eight with my first attempt, but left myself a split for the second and ended up with nine to her spare. She then scored nine but ended up in the gutter with her second ball. I again scored nine — making it 28 to her and 18 to me.

"You had better not be letting me win," she warned me.

"Of course not. I'm just not into my rhythm yet."

Anne then scored a strike. She turned to me with a huge smile on her face. I caught her and gave her a kiss.

"Like that is it?" I challenged.

My next was a strike. I walked over to her and kissed her again. "Not trying, eh?"

"Right. That does it!" she grinned – her eyes sparkling.

She took careful aim and scored another strike, then came back to me for her reward.

"So, it's war, is it?" I asked.

I couldn't believe it. My next two balls went into the gutter. From then on, I couldn't do a thing right and failed to get another clearance. Anne, in contrast, seemed almost unable to make a mistake and ended up with 129 to my 84.

It was my poorest score for years. But I didn't care. I was with the most fabulous girl I'd ever met and she liked me. I couldn't believe my luck.

Out in the car park, Anne pulled me towards her and held my face between her hands. She looked me straight in the eyes and demanded to know if I had deliberately let her win.

I held her trim waist and admitted I hadn't tried 100 percent with the first two goes until she had warned me against letting her win — but swore from then on, I'd really being trying.

"You'd better have been, because I can't stand being patronised or given something on a plate. The only thing I hate more is guys who can't stand it when I do beat them fair and square."

Her arms slipped round the back of my neck as I pulled her close and kissed her.

"What would you like to eat?" I asked. "Burger, pizza or chicken — or a Chinese or what?"

"A pizza would be great."

We drove along the A4 and went in search of a Pizza Hut where we had a late supper before I drove her home. I kissed her goodnight and arranged to see her at the club the next morning.

The next day, I got my revenge for the previous evening's bowling by beating Anne by about a boat's length in the first race and by an even larger margin in the afternoon.

Apart from the fact my work restricted me to one free night a week, Anne pointed out we were working to save money for college and going out somewhere every evening would seriously reduce our potential savings as she insisted that she share some of the costs. She suggested we limit our excursions to my free evenings and just go for a ride on the bike, a walk or visit each other's homes on the other evenings. We could also continue with our sailing on the afternoons when I was on late shift.

By the end of the summer, we knew we were in love. But we accepted the next two years were crucial to our futures and being away at college in a mature, more relaxed atmosphere was bound to change us.

We agreed to write or phone regularly but to make no attempt to see each other before Christmas. In the meantime, there was no commitment and, if either of us wanted to go out on dates, we were free to do so.

Chapter 9. John — Easter 1985

I couldn't wait for the holidays and the chance to see Anne again. In spite of our agreement that we were free to date other people if we wanted to, I hadn't. And, from what Anne said during our weekly phone chats, neither had she. Not that we'd become hermits; we'd both been out as part of groups and attended parties but when it came to other girls none of those that hinted at a date came close to matching Anne.

Over the Christmas holidays, Anne and I had taken part in the 'Icebreaker' winter race series at the yacht club and gone out to friends' parties and for a couple of meals but, most of the time, we just met at each other's house. Christmas Day was spent with our own families but I went over to hers on Boxing Day and we exchanged gifts.

On our first evening together of the Easter holidays, Anne and I went dancing. As we held each other close, I kissed her. She pulled me tighter and responded.

"I've really missed you," she said.

"So, no-one else has swept you off your feet then?"

She grinned as she looked me in the eyes, "Well, there was one guy but that was when he crashed into me while a group of us went ice-skating."

"I've missed you, too," I told her. "I wish we could be together all the time."

"It would be dreamy — but we graduate in just over a year. And that is important for both of us."

"I know darling. But it doesn't stop me hating being apart."

She leant backwards in my arms just as the music stopped.

"That's the first time you've called me 'darling'."

"What? Well, you must know how I feel about you."

"And what's that?"

"Isn't it obvious?"

"Tell me."

"Anne, darling, I love you. There, are you satisfied now?"

She pressed her lips against mine in what I assumed was her answer before taking my hand and leading me to a table.

As we sat having a drink, I decided to take the plunge. I'd been toying with the idea for some weeks but didn't know if asking the question would put pressure on her and spoil everything.

"Anne, do you still want to keep our agreement not to make any firm commitment until we've finished college?"

"Do you?"

"That's not fair, I asked you first."

"Why?" she asked.

"Just answer the question."

She stared me straight in the eyes and I could see them twinkling. She tilted her head and licked her lips – teasing me. I took hold of her hands and she squeezed mine.

"Yes, I will," she announced after an interminable pause. It wasn't the answer I was expecting and I was confused.

"Will what?"

"Marry you, you chump. That is what you were leading up to wasn't it?"

"Well, yes it was. Wow. WOW. Are you serious? I can't believe it. WOW."

She smiled at me and pulled my head towards her until our noses nearly touched.

"Of course, I'm serious. I love you too you fool. But we must finish our degrees before we get married."

"Yes, of course we do. But we can get engaged straight away, can't we?"

"As soon as you can afford a ring," she grinned.

It had hardly been the most romantic of proposals. In fact, I'm still not sure whether it counted as me proposing to Anne or her proposing to me. But who cares?

It was still only just after 11 by the time we left the restaurant so we drove out past the airport again and found a secluded spot to park. Anne didn't object to me fondling her breasts as we kissed and, when I put my hand on the inside of her thighs, she opened her legs so I could stroke through the flimsy material of her panties. She then put her hand onto my bulge and fondled me. I started to try to remove her panties.

"Not tonight, not here," she said.

"Where then?" I asked.

"Sorry John. I'm not being the reluctant virgin waiting for her wedding night. But I don't want to our first time to be a fumbled grope in the back of a Mini with the risk of some peeping Tom seeing us. Can you understand?"

"Of course I can. And I don't mind waiting."

The next evening, I rode over Anne's house. Her mother was in the kitchen preparing dinner while her father was in the lounge.

"Would you like a drink, John?" he invited, "Anne says you want to ask me something."

"Yes sir. Thank you, I'll have a beer if I may."

"There you are. Now, what was it you wanted to ask me? It must be important otherwise Anne wouldn't be in the kitchen with her mother."

I took a deep breath then said:

"Anne and I want to get engaged and we'd like your blessing."

"You certainly don't beat about the bush, do you? Well Anne is over eighteen so she doesn't need my permission but if I don't give you my blessing, I suspect my life is going to be hell. I like you, John, and I know you and Anne love each other so of course you have my blessing. But I wouldn't like Anne or you to give up university and I can't see you being able to support her on a grant."

"Both of us want to complete our courses, naturally and we are quite happy to wait until we have before getting married."

"How do your parents feel about this?"

"I haven't told them yet. I thought you and Anne's mother should be first to know."

"I appreciate you coming to ask for my approval. Not many lads of your generation would bother. I suspect, though, you'd have gone ahead even if I'd said I wasn't happy — wouldn't you?"

"Probably, but I'd then have done my best to prove to you I was right for her and I know I'd have convinced you in the end."

Anne and her mother came into the room.

"I'm sure you and Anne are going to be very happy together," said Mrs Lucas as she hugged me. "Now, dinner will be ready in half an hour, so I suggest we have sherry or something to celebrate."

"I think I have something rather more appropriate," said Anne's father with a sparkle in his eyes. He reached behind his chair and pulled out a bottle of Champagne already cooling in an ice bucket. "Rather expected your news. And if you hadn't made any announcement, we would just have used it to celebrate your return from college."

After dinner, I took Anne back to my house and told my parents our news. They were as generous in their welcome to Anne as her parents had been to me. My mother suggested we invite Anne's parents to dinner the following evening. We both prayed our parents would get on together but we needn't have worried.

After dinner that evening, my mother pulled out the family photo albums and embarrassed me by showing Anne all of my childhood pictures. Worst of all were the ones of the Panto when I'd taken Carol's place and of the New Year's Eve Party. I was absolutely mortified. I'd forgotten the pictures even existed and, had I remembered, I would certainly have destroyed the evidence.

The next morning, I collected Anne and went for a ride in the country. My original Suzuki had now been replaced by a 350cc Honda, much more suitable for carrying two. I'd thought about buying a small car instead but had decided the additional running costs would be too high. We parked at a pub where we had a leisurely ploughman's lunch and a drink, then decided to take a walk in some woods behind the pub. It was a delightful spring day — but, then, I doubt if we would have noticed if it had been blowing a gale!

As we strolled along the paths, we came across a carpet of Bluebells. I was about to pick some for Anne when she told me they were protected and I should leave them for everyone to enjoy. I took her in my arms and led her to a secluded area where I pulled her to the ground. She didn't resist as I unbuttoned the top of her blouse and kissed her nipples.

When I put my hand down inside her jeans and fingered her, she moaned with pleasure. But she stopped me as I started to unzip her jeans.

"Not here, darling, please," she whispered.

"Where then?" I asked, sitting up.

"I don't suppose we can do it at your place could we?" she suggested.

"My mother is always in during the day. What about yours?"

"Mum helps out at the Oxfam shop on Mondays, Wednesdays and Fridays, but the neighbours are very stuffy and would be bound to tell them if they saw you coming and going. Dad is very old fashioned about sex before marriage and I'd hate to upset him even though we are engaged."

"What about a hotel?" I suggested.

"Too expensive — we need to save everything we can for college."

She sat up, rested her elbows on her knees and her chin in her hands, then tilted her head as she looked at me.

"There is one possibility, but I'm not sure you'll like it," she continued.

She paused.

"Well come on, what is it?" I demanded.

"It was those pictures of the panto that gave me the idea. If the neighbours saw me arriving with a girlfriend, they wouldn't think anything of it. With your long hair, you'd just need to pad out the top a bit — lots of girls wear jeans and t shirts. What do you think?"

Could I get away with it? Probably. But did I want to? I remembered the feelings I'd had when I dressed as Cinders? Did I dare risk where that might lead? But surely it was just a phase, wasn't it? And it would solve our problem.

"I don't mind anything if it means we can make love together," I replied.

"Look, I'll bring a spare bra with me tomorrow. You can put it on in somewhere and pad it out — then a bit of make-up and no-one will be any the wiser."

The next morning, we met near the club just after 9 o'clock and Anne passed me a bag. "There you are darling. I hope it fits. I've also put in a pair of stockings and a suspender belt in case Mrs T notices you're wearing socks."

I parked in a lay-by near some public toilets and found a vacant cubicle. Having locked the door, I removed my trousers and put on the suspender belt and stockings — and found a pair of panties with a note attached which said "just to complete the set. A xxx," I put them on as well then pulled up my trousers. I then removed my T shirt so I could put the bra on.

As I did so, I heard a voice say. "Very nice darling, what do you like?" The man in the next cubicle was leering over the wall.

"Piss off you pervert!" I shouted under my breath.

"Who's calling who a pervert?" he demanded. "You're the one wearing ladies' undies!"

I pulled my T shirt over my head and put my jacket back on, its bulk disguising my changed shape. The head had disappeared and I heard the toilet being flushed and the door of the cubicle being opened.

As I left, I saw the guy who had looked over the wall at me standing at the urinals looking down at the man next to him.

I quickly left the toilets, took my crash helmet from Anne and we rode off. We'd decided we couldn't arrive on my bike in case the nosey neighbours recognised it. Instead, we would drive to Egham, take a train to Virginia Water and walk to her house from there.

As expected, the train was virtually empty and we had no trouble finding a vacant compartment. It was then simple enough for me to remove my jacket and for Anne to quickly apply a little powder and lipstick to my face in the few minutes the journey took. She then pulled my hair back into a pony tail and clipped a pair of earrings in place.

She held up a mirror for me to check the transformation. We swopped jackets, Anne wearing my bulkier one while I left hers unbuttoned.

"Not bad, even if I say so myself," Anne remarked.

We handed in our tickets at the barrier and walked along with our arms linked, perfectly acceptable behaviour for 2 girls — but 2 men might well have been arrested doing the same.

As we walked up to Anne's house, we saw Mrs T in the garden next door.

"Hello love, how's that fiancé of yours?" Mrs T asked.

"He's fine, Mrs T. I don't think you know my friend Lorraine do you."

43

"Pleased to meet you, Lorraine."

I was saved from having to reply by Mrs T's telephone and we wasted no time in getting inside the house.

"That was close," I said as the door closed behind us.

"Nonsense, she was bound to see you sooner or later. This way she knows who you are — or thinks she does."

We climbed the stairs to Anne's bedroom and closed the door behind us.

I took Anne in my arms and held her close. We kissed and our tongues intertwined as I hooked my fingers into the elasticated waistband of her skirt and pushed it down over her hips. I then reached under the back of her T shirt, found the clasp of her bra and undid it. I lifted up the front of her T shirt to reveal her firm breasts. Her nipples were already erect as I kissed them.

I kicked off my trainers as Anne unbuckled my belt, undid the top button of my trousers then reached for my zip and slid it down. My jeans fell to the floor. She looked down and saw my penis bursting out of the panties she had put in the bag.

"I wondered if you'd wear them as well," she remarked with a smile.

Anne's T shirt soon joined her skirt and was, in turn, followed by her bra. All she was now wearing were her suspender belt, stockings and panties. She hooked her leg behind mine and slid it up and down. The sensation of her stockings rubbing against mine was fabulous. Then I felt Anne removing my panties and releasing my penis. I led her to the bed and we lay down together. I kissed her on the lips, then took each nipple in turn in my mouth. She lifted her hips so I could remove her panties and she took my penis in her hands.

"You did say you were on the pill, didn't you?" I asked.

"Yes darling," she replied.

As nineteen-year-old undergraduates, we probably both assumed the other had had some sexual experience but the menace of Aids was still virtually unknown in the UK at this time and neither of us considered any other protection was needed.

I hoped I was being gentle as I penetrated Anne, but she still moaned.

"Sorry, did that hurt?" I asked.

"Just a bit," she confessed, "but it's fine, honestly."

I withdrew then pressed forward once more. It felt easier this time and, as we increased the tempo, Anne's moans became those of pleasure rather than discomfort. All too soon, I found myself ejaculating and just couldn't prevent it.

I kissed Anne and tried to remember some of the suggestions I'd read in a book on lovemaking about how a sensitive partner should continue with fondling after he has come. I was conscious Anne hadn't had any opportunity for real satisfaction before I had finished. I shuddered to think of her opinion of my sexual prowess. A score of 1 on a scale of 10 — if I was lucky.

I eventually withdrew from Anne and whispered I was sorry.

"For what?" she asked. "We both wanted to do it."

"Not for doing it at all, but for not controlling myself long enough for you."

I reached for some tissue on the dressing table and started to wipe the semen from between Anne's legs. I then noticed some blood.

"You're bleeding, did I hurt you?"

"Just a bit at first, but it was fine after that."

It then registered Anne had been a virgin.

"I'm sorry I wasn't any better for you, John," she said, "but I'm sure you can help me to learn."

"I can honestly say you were the very best I've ever had," I replied.

Anne looked at me. "It wasn't your first time too, was it?"

"Yes darling."

We lay in each other's arms.

Anne pulled my bra strap and released it so it twanged against my back. "That colour suits you," she said.

"I'd forgotten I was wearing it," I told her.

"Fancy a cup of coffee — or something while we both recover?"

Anne made us coffee, but it was cold by the time we got around to drinking it.

I had to be at work by 4 and it would take about 40 minutes to retrace our steps to Egham, where I'd left the bike. Leaving the house was as easy as arriving. Mrs T was nowhere in sight and a few minutes' walk brought us back to Virginia Water station.

We caught the train and I de-padded my bra and removed the make-up which Anne had retouched before we'd left her place. My hair was soon combed back into its usual style and I quickly put my socks on over the stockings I was still wearing. I could change properly at the hotel.

My cousin Carol was now also at university. In her case it was Manchester where she was taking Business Studies. She was spending the holiday with her boyfriend and his family, who was on the same course, lived about 10 miles from us in Esher. When she heard our news, she telephoned to congratulate me.

"So, Cinders has found a real Prince Charming, has she?" teased Carol, when she called. "Does Anne know you dress as a girl? Can't wait to meet her!"

If Carol thought she was putting me on the spot, she soon learnt she was wrong when I told her Anne already knew I'd taken her place in the panto — and how we had managed to spend time together.

We arranged to go out together for a drink the following evening. As I'd expected, Anne and Carol had a lot in common and I got on well with Steve. We discussed what we were planning to do during the long summer break and agreed to try to find some way of getting together. Anne suggested we might be able to get jobs at a holiday camp. She agreed to investigate this possibility.

Chapter 10. John — Summer Term 1985

I was apprehensive as I opened the door to Oliver Jones Associates. Oliver Jones, the owner, had offered me the opportunity for work experience with the advertising agency. The receptionist smiled as I approached her.

"Good morning, I have a ten o'clock appointment with Mr Jones," I told her.

"Good morning, it's John, isn't it? OJ told us you were starting this morning — no-one calls him Mr Jones. I'm Penny. I think he's in the studio, I'll take you through."

Chapter 10 – John Summer 1985

She showed me into the studio. OJ was standing next to a guy sitting at one of the three drawing boards positioned to get maximum light from the north facing windows.

"Ah, John, good to see you. Let's get you settled in. This is Malcolm our Head of Creative. The title sounds good when talking to clients but at the moment 'creative' is just the two of you. This is your board. I take it you've got your own drawing instruments?"

He didn't give me chance to reply before continuing. "Come on through and meet the others."

We walked back into the reception area.

"You've met Penny. She's our receptionist, secretary, book-keeper, administrator and chief coffee maker. In other words, the most vital part of the operation!"

OJ opened the door to another office.

"Paul, this is John. Paul handles our client liaison — and writes most of the copy, although we're hoping you can take some of that work off his shoulders to allow him more time to go out and get more business. That, at the moment, is the team. But, as I said when we met, I'm looking to expand as quickly as we can."

OJ Associates wouldn't, to be honest, have been my first choice for a full-time job, but for work experience it was fine and would enable me to develop both my writing and design skills.

"Right, John. We are currently pitching for a new client — nothing exciting I'm afraid. It's a double-glazing outfit. Usual situation, their products are hardly any different from the other hundred and one similar companies, they aren't the cheapest or the most expensive. Their main advantage is a reasonably well motivated sales force. We have to come up with proposals to generate enquiries. We're having a brainstorming session in my office at 10, so why don't you get settled in, have a coffee and I'll see you there."

Half an hour later, OJ, Malcolm, Paul and I were ensconced in his office, dominated by a board table forming a T with OJ's desk. The door to reception was open to allow Penny to contribute while still manning the switchboard.

"Right, let's consider the options. The products are double glazing, replacement windows and doors and conservatories. The target market is owner occupiers, probably C1/C2 and possibly D demographics. Age range 30 plus. Our objective is to generate enquiries. So how are we going to get potential customers to call Plasglaze?"

Various ideas were tossed around and evaluated, most to be discarded, others to be added to the list on the flip chart.

After a couple of hours, OJ summarised the plans.

"OK. So, we'll propose display units which can be taken to high footfall areas, demonstrators to distribute leaflets and questionnaires about householders' plans to install double glazing; producing a script for telephone canvassers. Anything else? Right, let's get cracking on some designs."

Two weeks later, OJ, Paul and I had an appointment with the client to present our proposals.

After asking a few pertinent questions, Anderson, Plasglaze's Sales Manager, thanked us for our time and told us he would be in touch. We already knew we were competing with a couple of other agencies for the work and hadn't expected an immediate decision.

"That went as well as we could expect," said OJ as we drove out of Plasglaze's car park. "Now we just have to keep our fingers crossed."

It might have been better for OJ if he'd not won the account. But he did.

The work took nearly three months to complete and occupied most of our time during this period to the detriment of some smaller jobs for other clients.

The agency's bought in costs quickly mounted; and this was without time costs being taken into account. OJ had asked Anderson for an advance payment and had been promised ten thousand immediately and a further ten thousand a month as the project progressed. The first instalment had taken a month to come through and we were still waiting for the second payment.

If OJ had been a better businessman, he might have recognised the signs and taken appropriate action. But he didn't. He was more concerned with getting the job completed on time — in spite of the client's constant changes and requests for additional work. All of which added to the original cost.

Chapter 10 – John Summer 1985

Suppliers of the trailers and display material were pressing OJ for payment of their bills and other clients, tired of waiting for prices and proposals for new jobs had taken their business elsewhere.

On the Monday evening of my final week with OJA, we were providing a briefing meeting for their sales reps, telephone canvassers and the demonstrators.

One of the trailers and one of the indoor display stands had been set up in the conference room at a local hotel. The other trailers were standing in the car park hitched to three of the eight identical sign written Escort estate cars bearing sequential registration numbers. A photographer would be along later to record the picture for some press releases.

Anderson, was late. The sales reps, always ready with their glib tongues, were chatting up the eight attractive demonstrators and the 4 tele-canvassers.

OJ was concerned. He went to telephone Plasglaze's offices and see if Anderson had been delayed.

He came back looking bemused. "He's been held up, but he's asked me to start the briefing."

With the briefing completed, we moved outside for the photograph. I suggested to OJ that, in the absence of Anderson, he should be seen hitching up the final trailer and the PR could then be used to promote his business as well as Plasglaze's.

The next morning, Anderson called OJ and said he wanted to see him. OJ returned from his meeting three hours later looking badly shaken.

He called the staff together. "Anderson has complained their corporate colour on the display material is the wrong shade. I tried to tell him it was as close as we could get with the methods we'd used to meet the deadlines — but he's insisting it be changed. He's refusing to pay our bills until it is. He also told me he's heard our costs are far higher than they should be. When I reminded him this was because of all the changes that he made, he wasn't prepared to listen. He's told me unless we redo the displays and cut the price by fifteen thousand, he'll fight the case in court.

"I know who's behind it. It's my former partner, Nigel Hall. Every time we win any significant account, he finds some way of getting at the client. We split up because I couldn't stand his unscrupulous methods."

There was no way OJA could afford to cut its price and replace the display material. The suppliers were already unhappy about the delay in settling their invoices. If the case went to court, OJA would certainly win — but it could take a year to eighteen months for it to be resolved.

"I'm sorry everyone, but I don't see any option but to close the company. I've written your pay cheques out and I suggest you get them specially cleared."

He turned to me, "I'm grateful for the work you've done this summer, John, and wish I could have given you a bonus I'd intended. As it is, I have to give priority to Malcolm, Penny and Paul — I'm sure you understand."

A week later, he was dead.

He'd told Mary, his wife, he was taking his Wayfarer dinghy out for a final sail before selling it the next day. The dinghy was found drifting in the Solent with traces of blood and hair on the boom. His body was recovered later that evening with a graze on the side of his head.

The conclusion was he had probably gybed unintentionally, the boom had struck him and he had fallen overboard and drowned. OJ's life-jacket was still uninflated but this was hardly surprising if he'd been stunned when falling overboard.

Questions were asked at the inquest about the advisability of using the sort of buoyancy aid OJ preferred and about the likelihood of falling off a relatively stable Wayfarer after being hit on the head. The verdict was misadventure. But Mary blamed Nigel Hall.

My first period in an advertising agency had taught me some very hard lessons. Lessons which were to prove very valuable in the future.

Chapter 11. Mary — July 1985

I couldn't believe my eyes when I saw Nigel Hall at OJ's funeral. Diane felt me stiffen as she helped me from the car. She held me tight — which was just as well as I might have attacked him.

"How dare he come here today, mum?" Turning to her husband, she said. "Get rid of that evil monster, darling."

Charles did as he was bid and strode along the footpath and held his arms out to his sides blocking Hall's progress.

Charles' firm voice carried clearly to us. "You were not invited and you are not welcome, Hall. This is a gathering of OJ's friends and you were never one of those. Now leave immediately."

Hall turned on his heels and walked away.

"What barefaced effrontery!" declared Charles as he came back to us.

"That man is a bastard. He's responsible for OJ's death and if I ever have the chance to pay him back I will," I told him.

A few days after the funeral, I went to see our solicitors. James Harrison had handled our affairs for years.

"Mary, come in to my office please. How are you feeling? This is just a formality, of course, Oliver has, as you know, left everything to you and as far as I can see, thanks to his insurance, you are well provided for — not that that makes up for his loss. But we'll go through the details in a moment. First let me organise some coffee — unless you'd prefer something stronger?"

"Coffee would be fine, thank you, James."

"Now as far as Oliver's estate is concerned, it will, of course be subject to probate and there may be some tax liability. However, the mortgage on your house was covered by an endowment policy which has substantial bonuses attached. There is, of course, also his 50% of the shares in OJA which makes you the sole shareholder but in view of the circumstances, they won't be worth very much I'm afraid."

"What about the business debts?"

"As the company was limited, there is no liability other than any which he might have personally guaranteed. As far as we can tell, it was only the bank overdraft which he had guaranteed."

"That's right. But are there any other business debts? I know he would have wanted to settle them."

Chapter 11 - Mary July 1985

"There are bound to be. But they will be the responsibility of the liquidator. He will chase Plasglaze for payment of their debts and, if they settle in full, should clear the full amount owing to creditors. I have to say, however, I consider that to be unlikely. Nevertheless, I anticipate they will settle enough to clear most of what is owing."

"Would it be possible to keep the company going if I settled any difference from the insurance?"

"It would, but why would you want to do that?"

"Penny and Paul have been very loyal. They have continued to work in spite of the fact there was no guarantee they would be paid in order to complete projects for clients. I would like, if possible, to let them take over the company as a going concern."

"I see. The alternative would be for them to set up their own company and offer a realistic figure for the assets and good will. I suspect that would be easier and quicker."

I thought about the suggestion for a moment. It didn't really matter to me whether OJA carried on or they set up in their own name so long as their loyalty was rewarded.

I drove across town to the old offices of OJA.

"Hello Penny, Paul. Are you busy?"

"Nothing that can't wait a few minutes," replied Paul. "Coffee?"

"Lovely, thanks."

Once we were sitting down, I jumped straight in."

"What would you say the company's assets are worth?"

"The book value is £7,645," replied Penny. "That's mainly the camera and processor in the darkroom and Paul's car. But they wouldn't fetch that much if sold."

"So, what do you consider they would fetch, Penny?"

"Probably around £5,000. Why? Are you thinking of selling the company?"

"Something like that."

Penny and Paul looked at each other.

"Where will your plans leave us?" Penny asked.

"That rather depends on you two. What I had in mind was to sell you the assets. You can then set up a company in your own name. That way you won't be burdened by anything that might or might not happen in the Plasglaze case."

"How much did you have in mind?"

"I thought £5,000 would be a realistic figure. And you have confirmed the assets are worth that much."

"It is reasonable, but I'm afraid we have to pass up the offer. We just can't raise £5,000 between us, especially as we would also need some working capital."

"I didn't expect you to be able to find it immediately. I suggest you pay it off in 10 quarterly instalments of £500. Obviously, you'll need to think it over and talk about it. Come over to the house this evening for dinner and give me your decision. OK? I'll see you about 7.30."

Penny and Paul arrived as the long carriage clock in the hall struck 7.30. I asked them in, took their coats, then took them into the lounge and offered them a drink.

"Well, have you reached a decision?"

"Yes, we have. And the answer is yes, we would like to take up your offer. But we would like you to have a shareholding in the company," replied Penny.

"That really isn't necessary," I told her.

"Then we decline your offer."

"Now that is quite silly."

"If you won't accept a shareholding, then we won't accept your offer," remarked Paul.

"I see. What did you have in mind?"

"We thought the shares should be spilt evenly," said Penny.

"That won't work, we would end up with 33 1/3rd each. No, I'll accept 20% and no more. You two will be doing all of the work so you deserve more."

Penny and Paul looked at each other. Penny nodded to Paul.

"OK, that's settled," agreed Paul.

"Not quite. If I'm to have 20% of a company worth £5,000, I'll provide £1,000 worth of working capital to be repaid after the equipment payments have been cleared. If necessary, I will also guarantee the company's bank overdraft up to £5,000 secured against the equipment."

The terms were accepted.

Chapter 12. John — Summer 1985

The start of the summer holidays found the four of us as 'Greencoats' at Greenbreaks, a newly refurbished family holiday centre near Torbay. Anne and Carol were Badger club leaders, looking after seven to ten-year olds; Steve was a swimming coach while I assisted with the sailing.

The afternoon we arrived, we joined other new staff for a briefing on our duties and the village regulations. This included dire warnings about boys visiting the girls' staff quarters and vice versa.

"We'll have to see about that!" Anne whispered to me. I squeezed her hand in agreement. I could see Steve and Carol had the same reactions. Did they think this was still the 19th Century?

Once the general briefing was over, we split into departments.

The sailing centre was open from 9.30am until 7pm, but we had to be on duty beyond these hours in order to prepare the craft and secure everything away each evening. Afternoons were the busiest so we operated a shift system of 9 to 5 and 12 to 8 with one day off a week.

We all met up in the staff dining room after the departmental briefings and compared notes. Steve's swimming lessons were mainly restricted to mornings but he also had to cover as a lifeguard during the afternoons and occasional evenings. As the Badger Club operated from 9 to 5, the girls were free every evening unless they wanted to undertake some overtime in other areas. They decided when Steve and I were on late shift, they would take on some overtime but, otherwise, we would leave our evenings as free as we could.

After a meal and a walk, we were all bushed and decided we'd have an early night.

Chapter 12 – John Summer 1985

"We'll have to find a way around the segregation rules, darling," said Anne as we kissed goodnight.

After work next evening, we planned how to do it.

The Greencoats' uniform tracksuits and trainers were unisex so, each evening, Carol could leave the women's quarters and I would leave the men's and we would go jogging. At some convenient place we could meet up. I would tie my hair into a pony tail, apply make-up and pad out my top. She would wear a tight T shirt to conceal her breasts. With her tracksuit hood up, and its bulk concealing her shape, it shouldn't be difficult. I'd open the top of my tracksuit and keep my hood down as I went in to show as much of my altered shape as possible.

Once inside the block, it would be relatively easy. The quarters comprised twin bedded rooms with adjoining bathrooms and toilets. The next morning, we would reverse the process. A piece of cake. Or so we thought.

The next morning Steve and I met the girls for breakfast. As they came out of their block, they looked glum.

"What's up?" I asked.

"We're going to have to think again about how you get into our quarters. One of the other girls and her boyfriend tried the idea of dressing in a tracksuit but they got caught by the supervisor. Seems the old battle-axe is on to that idea and checks everyone wearing unisex clothing especially tracksuits and hooded tops."

"Shit. We'll have to find a plan B then."

"Looks like you may have to go back to your old tricks again. John, it'll have to be the full works to throw her off the scent," said Carol.

"No point looking at me," said Steve. "I don't look anything like either of the girls."

"True; and that fuzz on your top lip would be a bit of a giveaway in any case," I pointed out.

"Don't you go dissing my moustache," Steve protested.

Carol leaned over and stroked his top lip. "I think it looks great, babe," she said, adding a kiss for good measure.

Chapter 12 – John Summer 1985

It was obviously going to be down to Carol and me to swop. We were almost indistinguishable, apart from a couple of obvious differences, thanks to our parents being two sets of identical twins.

Carol held Steve's hand as the other three looked at me. I shrugged my shoulders. I no longer had any qualms about cross dressing. In fact, though I was reluctant to admit it to the others, I quite enjoyed it.

"OK, let's work out how to do it," I said.

"What about the swimming pool? The changing cubicles are all in one block between the central complex and the pool itself and everyone uses the same ones. The pool is also open until 10," suggested Steve.

"It could work," I agreed. "We could have a swim, then Carol could collect her things from my locker and I could collect hers. What about clothes though? I'm a bit taller than Carol now but I don't think that'll be too noticeable. You'll have to flatten your, err, top though Carol." Struggling for a moment to find an acceptable expression.

"I could wear a tight T-shirt under a looser shirt," she suggested. "Not that I'm that well-endowed anyway, unfortunately."

She looked at Steve who just held up his hands. "I'm saying nothing darling. I love you just as you are."

"Get a room you two," laughed Anne.

"I thought that's what we're trying to work out," pouted Carol.

"Right. That should work. If you wear my baseball cap, that'll cover part of your hair and the peak will hide a bit of your face as well," I said, trying to get us back on track.

"Great. What size shoes do you take these days?"

"Eights."

"That may be a problem. Mine are sevens. I don't really want them stretched out of shape," Carol said. "I know. The shop sells flip-flops. We'll buy a pair each of the same colour."

The plan was coming together.

Chapter 12 – John Summer 1985

We returned to our rooms and collected our swimming costumes and met up again in the central complex where we popped into the shop and bought the flip-flops.

The pool was still quite busy and we spent half an hour on the various water shoots. As we splashed around in the waves generated in the main pool, Carol and I swopped locker keys.

Anne and I left the pool first, retrieved our bags and went into the changing cubicles. It was a tight squeeze with both of us in the same cubicle but I needed Anne's help to do my make-up.

I padded out the bra and put her dress on. I rough dried my hair and brushed it back into a pony tail and Anne swopped my ear studs for a pair of Carol's much larger earrings.

Wearing Carol's cardigan over my shoulders, I opened the door to the cubicle and stepped out.

"Hi girls, coming for a drink?" It was Hazel, one of the other Badger Club leaders.

"No thanks, we're meeting the boys," Anne answered.

"OK, see you at breakfast," she replied, walking away.

I looked at Anne and let out the deep breath I'd been holding for the last couple of minutes.

"Phew! That could have been awkward."

Anne slipped her arm through mine. "No problem, you and Carol look so alike and having damp hair after swimming changes your appearance anyway."

"We may look the same but we certainly don't sound the same. If I have to say anything, it'll be a total giveaway."

"Mmmm, good point. You'll have to speak more softly and try to raise your pitch a little bit. If you do have to reply to someone who knows Carol, pretend to cough as though you've got something stuck in your throat. That'll explain any difference."

"Good idea. Oh well, fingers crossed it won't be necessary."

"It'll be worth it, anyway, love." Anne smiled at me and I almost kissed her before remembering I was now 'Carol'.

Back at the accommodation block, we showed our passes to the supervisor who barely glanced at them. Wearing a dress had worked and we were in! We linked arms then almost ran to Anne's room.

As we closed the door to Anne's room behind us, we almost collapsed in a fit of laughter.

"We did it! She was totally fooled. Well done *Carol*. Now come here."

That night we made up for lost time. It was snug, to say the least, sharing a single bed but we weren't complaining.

The next morning, I put on the tracksuit and trainers and trotted off to swop places with Carol. We met up, as arranged, near the boating lake then separated before returning to our own rooms to shower and dress for breakfast.

It had worked! And there was no reason why it shouldn't continue to work. Or so we thought.

A few days later, as Anne and I were about to go into the same cubicle after swimming, we were seen by one of the managers. In spite of our protests that we were engaged, he was adamant we must not share a cubicle.

Obviously, with him around, it would be dangerous to swop roles that evening. Fortunately, to facilitate cleaning, the cubicle walls did not reach the floor — so I was able to pass Carol's clothes back to her and retrieve my own.

We went and had a coffee and consoled each other.

"You'll just have to do your own make-up, darling," whispered Anne as she caressed my leg.

I'd been taking notice of how she had done it each evening, but knew I'd need to practice to achieve the finish she did.

"It's about time you bought your own cosmetics in any case," joked Carol. "My powder and lipstick have been going down fast recently. I hate to ask it, but would you mind getting your own undies too? Mine are getting a bit pulled out of shape."

Chapter 12 – John Summer 1985

"We need a shopping trip," said Anne. "and, as you'll be buying make-up and undies, you need to go as Carol."

I wasn't convinced that this would be necessary but I liked the thought of spending a day cross-dressed with my fiancée's encouragement. I was beginning to wonder if she got a thrill from it as well.

Both Anne and I were off duty the next day. I borrowed some of Carol's clothes and put them on under my tracksuit.

We drove out of Greenbreaks and found a secluded location where I could remove my tracksuit. Anne did my face and we headed for Plymouth.

"Those flip-flops really aren't right for shopping, darling. We need to see about some proper shoes for you."

I wasn't going to argue.

As we drove along, Anne took out a cassette and slid it into the car stereo. Olivia Newton John sang out. "Right, sing along babe. Try to raise your pitch to match hers. It'll help you sound more feminine."

I was sceptical but did my best. By the time we reached the outskirts of the city, I felt that I had lifted my pitch a little. Combined with speaking softly, it might just pass.

After parking the car, Anne hooked her arm through mine and pulled me to a sale rack on the pavement outside one store. She picked up a navy high heel and held it to me. "What about these, Carol. They're an eight and a bargain at just five pounds."

The heel looked so thin and high; I wondered if I'd ever be able to balance on them.

"I think I'd prefer something a bit lower with a thicker heel."

"Well, let's see what they've got inside, but you can try these on as well."

I took a deep breath as Anne pushed the door open and we stepped inside.

Anne seemed to in her element looking through the stock on display and offering suggestions. When we'd found several possibles, she told me to ask the assistant for the shoes in my size.

"Go on," she insisted. "You can do it."

59

Chapter 12 – John Summer 1985

Using my best 'ONJ' voice, I did as instructed.

We then sat down to wait for the assistant to return. She handed me some pop socks to wear while I tried on the shoes.

The navy heels weren't easy to walk in but I did like the way they made my legs look.

"You'll get used to them," Anne whispered. "They do look great."

"I don't know," I told her. "When would I ever wear them? We only need something for shopping."

Anne looked at me, arched her eyebrows and smiled. "Really?" she asked.

By the time I'd tried on six other pairs of shoes and sandals, it felt quite natural to walk up and down and look at them in the mirror and sweep my skirt from underneath me as I sat down. I no longer felt self-conscious speaking to the assistant. After one exchange, I looked at Anne who was had a slight smirk on her face.

"What?" I asked.

"Nothing," she said innocently.

In the end, I bought a pair of sandals with two-inch heels which felt really comfortable. I also bought the navy high heels. I wore the sandals out of the shop and put the flip-flops into the bag with the high heels.

We then went into Boots where Anne selected some make-up for me.

She tried different foundation pan sticks on the inside of my wrist to find the best shade then selected matching powder. A green colour correction stick to hide redness, a palette of eyeshadows, mascara, eyeliner, blusher and a lipstick joined them in the basket along with brushes, a mirror and some cleansers and tissues — and a make-up bag to keep it all in.

Then it was across to Marks and Sparks for some matching sets of bras and knickers and some hold ups. Before we returned to the car, we also picked up some supplies for a picnic.

Shopping completed, we drove north out of the city onto Dartmoor and parked at a secluded spot. Anne then took out the purchases and unpacked them — explaining how each should be applied. "Just use the foundation, powder, lip stick and mascara to start, as little as possible and avoid smudging," she instructed. "Leave the blusher and eyeliner for now. You can practice those in the chalet."

The foundation and powder were relatively easy to learn; getting the eyeshadow evenly applied took a bit more practice — as did applying the mascara without constantly leaving black marks below the bottom lashes and on the eyelids.

Two hours later, Anne declared herself satisfied with my efforts. "You've got the hang of it now, darling." We then drove back to Torbay after I had cleaned off my face and put my tracksuit back on.

That evening, I took longer than Anne had to do my make-up, but the end result wasn't too bad. With my hair in a ponytail, I would still pass muster. I felt quite proud of my efforts.

"Well done," whispered Anne who was waiting for me outside.

"No fiancé tonight?" asked the manager who had previously seen us going into the same cubicle.

"The boys are just coming," Anne replied. Nodding towards them as Steve and 'John' emerged from their cubicles.

As we walked out of the complex, Anne raised a point that I'd been wondering about as well.

"People know John and I are engaged and it must look strange if we are never seen walking back to the chalets together. Same with you and Carol, Steve."

"You've got a point there," Steve agreed. "But I'm not going to kiss this Carol goodnight. I'll hold hands or put my arm around your waist, but I draw the line at kissing," he said to me.

I fluttered my eyelashes and pursed my lips at him and got a dig in the ribs in return. But the point had been made.

That evening, Steve held my hand as we walked to the rooms and Carol had her arm around Anne.

We then noticed some bushes at the side of the block. I pulled Steve with me.

"What's going on?" he protested.

"Be quiet," I told him. I kissed the palm of my hand then pressed it against his lips. My own lipstick now looked as though we'd been doing what engaged couples are expected to do — and he bore evidence of the same activity.

"Good thinking," said Anne, following suit.

The supervisor was well used to us by now and no longer even asked to see our id cards.

Part Three. Autumn 1985 – December 1997

Chapter 13. Mary — Autumn 1985

After sorting out OJ's affairs and helping Penny and Paul to set up their own company, which they called 'The 2 Peas', I decided to take a holiday in Italy.

I missed OJ, of course. You can't lose someone you've been married to for nearly twenty years without them leaving a void. But I have to admit I enjoyed the hustle of setting up a new company and helping it through the first critical months; keeping occupied had certainly helped me too.

Although I had been personal assistant to the Managing Director of an engineering company from the time our daughter, Diane, had started secondary school until ten years ago, OJ had kept me at arm's length when he had been running his business. I was the woman and it was his job to be the provider. Before joining Hall, OJ had earned good money — more than enough to give us a comfortable lifestyle. Even as Hall's partner, he'd continued to draw an excellent salary. It had been after splitting with Hall he had found the going tougher. In spite of the problems he had encountered, he refused to discuss them or give me the opportunity to help. I suppose, on reflection, I could have been more insistent, but I was probably too ready to accept his explanation they were simply the usual ones of starting up a new business.

While in Venice, I spent time considering what I was going to do with the rest of my life. I had no need to work thanks to OJ's insurance. But, at 46, I wasn't prepared to spend all of my time on charity committees, in beauty salons or even just around the house. Diane had left home 2 years ago and was now living, with her husband, Charles, in Bath.

On my return, Penny and Paul welcomed me back and were happy for me to continue helping with the admin side of their agency. Penny had revealed a hidden talent for creative work although she had had no formal design training. Her ideas had proved popular with clients and they had sub-let part of the studio to a freelance artist who could develop her basic concepts and produce finished visuals for presentation to clients and then prepare the artwork ready for printing.

However, there really wasn't enough work to occupy me for more than one day a week; especially as we'd installed one of the latest computers which enabled us to do all of the accounts work, media schedule planning and word processing in a fraction of the time it had previously taken.

Chapter 13 – Mary Autumn 1985

After a '2 Peas' board meeting, a rather grand title for the three of us discussing work in progress and future prospects, Penny asked if I had considered offering the same business management and secretarial service to other small companies.

"Who knows, it might also get us a foot in the door for other work," she had suggested.

"It's certainly worth considering," I agreed.

"You could use your existing office and hold client meetings in the boardroom. You haven't let us pay you for the work you've been doing for us, so we'll come up with some ideas for a direct mail shot to promote the service if you decide to go ahead."

At first, the bureau picked up odd bits of work here and there, but it gradually increased. We were one of the first companies in the area to offer a fax service and this quickly built up the number of customers coming in to see us, leading to other work for several of them.

The word processing side also generated substantial business — especially as we were able to offer a personalised letter service. This linked naturally into the agency's work and resulted in orders for leaflets to accompany these direct mail letters.

By the end of the year, we were becoming stretched for space for both the agency and my bureau so we looked around for alternative premises and found a shop with offices on two floors above.

The shop front was ideal for the secretarial bureau as it was less imposing and far more accessible than a traditional office. It was available on either a lease or could be bought outright. I discussed the alternatives with both our accountant and James Harrison and decided it was a secure investment.

Penny and Paul insisted 'The 2 Peas' should pay a realistic rent for their share of the offices. They pointed out the secretarial bureau was feeding more than enough work their way to cover the cost.

With no need to arrange a mortgage, the formalities were quickly resolved. I told James to inform the vendors we wanted to start refurbishment immediately and if they didn't like it, we would find alternative premises. Our offer was accepted without further ado.

Chapter 14. John — 1986 – 1991

Anne and I got married on 1st July 1987. As our finances were rather stretched after 3 years at college, we spent our honeymoon as guests at the holiday village where we had worked the previous summer — taking advantage of the staff discounts to which we were entitled.

For almost the first time, it was not necessary for me to dress as a girl in order to spend the night with Anne! Even during the last couple of holidays at home we had returned to our previous subterfuge to avoid the risk of gossip for Anne's father's sake.

We took full advantage of all of the entertainments the centre had to offer and joined in the spirit of the crazy games before returning to bed each night and staying there until mid-morning.

Friday evening was "Topsy-Turvey" night — with prizes for the most convincing cross-dressed couple.

Friday morning, Anne left me to go into town.

She returned just before lunch with some packages which she tried to hide in the cupboard while I wasn't looking. I decided to let her have her fun.

Later that afternoon, as we walked back to the chalet, I asked her what weird and wonderful scheme she'd thought up for that evening.

"Wait and see," was all she would say.

Back in our room, she took out the packages. One was a dinner suit with shirt and bow tie; the other a long evening gown.

"No prizes for guessing who is going to wear which," she announced. She then unpacked the underwear we'd bought for me to wear the previous summer and laid it out on the bed together with a new pair of sheer stockings. I'd never grown much body hair — even on my legs and the little I did have was fine and hardly visible as I was naturally blond.

The final items she unpacked were a pair of high heel shoes in my size and a set of false nails.

After I'd had my bath, Anne put heated rollers into my hair. While these did their work, I started to dress and Anne got into her own outfit.

I put on my underwear — and realised I had missed the luxurious silky feel of the feminine garments. Anne had also bought a long slip for me to wear under the dress and once I'd put it on, I sat down at the dressing table and let her apply my make-up. She took the nails and glued them to the end of my own before buffing the join until it was smooth, telling me not to touch anything which might dislodge them before they were set.

Once I had put on the evening dress, she removed the heated rollers and brushed my hair into place before applying hair spray. She then swopped my small gold studs for long diamante earrings, fastened a necklace around my neck and a matching bracelet around my wrist.

The final step was to varnish my nails to match my lipstick and, as a finishing touch, lightly dabbed perfume to the inside of my wrists and behind each ear.

"We are going to knock them dead, darling," she assured me.

I was totally unsurprised when we won the competition. I'd have been amazed if anyone else had done so.

"You really enjoyed this evening, didn't you?" asked Anne as we walked back to our room.

"Yes, darling, I did," I confessed.

"So did I. And I'm sure quite a few of the men there fancied you. Did you see the bloke in the green blazer? He could hardly keep his eyes off you."

As we undressed for bed, Anne told me to keep my undies on as she loved the feel of my things against hers. I was happy to comply. We made love with even more passion than usual that night as our undies rubbed against each other's.

"I'll have to get you dressed up more often," she told me as we lay in each other's arms.

"Whenever you like," I replied.

After the honeymoon, we returned to London and a small flat we found to rent.

It wasn't much, just a bedroom, living room, kitchen and shared bathroom in a turn of the century house in one of the squares in Islington. We had deliberately chosen to live near the city as I'd been offered a job with an advertising agency off Tottenham Court Road and Anne would be working for an international bank near Moorgate. After 12 months' service, she would be entitled to a subsidised mortgage from her employers. That, and the fact we could both expect reasonable increases in salary after a year, meant, by waiting, we would be able to afford a much nicer place than we could currently buy.

On the Monday morning, I walked with Anne to the Angel tube station where she would take the Northern Line to her stop at Moorgate. I then caught my train in the opposite direction before changing onto the Victoria Line at Kings Cross.

I quickly became part of the creative team at the agency — working mainly on press advertising for a chocolate count line, the launch of a new car and a range of consumer electronics.

Anne and I had sold our individual Lasers and had bought a 2-man Laser 2 which we crewed together at King George's Sailing Club in North London. At first, we adopted the usual chauvinistic arrangement of the man helming. But, after a crew's race in which Anne helmed and I took over the trapeze, we realised this was a far better arrangement. My extra weight gave us more balance for stronger winds and she had a finer touch on the helm. I could also concentrate on the tactical decisions of the course to steer and when to tack, while she ensured the sails were set correctly and the boat was sailing as fast as it could.

At home, we settled into married life and made plans for the future. We were earning nearly £8,000 a year between us and could expect this to rise significantly over the next couple of years.

After a year, Anne would be entitled to a subsidised mortgage and, after a further years' service would also be entitled to 6 months maternity leave with a guaranteed job to return to. In a year's time we'd have enough to put down as a deposit on a house and could expect to get a mortgage for the balance. We could then start a family in a couple of years — by which time I anticipated earning as much on my own as we were now earning jointly.

As we were both working, it was reasonable for us to share the work around the house. Whoever arrived home first would start to prepare dinner, then we would share the washing up. Being small, the flat took very little cleaning — a quick tidy, a few minutes with the vacuum and bit of dusting and it was done.

Our sex life was uninhibited and I often wore feminine underwear as I knew Anne enjoyed the sensation of our stocking clad legs rubbing against each other's and the feel of the silky garments she had bought me. Frankly, so did I. Our particular favourites were matching teddies with built in suspenders.

Chapter 14 – John 1986-1991

As I cleaned and dusted the flat one evening while she did the ironing, Anne said she thought I ought to have a maid's outfit to do the housework.

"Why?" I asked. "You don't wear one while you do it."

"I just think you'd look very sexy in a short skirt, black stockings and high heels, darling," she replied. "I'd be able to see your lovely bottom when you bend over."

She walked into the bedroom and called me a few minutes later. "Try these on," she suggested, handing me her own white blouse and black mini skirt. I took out my teddy and stockings, donned the skirt and blouse she had left on the bed then put on the high heels she had bought for me to wear for the Topsy Turvey night.

"That's very sexy," she remarked as I resumed the dusting. "But you haven't done your make-up! Where did we put that make-up we got for you at Greenbreaks?" She took me into the bedroom again and quickly did my face.

"You like seeing me dressed as a girl, don't you?" I asked.

"Yes, it reminds me of when we first made love together," she replied.

While Anne finished the ironing, I made us a coffee. We sat together on the sofa and cuddled up.

"Do you like dressing up?" she asked.

"I don't mind," I told her.

"That's not what I asked. I know that, apart from the panto, you started because it was the only way we could get together. And I know you know I love the feel of our undies against each other. But do you enjoy it?"

"I enjoy anything that gives you pleasure," I told her.

"But, would you do it if you were on your own? Do you get a kick out of being transformed? Do you like the feel of wearing feminine things?"

It was a question I'd been asking myself for a while. At first, I assumed it was because it was associated with making love with Anne. But, if I was being honest, I did get a thrill out of seeing a feminine version of myself and I enjoyed the sensation of a skirt swirling about my legs and the feel of wearing high heels.

68

Chapter 14 – John 1986-1991

"I don't know whether I would do it on my own. But yes, I do enjoy it. Why do you ask? Does it bother you?"

"Goodness, of course I don't mind you enjoying it. Why shouldn't you. You don't think any less of me when I slum around in jeans, T-shirts and trainers. So why should I object if you enjoy doing the exact opposite? You can dress up as often as you like. I'll even help you buy some things of your own if you want to. Why don't we go over to Brent Cross tomorrow?"

I took Anne at her word. The next morning, I shaved very carefully and dressed in one of the bras we'd bought in Plymouth and the blouse and top I'd worn the evening before. I borrowed a pair of tights and Anne brushed my hair into a feminine style then did my make-up and varnished my nails.

"I think I had better drive," she remarked as we walked to our car parked in what had been the garden at the back of the house.

We started by buying a firm controlling pair of panties as there was a danger of my penis getting out of control. Then we went into Fenwicks and found a dress, a skirt and a blouse which would be enough for the time being.

"You really need some make-up of your own, my foundation, powder and lipstick aren't quite right for your complexion," Anne told me.

We went into Boots where Anne helped me choose the right shades.

"Those shoes are a bit over the top for day wear; let's see if we can find something a bit more suitable."

"Aren't we spending a bit much?" I asked as we left Saxones having purchased a pair of plain black courts with a one and half inch wedge heel.

"It's coming out of your pocket money for the month," Anne replied.

Back at the flat, I removed the make-up Anne had applied earlier and under her instruction, practised with the items we had bought earlier. I then changed into my new dress.

"That dress really suits you, darling," Anne told me. "Come on; let's go out for a meal. We can find a Berni Inn or something."

I felt completely relaxed dressed as a girl and even enjoyed it when a car pulled alongside us at some traffic lights and two guys tried to persuade Anne and me to join them for a drink.

69

Chapter 14 – John 1986-1991

As they drove off, their invitation having been politely declined, Anne turned to me and laughed.

"You need a name for when you're dressed. Any ideas?"

"How about Angela?"

"Why not? Though I'm not sure you're Angelic."

That night, as we made love, Anne pulled away from me. She stroked my face and said "Your chin feels a bit rough, darling."

"Do you want me to shave?" I asked.

"No, it's OK. I was just thinking, though, if you're going to dress more as a girl, maybe you should get electrolysis and wax your legs. It would make things easier for you."

IF I was going to dress more as a girl? Was that even a question? If Anne didn't mind, then I knew I would. At least in private — or where there was no chance of being recognised. Having friends or colleagues see me was a different matter. Of course, the family knew about the panto incident — but that was very different to going out in public.

"OK, love; if you think I should." I was still a bit uncomfortable about letting her know how much I wanted to 'dress' — but maybe that was me thinking it was wrong. In any case, it felt safer to give the impression I was going along with her ideas.

"I'll look into it for you, darling. Now, where were we? Oh yes." She pulled me to her and fastened her lips onto mine.

The following week, Anne called a number of beauty salons and asked if they would be prepared to do the electrolysis and waxing for a man. After several refusals, one was quite obnoxious, she located a salon near Swiss Cottage which was prepared to treat me and made an appointment for 6.30 on the Thursday evening.

Instead of my usual Victoria and Northern Line trains from Warren Street that evening, I caught the tube to Swiss Cottage and walked down the hill to the beauty salon. This was new territory for me in more ways than one.

All the way down the hill, I glanced around in case there was someone I knew. More than once, I was tempted to turn around and go home; but the thought of having smooth legs and not having to shave or apply beard cover forced me to continue.

I nervously approached the salon, but was reassured by a signboard on the pavement which announced "Beauty treatments for men and women." Bracing myself, I opened the door and stepped inside.

As I entered, I was greeted by one of the staff. "I won't keep you a moment," she announced. "Please take a seat."

I sat down while she finished accepting a cheque from another customer.

"Mr Parker, is it? I'm Sara. Can I just take down a few details? Is it OK to call you John — or is there another name you'd prefer"

Anne had told me she hadn't given my real name in view of the treatment I was seeking.

"Have you had any electrolysis before? Do you suffer from any skin disorders? Or any heart trouble?"

I replied no to each of her queries. Why would she need to know if I'd had heart problems? Was the procedure dangerous — or so painful? Other than that, the questions seemed so routine and my concerns about how I might be treated started to disappear.

"Fine, would you like to come with me?"

I followed her up the stairs at the back of the reception area and into a curtained off cubicle.

"I'll leave you to strip off from the waist down — you can keep your knickers on, I'll do your legs first." The use of 'knickers' made me pause. Had she realised what I was? Or was it just that most of her clients would be female so it was the usual term for them. Oh well, it didn't really matter.

I lay on the couch and she spread the hot wax with a spatula then pressed strips of cloth into it. I hadn't realised how hot it would be.

As she continued to wax my legs, Sara outlined what was involved in electrolysis. She was quite chatty and I started to relax even more.

"You are likely to experience a tingling sensation which is perfectly normal, it's also quite normal for the skin to redden for about 24 hours after treatment.

Chapter 14 – John 1986-1991

There is a limit to the area we can cover in one session. There will also be hairs which are dormant during the initial treatment and which appear again afterwards. You should realistically expect to take up to a couple of years for the treatment to be completed. Even then we can't promise permanent removal unless you are on hormones."

"I hadn't realised it would take that long," I told her — wondering why someone might be on hormones.

"You won't need to come weekly after the first ten or twelve sessions — once a month for us to deal with any new growth should be enough. So, you are looking at thirty sessions in all for the year. If you want to pay per session, that's fine, but we offer a discount if you pay for the whole years' treatment in advance. You can pay for the full course next time if you wish."

"I'd like to be certain there are no side effects and I can tolerate the treatment before I commit myself" I told her.

"Of course. Now this will be like removing a plaster, only rather larger," she warned.

"Ready?" she asked.

For what I wondered — removing a plaster wasn't that bad. Then I found out as she ripped the cloth off my leg — taking, I was sure, a strip of skin with it.

"Jesus wept," I screamed.

Was this some sort of punishment that Anne was inflicting on me for enjoying cross dressing?

"No pain, no gain, John. Girls have to suffer for our beauty."

My eyes watered as she checked her handiwork. "That's fine, but your hairs will grow again and you'll need the treatment repeating every few months."

She then prepared the electrolysis equipment for use. "I'll start with the top lip and chin," she said. "Those tend to be the most difficult to get really smooth when you are shaving and which usually show through make-up."

I must have looked quizzically at her.

"Sorry, I assumed you are a cross-dresser," Sara remarked, "we do occasionally do electrolysis for men who are fed up with shaving, but they don't normally ask for their legs to be waxed."

Cross-dresser? It was a term I'd always associated with perverts. But I had to face the fact that I was a cross-dresser and that I enjoyed it. I had no desire to go to bed with a man or parade around in tiny miniskirts or wear outlandish make-up like drag artists; but I did enjoy presenting as female and even shopping at Brent Cross had been great once I'd overcome my nerves. Sara didn't seem to care if I was.

I acknowledged, for the first time to someone, I was a cross-dresser and asked if they had many such customers.

"About a half a dozen regulars and some who just come the once for some treatment or who want us to teach them how to do their make-up. It was your wife who made your appointment, wasn't it? You are one of the lucky ones. Most TVs daren't tell their wives.

"How are you feeling? Not too bad, is it?" She asked as she paused the electrolysis. If what I was experiencing was 'tingling' I hated to think what Sara might regard as 'pain'. But having wimped out over the waxing, I wasn't going to complain again.

"No, I think I'm getting used to the sensation."

"If you want some lessons on make-up or a make-over at any time, don't hesitate to let us know. But give us some warning if it's on one of the Tudor Lodge nights, they tend to be our busiest afternoons."

"What are the Tudor Lodge nights?" I asked.

"The TV balls at the Tudor Lodge. Haven't you heard of them? Do you know about the meetings in Islington?"

"No. I haven't been involved at all in that sort of thing, just with my wife." I explained to Sara how I had started dressing as a girl to get into the women's quarters at the holiday camp but now wanted to go out dressed.

"I'll give you a copy of Glad Rag, the magazine produced by the group that meets in Islington; I advertise in it so they send me a few copies. It gives you details of their venue and times and has an advert for the Tudor Lodge."

Chapter 14 – John 1986-1991

I wasn't sure if I wanted to go to any meetings or attend the balls — I had no idea what went on at them. Were they glorified orgies? Would the other cross-dressers be outrageous? Would they belittle me, recognising that I was a newcomer? Would they laugh at my appearance or criticise?

Anne had arranged to meet me at the salon at 7.30, having picked the car up from the flat, and was sitting in reception waiting for me. I paid my bill and confirmed I would be back the following week.

"How did it go?" asked Anne, fastening her seat belt, "was it painful?"

"Yes. No, not too bad," I replied, not wanting to appear a wimp. Then I decided to tell the truth "Actually yes. You could have warned me," I said as I started the engine, then pulled out from the kerb. "Sara, the beautician, told me about a club for cross-dressers which meets in Islington and about some gala events held at the Tudor Lodge. She gave me a copy of the group's magazine — here, have a look at it."

"The address is just down the road from us, darling. They meet on Fridays & Saturdays, do you fancy going along to see what it's about? They say partners are also welcome."

"What, tonight?" I felt I'd stepped onto a fairground ride that I couldn't get off even if I'd wanted to. But did I want to get off?

"Why not? It shouldn't take us more than 20 minutes to get home and half an hour to get changed. We could be there by nine at the latest," I looked across at Anne, she squeezed by knee – "Come on, you know you want to. It should be fun."

I rested my hand on hers and said, "OK."

At home, Anne called the telephone number given for the club to check it was open while I had a quick shower and shave, put on my undies and did my make-up, pulled on my new dress and stepped into my heels. I brushed my hair into a more feminine style and sprayed some lacquer to keep it in place and slipped on some jewellery and stuck on false nails.

Anne then lent me a jacket and hand bag and we left the flat for the short walk to the group's meeting place. It was scary walking down the street past pubs spilling revellers out onto the street. As we passed one, a guy stumbled out of the door and nearly collided with us. "Sorry ladies," he remarked as he stepped aside for us to pass.

I looked at Anne and we both laughed but as we approached the door to the support group, my nerves failed me.

"I've changed my mind. Let's go home." I went to grab Anne's arm but she was already ringing the bell. The door buzzed and she pushed it open.

"We're here now. Come on. We can always leave immediately if you aren't comfortable."

"What if there's someone here we know — or from work?"

"If they're here, it'll be for the same reason as you. What is there to worry about? They won't say anything about you and you won't say anything about them."

Inside the club, we found ourselves in a room with a bar offering a choice of coffee or wine. Just past the bar were steps leading down to another area with a separate room beyond used by some of the members for changing. There were about eight or ten others standing at the bar or sitting at tables. At least my worries that it might be a sex party were unfounded — it all looked relatively normal.

A tall cross-dresser came over to us. "Hello, I'm Yvette. You must be Anne and Angela — we don't use surnames here; we spoke on the phone. What would you like to drink?"

We accepted a glass each of wine and sat at one of the tables with Yvette. Yvette explained she had helped to form the club some years earlier to provide support for cross-dressers and transsexuals. It was a constant struggle to survive and there was a continuous turnover of members.

I scanned the room. There were some who were very obviously men dressed as women but I couldn't tell if some of the others were or if they might be the cross-dressers' partners. As I looked around, I realised that my own presentation was more convincing than most. Anne squeezed my hand smiled at me and gave me a wink.

"Obviously not all members can get here every week. We have some who just want to receive our monthly newsletter and probably just fantasise about coming out. Others come here for the few times when they are just starting dressing then drift away when they feel they don't need us anymore. They don't consider the fact that is when they could be in a position to help others and repay the advice they've received. Sorry, I'm on my pet subject there."

"So, tell me about yourself, Angela. As much or as little as you want to reveal. We respect other's confidences and understand any reluctance to give out too much personal information."

I told Yvette why I had started dressing, that I enjoyed it and saw no reason not to continue even though I no longer needed to do it to spend the night with Anne.

"You're very lucky, most of our members' wives don't know their husbands are TVs and they are too scared to reveal the fact. There have been too many instances when the wife has been unwilling to accept their husband's transvestism. Some regard it as a perversion, others think it means their husband is gay, some have felt challenged by the husband dressing as a woman. They think it makes them less than a total woman — yet they are quite happy adopting part of a man's role, working, driving, being involved in decision making and wearing trousers. Those would have been the man's prerogative even thirty years ago." Yvette paused to take a sip of her wine and light a Peter Stuyvesant cigarette.

I realised that I was, indeed, very fortunate with Anne who not only accepted me as Angela but actively encouraged me and joined in.

"Where was I? Oh yes. Over the course of this century, women have started to do nearly everything a man would. They regard it as equality and I don't have anything against that. But to then complain if a man dresses as a woman, the wife's femininity is challenged is ridiculous."

Yvette waved to another girl who had just come in. She would have been around six feet tall even without the five-inch heels she was wearing. Her wig was long, straight and blonde. I realised that most of those present were blonde with one auburn and one jet black. I thought, apart from me, only one of the other trans people had their own hair. It was quite apparent that the wigs made it obvious that they were trans.

"Some wives do accept their husband's transvestism. Some will actively support it, but they are in the minority. Others tolerate it, but won't get involved and some will just ignore it completely. I suppose the worst problems arise when it's been a secret for a very long time. The wife then feels cheated because her husband didn't trust her enough to tell her the truth. Or because he will have lied to her to cover up his activities. Or even because he's probably spent a fair bit of money on clothes, wigs, make-up and other bits and pieces."

"I can understand that point of view," I said. I hugged Anne to show my appreciation for her support.

"So can I, Angela, but it's because they are scared of their wives or colleagues and friends' reactions' most TVs keep their dressing secret. And that is why places like this exist. To give TVs somewhere where they can come and relax. Where they can dress as they like, get advice if they need it and, most important of all, know they are not alone. You wouldn't believe the number of people who thought they were the only one who cross-dressed, who didn't even know there was a word for it, let alone there are support groups and shops which specialise in TV accessories."

Yvette continued with what was clearly a speech she gave to all newcomers.

I asked how many other clubs there were in the UK. When she told me there were five other similar clubs that she knew of, plus a national organisation with members all over the country, I realised that I was far from alone.

"It must be difficult to run a group like this. Don't you get unwanted attention? What do your family and friends think?"

"I live on my own in a tower block and my neighbours know I go out dressed as a woman. If they don't like it, I tell them to just ignore me."

I was amazed. I couldn't imagine having the confidence to just walk out of the flat not caring what others thought. Maybe I'd get there some day. Then I realised that I had left our flat as Angela and walked here. God knows where I'd got the courage from to do it.

"What's this in the magazine about the Tudor Lodge balls?" asked Anne.

"They're events for trannies and drag queens — and the guys who fancy them. Everyone gets dressed up to the nines — and over the top."

"What's the difference between drag and cross-dressing?" asked Anne

"Most cross-dressers dress to imitate women, often their idea of a sexy woman. It doesn't always work, I mean a six-foot, eighteen-stone bricklayer doesn't look sexy in a short mini-skirt and thigh-high boots. But in their mind, they should be on page three of the Sun. Drag is a parody of women, much more theatrical and some do go on the stage in pubs and clubs."

She then excused herself to have a word with one of the other members.

"Sorry about that," she said when she returned. "I wanted to check if Michelle was going on to the Philbeach later — are you coming, we usually get a couple of cabs?"

"What's the Philbeach?" I asked.

"It's a gay hotel in Earls Court, there's a disco and a late bar. There's usually a few guys hanging round looking for trannies which is why Michelle likes it."

"Are many cross-dressers gay?" asked Anne.

Yvette took another sip of wine before continuing.

"There is no actual link between being a cross-dresser and being gay — any more than being blue eyed makes you right-handed. Because we are both subject to bigotry, we tend to be more tolerant of each other so it's almost inevitable we mix in a lot of areas. We share these premises with a gay help-line, for example. Some gay clubs will admit TVs — but by no means all. But this means TVs are likely to be seen around or in the company of gays. So, people assume TVs, or a large proportion of them, are gay. We don't ask members about their sexual preferences. That's their business. But some are completely straight, others are bi-sexual, some are a-sexual and some are gay. Some wouldn't consider sex with another man when they are dressed in male clothes but like to be treated as a woman when they're dressed as one. Some will go out with men on dates, others will let men kiss and caress them and others like to have sex with men because they consider it's the ultimate feminine experience they can enjoy."

I saw Anne's eyebrows raised at this comment.

"Then you get male prostitutes who dress as women only to attract customers who don't want to admit to themselves that they are gay. Some of them live all the time in the female role and think that's the only way they can earn money to live on."

Yvette paused to stub out her cigarette.

"Anyway, I've talked enough for now. Let me introduce you to some of the others."

Chapter 14 – John 1986-1991

We spent the evening being given information about shops which specialised in TV products, including false breasts, and about events such as the forthcoming ball at the Tudor Lodge and weekends away in Weston-Super-Mare. I noticed Anne writing some of these details into a small notebook.

We decided to go on to the Philbeach and, as she'd only had one glass of wine, Anne went back to the flat to collect our car and returned a few minutes later.

We gave two other TVs, Michelle and Kym, a lift to the hotel so they could direct us if we lost touch with the other car.

At the hotel, Anne and I danced together at first, but when Kym asked if I minded if she danced with Anne, I raised no objection.

At first, I sat on a bench seat talking to Michelle while they danced. Michelle was then invited to dance by one of a group of men which had arrived shortly after us. Another of the group walked over to me and sat down.

"Fancy a drink, love?" he asked.

"No thanks. I've just got one," I replied wishing he'd leave me alone.

"Cigarette?"

"I don't smoke thanks."

"Mind if I do?"

"Please yourself."

He reached across to take the ashtray and his leg touched mine as he did so. He then shuffled to make himself comfortable, moving closer to me as he did so. I shifted along the seat to create a space between us. Where was Anne when I needed her?

"On your own, darling?"

"No, I'm here with my wife and some friends."

He looked shocked. "Sorry, I didn't realise you were a bloke."

As we'd been told this was a gay hotel, I wasn't sure what else he had expected.

Out on the tiny dance floor, Anne was still dancing with Kym. In spite of the quick tempo, Michelle was in a clinch with her partner whose hands were fondling her bottom. I saw Michelle lift her head away from her partner's and watched as they kissed. They then whispered something to each other and I saw a look of horror appear in the man's face as he let Michelle go and walked back to his friends.

Michelle then returned to the table. "Silly sod thought I was a woman. Seems it's a stag party and the best man thought it would be amusing to play tricks on some of the others as well as the groom! Damn! I thought I was in with a chance there!"

Kym and Anne came back to our table, then Michelle and Kym returned to the dance floor.

"What was all that about?" Anne asked as she sat down. I explained what had happened and she laughed.

"I can see why he might have thought you were a girl, but Michelle? She's five foot eleven if she's an inch and must weigh fifteen stone. Still, it's not that light in here."

Anne's hand slipped under my skirt and fondled the top of my stockings. "Ready to go?" she asked.

I picked up my handbag and coat and went over to Yvette and the others to say goodnight. Yvette kissed me on the cheeks — "Don't worry, it's no more than French men do to each other. Hope to see you again next week."

Anne and I climbed the stairs to the front door of the hotel and walked to our car.

As we drove up Warwick Road, Anne asked me if I had enjoyed myself. I told her I had and asked what she thought about the evening.

"Great. I learned a lot tonight, and it's given me plenty to think about. I have to admit I'd been a bit concerned about the possibility of you being at least bi-sexual because you enjoyed dressing as a girl and I'm not sure I could handle that. But I can now see the two are unrelated and that's set my mind at ease."

"Then you wouldn't mind if we keep going to the group, or on one of the weekends or Tudor Lodge."

"Not at all. But I have a feeling the Weston weekend is the same dates as my company conference so you may have to go on your own."

Chapter 14 – John 1986-1991

Over the next three years, I continued my dressing and Anne usually accompanied me to the drag balls and some of the weekend events. She wasn't particularly interested in attending the group evenings but encouraged me to go on my own — especially after we moved out of Islington to our own house near Harlow.

I'd realised soon after joining the ad agency, I was a competent designer and reasonable copywriter, but hardly likely to win awards or graduate to Art Director with one of the leading agencies.

I had, however, found I was good at presenting work and interpreting clients' instructions. So, I enrolled in an Advertising course at a college on Leicester Square. At the end of my first year, I applied for an Account Executive's position with another agency and was accepted. This move meant a big pay rise plus a company car.

By the end of the course, I'd been promoted and given another rise and was on course for a substantial bonus based on my clients' spend. Anne was still working for the bank having miscarried some three months earlier. We were concerned about the possible contribution the travelling might have had to losing the baby and she had applied for a vacancy with the regional headquarters of one of the High Street banks. As they were looking to set up a service similar to the one she was already handling, she was able to negotiate an excellent remuneration package which meant our mortgage payments would remain the same.

We even considered moving house to a larger one on the grounds that property prices were increasing rapidly. Instead, Anne suggested we should invest in a second house which we could rent out.

I was now responsible for three of the agency's clients. A leading computer company, a confectionery count line and the holiday centre where Anne and I had worked. In fact, my personal experience of working at the holiday village had been a contributing factor to the agency's acquisition of the account.

Since moving onto the account handling side, I had realised I needed to learn more about marketing and had enrolled for a two-year Diploma course. This would not only help me to appreciate more about the way our clients' advertising fitted into the overall marketing strategy, it would open up some additional opportunities for future career moves.

Chapter 15. Mary — 1986-91

Our campaign to promote the bureau by distributing leaflets to hotels in the area proved very successful — but, then, it would have been a pretty poor show if the 2Ps hadn't produced effective work for it.

There was an average of more than one call per day for some form of secretarial work, usually transcribing Dictaphone tapes, preparing reports from handwritten notes or telexing or faxing messages back to their head offices throughout the world. Few of the jobs amounted to more than £50 but, together, they generated a significant turnover.

Occasionally we were asked to provide a secretary to take notes at business meetings and provide minutes. We prided ourselves on a fast, efficient service and aimed to get the reports back to clients within a couple of hours.

In March 1986, we were asked to cover a meeting involving an American who was finalising negotiations with Conroys, a local company, to distribute its products throughout the UK. We prepared an agenda for the meeting and, as usual, were able to type and print off the required number of minutes and deliver them back to the hotel before those involved had finished celebrating their deal in the bar. I decided to take the documents to them personally and was invited to join them for a drink.

"This is mighty fine work, Mary," Neil Patterson, the American, commented when checking the notes. "I'll be sure to recommend you to any of my associates in the states when they come over here. I don't suppose you know of an advertising agency which could handle the launch do you?"

"As it happens, I do. I'm involved with a local agency here in Southampton. They really are very good," I told him.

"Is that so? Well, if they're as good at their job as you've been at yours, we'd better see them. I don't suppose they'd be available now, would they?"

"I'll give them a call and find out."

Penny answered the phone and I explained the position. I heard her check that Paul was free, then she told me they would be right over. Within half an hour, Paul was showing Neil, Trevor and Stuart the agency's portfolio.

Neil asked some relevant questions about the briefs provided for each job and how the results had been monitored. Paul answered each query as honestly as he could, but said many clients were reluctant to pass on information about responses to advertisements or how successful individual leaflets had been.

"I sometimes wonder if they think we'll put up our prices if they tell us the creative work has been particularly successful," he remarked.

His replies seemed to satisfy Neil and the guys from Conroys.

"This work is certainly better than some of that done by our existing agency," commented Trevor. "If the launch goes as well as I expect, we'd better talk to you about our other campaigns. What do you think, Stuart?"

"I couldn't agree more," replied Stuart.

Neil then turned to money.

"We've allocated a budget of around £200,000 to launch the product. Is that the sort of account you can handle?"

I saw Penny raise her eyebrows at the amount and glance at Paul.

"It would be the largest individual account, but, yes, we can handle it," Paul answered. "If you'd been talking about much more, we might have been considering some television advertising and that's an area we don't have experience of. But at that level, we'd almost certainly be thinking about press, direct mail, literature and PR. And we have experience of all of those areas."

Neil looked over at Trevor and Stuart.

"Would you excuse us for a few minutes?" He asked.

The three of us left them to discuss the matter.

As we waited in another part of the bar, out of sight of them, Penny and Paul were apprehensive. "This will nearly double our turnover, if we get the account," said Penny.

"Worried?" I asked.

"A bit. It's a huge jump and I wouldn't want to be so heavily dependent on one client."

"Could be a springboard to bigger things though," said Paul.

I had every confidence in their ability to do the work and told them so.

"Well, fingers crossed anyway," said Penny.

I knew, from the documents we had typed, Neil was putting up the launch budget so, obviously, he had the main say in who would handle the account. He'd seemed impressed with Penny and Paul, nevertheless, he also needed to be certain Trevor and Stuart were happy.

A few minutes later, Neil signalled us to re-join them.

He held out his hand to Penny.

"Looks like you've got yourself an account."

"Thank you very much. I'm sure you won't regret it. However, we will need to take up some references and do a credit check on Conroys. I'm sure you understand."

"I would have been disappointed if you hadn't done so. Please go ahead. I think you'll find my company is reasonably sound and I took the same precaution with Conroys before even meeting them," replied Neil. "Now, how about joining us for a meal?"

The credit checks came through with a couple of days. Penny was horrified when she saw the report on Neil.

"I had the nerve to ask if he was OK for £200,000. His companies have a net value of $35 million and his personal fortune is estimated at more than eight million."

The 2 Peas prepared launch proposals for Conroys and offered a freelance PR consultant desk space and an account executive to work on both the new and existing business. They were determined not to make the mistake OJ had of concentrating on the new account to the detriment of existing clients.

But the contract with Conroys was not the only consequence of the bureau's prompt service at the original meeting.

Three months later, at the beginning of August, I had a telephone call from the US.

"Mary Jones? Hi. My name is Arthur Wilkes. A friend of mine, Neil Patterson, suggested I call you. I'm coming over to the UK next month and need some secretarial work. I'm over for around three weeks visiting various parts of England — London, Bristol, Cardiff, Liverpool and Glasgow. I need someone who can also drive me around as I hate driving on the wrong side of the road. I'd want a decent size car, doesn't have to be American, say a Jaguar or something small like that would do. Can you handle that?"

His Texan accent had grated. A Jaguar — small? And I wasn't at all sure the Welsh or Scots would consider Cardiff and Glasgow to be part of England! But business was business and if Neil had recommended us, I didn't want to let him down.

"Three weeks you say. What are the exact dates?"

"I'm arriving Heathrow on Concorde on September 3rd and leave again on September 24th."

I checked the diary and thought about it. I knew none of my staff would want to spend three weeks away from home. But there was no reason why I couldn't do it myself.

"May I make one thing perfectly clear, Mr Wilkes? We can provide a secretarial service and drive a car for you. But that is all. I'm sorry to mention it, but we have had some overseas visitors who think that more personal services might be included but they are not."

"Hell, sorry ma'am, I understand perfectly. I hope you don't object to me buying your staff dinner. I hate dining alone."

"I'm sure that would be acceptable. In fact, I would be the one to accompany you."

"That's fine Mary, I hope you don't mind me calling you Mary?"

"Not at all Mr Wilkes. Can ..."

"Please call me Arthur," he interrupted.

"OK, Arthur. Now can I take down some details of where you wish to stay and when and the sort of hotel you prefer. Or have you already dealt with that?"

"My secretary has booked the hotels. I had her reserve two rooms at each one. Do you have a fax?"

I gave him our number.

"Fine, I'll fax my schedule to you."

"Don't you wish to discuss our fee for the trip?"

"No. Neil said you were reliable and fair. You work out what you think is appropriate and I'm sure it will be fine. I'll settle the bills for hotels, car hire, gas and any other incidentals."

"Fine. I look forward to receiving the fax. Goodbye."

"Talk to you soon, Mary."

I thought about what to charge. Our usual rates were £6 per hour, plus travel. Clearly travel costs wouldn't come into it but how many hours should I charge for each day? I was sure they would be long days but I didn't want to look greedy — this trip could lead to others if I handled it sensibly.

Arthur's fax arrived as I made the decision to set the fee at £1,000.

The schedule not only showed dates and locations but detailed individual meetings. There was a note at the foot asking if I could find suitable restaurants for lunches and, in a few cases, somewhere to entertain his clients.

The telephone rang again as I finished reading the message.

"Mary? Arthur Wilkes. Did you get the fax?"

"Yes, I've just been looking through it."

"Any problems?"

"None I can see. I have assessed the fee for the work and I'm afraid it will have to be £1,000 plus Value Added Tax."

"From your tone, you figure I might think that's high. Am I right?"

"Yes, but I've based it on eight hours per day and no additional charges for weekends."

"I guessed as much. Well, I figure you'll be looking at more like twelve hours a day as I expect to be on the road by eight thirty at the latest and I don't see you finishing meetings until gone seven or eight at night, later some nights. My policy, Mary, has been to ensure I get a fair deal, but not to screw suppliers or staff. That way people work harder for me and I end up the winner. Doesn't always work. I sometimes get screwed instead, but only the once and I then pass the word around. Now I reckon you'll earn every penny of double the fee you suggested.

Let's face it, you're going to do two jobs, driving and secretary. So, I'll pay you £2,000. Is that fair enough?"

I wasn't about to argue.

On 3rd September, I collected a Jaguar from a car hire firm in Southampton and drove up to Heathrow. I was dressed in my usual business attire of a skirt suit and blouse.

At the airport, I took the sign the 2Ps had produced for me with Arthur's name and made my way over to the arrivals area. Concorde was not due to land for an hour as I had allowed plenty of time for the drive, in case of delays. I decided to have a coffee and review his itinerary while I waited.

I hadn't been sure what to expect. From his Texan drawl, I had visions of a cowboy or an oilman. But the distinguished man that walked up to me might well have bought his suits in Saville Row. His six-foot six frame made me feel dwarfed.

"Mary? I'm very pleased to meet you." His handshake was firm but not crushing.

I enquired about his flight as we walked back to the car and placed his suitcases next to mine in the boot. He had, apparently, been in Washington for a meeting with a group of Senators concerned about the Japanese penetration of US markets.

As we drove out of the airport, he expounded on his opinion of the Japanese and their marketing activities.

"To some extent, I sympathise with them. They need to develop overseas markets; they produce products people want and at prices they can afford to pay. But they then do everything they can to limit imports and that's going to result in a backlash sooner or later."

I concentrated on my driving as I was still not completely used to such a large powerful car.

"You British are going to suffer more than most from the Japs. They've already killed your motorcycle industry and are hitting consumer electronics hard. You invented television, but you don't now have single British owned manufacturer. Foreign companies have bought up all of them or have set up their own plants. It's not just the Japs. As well as Sony in Wales, Toshiba in Plymouth, Sanyo in Lowestoft and others about to do the same, you've got Phillips running the remains of most of the original UK manufacturers. Frankly, I don't understand what your government is playing at."

I had to agree with Arthur. But I wondered what his plans were. He must have sensed my unspoken questions.

"I own a group of companies in the states. But I've got a lot of respect for British inventiveness. I'm here to see where we can invest in new ideas in all sorts of fields. I'm also interested in setting up some research centres to look into possible applications for new technologies — lasers, computers, bioengineering, whatever. Take computers for example. Ten years ago, a computer meant a special room with programmers and operators working round the clock to justify the multi-million-dollar investment. Five years ago, Mini computers started to penetrate the market, but you were still talking upwards of thirty thousand dollars and something the size of a desk. Now you can buy a computer to sit on a desk for around a thousand dollars. Within the next ten to fifteen years, you'll see them on nearly every office desk. You probably think I'm mad, Mary. But I'll be proved right."

"I don't doubt you. We've had an IBM personal computer for a year now and wouldn't be without it. I can certainly see most companies investing in at least one."

"Hell, I'm not just talking about one per company, I'm talking about one for every executive and his secretary. And they'll be able to do almost as much as some of the mainframe models sold today. I've seen some of the research that's being done. Your machine will be obsolete within five years and the one that replaces it obsolete within three. Each step will more than double the processing power. By the middle of the next decade, you'll have desktop computers handling data 20 times faster than yours. Built in hard drives with a capacity of 100 times the 10 megabytes yours probably has; floppy disks taking ten times as much data. And programmes will be so much more powerful than today's they'll need that storage capacity. Programmes we can't even dream of at the moment."

We had arrived at the hotel in Kensington High Street. I pulled up the ramp in front of the entrance and a green coated doorman came over and opened Arthur's door. I opened the boot and he took our cases into the lobby. Arthur followed him to register while I drove the car down the spiral ramp to the underground car park.

Chapter 15 – Mary 1986-1991

As I threaded the car through the narrow confines, I wished I'd been driving my usual Mini. But I eventually managed to manoeuvre it into a space and, having locked it, I took the lift back up to ground level and met Arthur again in the lobby.

He handed me my key and told me my bags had been taken up to my room. The lifts were just to the right of the reception desk.

"Order what you want from room service. I'll meet you for dinner at 8 in the rooftop restaurant then we can go over tomorrow's schedule. I'm going to have a bath and a nap. OK?"

The next two weeks involved meetings, often two per day, with companies and individuals with ideas, but not the resources to develop them. At this stage, Arthur was gathering information and, more importantly, assessing those involved in the projects.

"A guy with drive and a halfway decent idea is more likely to succeed that someone with a brilliant idea but no drive," he explained.

In the final week of his tour, we revisited six of the projects to discuss possible arrangements in more detail. In each case, Arthur offered to provide limited financing to allow the ideas to be developed. Further injections of capital would be made available if progress was satisfactory. Only one of those approached declined his offer in favour of a selling their basic concept to a Korean company.

When he returned the following April, we revisited the companies in which he had invested and reviewed progress. He hadn't expected any of them to have reached fruition, but was clearly frustrated with one project. The team had had an excellent idea, but had made far less progress than might have been expected. It wasn't they had encountered unforeseen problems; rather they hadn't given the project the commitment they had promised.

As we drove away, Arthur turned to me and said, "What I need is someone to keep a regular eye on these projects. It's all very well having monthly reports, but it doesn't convey the attitudes of the people involved. How would you feel about attending monthly progress meetings on my behalf?"

It would amount to around five days per month which I could fit into my schedule if I took on another secretary in the office. As Arthur's fee would cover her salary, I agreed.

Chapter 15 – Mary 1986-1991

Over the next three years, Arthur's interests rapidly increased and I found myself spending nearly all of my time on his business.

Arthur still visited the UK but only once a year; leaving me to evaluate initial proposals, decide on investments and monitor progress. Once a month, I flew to Washington by Concorde to report to him, returning the next day.

It was a hectic schedule but I thrived on it.

In 1991, Arthur tried to persuade me to join the main board of Intertrade Developments Inc. in the USA. His Vice President was due to retire at the end of 1992 and he wanted me to take his place.

I asked him for time to consider and talk to my family and promised to give him my decision the following month. Diane her husband Charles and their two children said they would miss having me around but, if I wanted to go, then they would visit regularly.

I accepted Arthur's offer the following month. I pointed out it would take a couple of months to sort out my affairs and said I would join him in January 1992.

Chapter 16. John — 1991-5

On the third of July 1991, two days after our fourth wedding anniversary, Anne gave birth to a daughter.

Samantha had our blond hair and blue eyes — and Anne's determination to get her own way. She saw no reason why the entire universe shouldn't revolve around her and, if her grandparents had had their way, she would have been spoiled rotten.

Anne's original intention had been to return to work after having the baby. We could certainly afford to employ a live-in nanny to look after Samantha during the day, and we had ample room at the house, with its granny annex above the garage. Anne eventually decided, however, that Samantha's early years were likely to be far more interesting than dealing with international finance. Once her maternity leave expired, she went to see her former boss and resigned from the bank.

Her decision had come as no great surprise and the girl who had been employed on a temporary basis was offered the post full time, much to her relief as other jobs were becoming scarce as the recession started to bite.

Chapter 16 – John 1991-5

Apart from sleepless nights, and worrying about the slightest snuffle or cough, the next twelve months passed relatively uneventfully.

I was still travelling to the London agency which was involved in the usual battles to win and retain new clients and produce exciting creative work for some basically uninteresting products. Budgets were already being reduced and clients were demanding more and more for their money.

On the leisure front, Anne had given up sailing when she was expecting, but I'd been fortunate to find another crew when an old school friend had moved to the area. We had decided our combined weight demanded something rather beefier than the Laser II Anne and I had been sailing and opted for a 5-0-5, one of the fastest dinghies around at the time.

Although we were members of a local club, we tended to take the boat to open meetings around the country, competing against some of the best dinghy sailors in the world. Had we been prepared to forgo all alcohol, lose a couple of stone between us and train every day, maybe we would have been able to match some of the performances we encountered.

As it was, we were usually in the lower half of the top 20% of the results — which we considered acceptable.

Unfortunately, Ian moved jobs again after a couple of seasons which made it difficult to practice together when we were not away at an open meeting. By then, however, Samantha was old enough to be left in the club crèche so Anne and I resumed our old crewing arrangement.

In 1994, I had been at an exhibition in Cologne and was breaking my return trip with a stopover in Amsterdam staying at the hotel near the Leidseplein.

After a scented bubble bath, I put on some silky undies, did my make-up then put on a calf length black dress and an evening jacket and went out to a club that had been recommended by one of my TV friends.

I was invited to join a group sitting at one of the tables and was soon chatting away as though I'd known them for years. As well as two other cross-dressers, there were three guys. One of them asked me if I'd like to dance and I agreed. He led me to the dance floor and we were soon jiving to an old Elvis number. After a couple of other relatively fast dances, the tempo slowed. I allowed Erik to put his arms around me and I rested my hands on his shoulders. He started to caress my bottom so I moved his hands back up to my waist and told him I was quite happy dancing in his arms but I wasn't looking for sex. He accepted my comment.

We returned to the table after a few more numbers. I then noticed someone was taking photographs of the various groups and couples.

Erik took hold of my hand and kissed it. "You are a very lovely lady," he told me "and I'm very sad you will not let me treat you like one."

"I'm happily married," I told him "and do not go to bed with men."

"Are you scared of Aids?" he asked, "I'm very clean."

"Of course I'm scared of Aids — but that's not the only reason. I'm a cross-dresser, not gay."

"But you like being a lady, no?"

"Yes, I like being treated as a lady — but only so far."

"OK, I understand. No bed, but we can dance close, yes?"

"Yes. We can dance together if you wish."

"Come then."

We returned to the dance floor and with my limits made clear, I allowed him to hold me close and fondle me if he wished. I also allowed him to press his cheek against mine and even to kiss me gently on the lips, although I did pull away when he started to give me a longer, more passionate kiss. In spite of the fact it was a very pleasant sensation.

At the end of that dance, I told Erik I needed the toilets and he said he would get me another drink while I used the loo.

Having powdered my nose, I re-joined him at the table. I declined a cigarette he offered but told him to go ahead and smoke if he wanted to.

He rested his hand on my knee and fondled my leg, then put his arm around me and kissed me. I realised he was going to become ever more forceful in his attempts to bed me, so I told him I had to leave. I retrieved my jacket from the cloakroom and made my way to the exit. Erik was waiting for me.

"I will take you back to your hotel."

"It's only just across the bridge," I told him.

"It is not safe for you to walk on your own."

He put his arm around my waist as we strolled over the bridge and into the lobby of the hotel. I still had the key to my room so I walked straight to the lift.

Erik pressed the button and the doors opened immediately.

"I must see you to your room," he insisted as the doors closed behind us. I pressed the button for the second floor and stepped to the other side of the lift from Erik.

At my room, I turned to Erik.

"Thank you. You are a perfect gentleman; I have enjoyed your company but this is where you stop."

Erik then put his arm around my waist. "You will let me kiss you goodnight though?"

That seemed a reasonable request. "Just one."

He fastened his lips to mine and held me close as I rested my hands on his shoulders. His hands ran up and down my back and squeezed my bottom, and I could feel his erection pressing against my thigh as I struggled to break loose. As he tried to thrust his tongue between my lips, I opened my mouth then started to bite. This had the desired effect and Erik reluctantly released me.

I put the key into the lock and opened the door. Erik was still holding my waist.

"I told you I'm not interested in sex with you, Erik, so please go now. Otherwise I shall get angry and I shall hurt you."

"OK, Angela. I will go. But it is a pity, we could have made beautiful music together. Maybe some other time."

I leaned forward and gave him a quick peck on the lips then turned and closed the door behind me.

That, had been the furthest I had allowed any man to go. I remembered what Kym had said at the first Tudor Lodge Ball I had attended about being treated as a lady by men being part of dressing for her. I now understood what she had meant.

I went over to the bed and, after taking off my jacket and dress. As I sat down at the dressing table to remove my make-up, there was a knock at the door. If this was Erik again, I would be angry with him.

I put on my negligee and looked through the spy hole. It wasn't Erik but another man wearing a raincoat.

"Please open the door Mr Ives, it's the manager."

I put the chain on the door and opened it.

"What do you want?" I asked.

"Please open the door so I can come in."

"I don't believe you are the manager; you wouldn't be wearing a raincoat if you were," I told him.

"You are quite right, but unless you want photographs such as this one to reach your wife, you had better do as I ask."

The polaroid photographs showed me dancing in Erik's arms.

I opened the door and allowed him to enter.

"What do you want?" I asked.

"You have two choices Mr John Ives of 40 Tern Close, Little Willington, Essex. You can do as we ask and we will pay you £200 and we give you these pictures; or you can refuse and they will be sent to your wife."

"How did you get my name and address?" I demanded.

"Hotel staff are not well paid and a few guilders is all it takes to see your registration card. You really have been very careless this evening."

"What do you want me to do?"

"We have some bottles of special Advocat which some friends in England enjoy. All we ask is you take it with you and they will meet you shortly after you leave the ferry. Presumably you will be taking the Hook to Harwich?"

"Yes, I'm booked on tomorrow night's trip — or, I suppose I should say tonight's as it is now 2am. What is in the bottles? You wouldn't be going to all this trouble just for some Advocat?"

"That is not your business. Just do as you are told and you will be slightly richer. Refuse and you will have some explaining to do to your wife."

"How do I know you'll keep your side of the bargain? What if I'm arrested?"

"There is no reason for us not to pay you and return the photographs when you hand over the bottles. But you are quite right; you simply have no choice but to trust us. If you are arrested, you will go to prison. But there is little likelihood of that. Why should anyone suspect you? If you are stopped, I expect the discovery of your ladies clothing will explain any nervousness. Only opening the bottles will reveal what is inside."

As far as I was concerned, they could show Anne any of the photographs had been taken that evening, well, except, possibly, for Erik's goodnight kiss.

But I was certain I was being asked to smuggle drugs and it had occurred to me by going along with their demands, I could help customs to track down at least one distribution chain.

"I don't seem to have much choice, do I?"

"No Mr Ives, you do not. You will be given instructions before you leave tomorrow."

After my guest had left, I considered my next move. I needed to contact Carol so she could set up a reception committee. Although the hotel telephones were direct dial the print out would show I had made a call to England and the time of that call and that information might find its way to my visitor. Going out to a public call box would also be dangerous, as there was every chance I would be followed.

I would have to wait until the next morning when I would be able to use the portable I had left in my car.

I finished undressing, removed the rest of my make-up and applied some moisturiser before putting on the long nightdress I prefer to wear in bed.

The next morning, I showered to remove the lingering traces of perfume from the previous evening, dressed in a casual shirt and trousers and went down to the restaurant.

After a leisurely breakfast of rolls, cheese and ham and several cups of coffee, I returned to my room, packed my bags and checked out of the hotel, wondering why I had not been contacted.

As I walked over to my car, I saw there was a piece of paper under the windscreen. The note informed me I should wait where I was. I had hardly finished reading it when a girl in a short red skirt and white blouse and carrying a rucksack came over to me.

"Are you going to the Hook?" she asked.

"Yes, I am," I replied.

"Could you give me a lift please?"

"I'm sorry, but I will not be going directly there, my ferry isn't until this evening."

"That is fine, Mr Ives. I'm also on the evening ferry."

This, then, was my contact. Presumably the bottles were in her rucksack.

"I'm planning to do some shopping before I leave Amsterdam, so why don't you meet me back here at four o'clock?"

"My instructions are I'm to stay with you all of the time until we get on the ferry."

"That's going to pose some problems sometime during the day — unless you are planning to accompany me to the toilet — or expect me to change into a dress and use the ladies."

"That, we will deal with later."

"Well, I don't know what your plans were for the day, but I'd intended to leave my car here and take the tram to the flea market at Noordemarkt. Do you want to dump your rucksack in the boot or are you going to carry it around with you all day?"

"I will leave it in the boot," she answered.

As I put her rucksack inside, I took both my sunglasses and my portable phone out of my briefcase. I then reached for my jacket which was lying on the back seat and transferred the phone to the inside pocket.

"Later, as we leave Amsterdam, we must collect a package from Harlem," she told me.

I'd been surprised at her willingness to leave her rucksack in the car if she already had the package I was expected to smuggle, but if we were to collect it en route, that explained matters.

My priority now was to find a suitable opportunity to get away from my companion to make my call to Carol. I could almost certainly lose her easily enough — but that would just raise suspicions and I could hardly use the toilet quite so soon after leaving the hotel.

It was a pity I hadn't made the call earlier. I could have picked up my phone from the car before having breakfast — but I hadn't anticipated being given an escort. Not that Carol would need very long to set up a reception committee, so, even if I failed to get through before getting to the Hook, I felt reasonably confident I'd have an opportunity there.

As it happened, my companion gave me the opportunity I needed while we were looking round the flea market. A 1960's minidress and matching boots on one of the stalls caught her eye. I could see the dilemma in her mind as she tried to decide whether or not to risk leaving me alone for a few minutes while she tried it on in the back of the stallholder's van.

She looked around and ensured there were no public call boxes nearby and said "If you are not here when I come out, I will have to report you ran off from me. You know what will happen then."

"I will be over by that stall there," I told her, indicating one selling old records.

As soon as she disappeared into the back of the van, I took out my phone and tapped in the numbers for Carol's direct line.

"Come on, come on," I mumbled as I waited for an answer.

"Carol, it's John. Listen, I don't have much time to explain. I've been asked to bring a package into Harwich on the overnight ferry, two bottles of Advocat, presumably containing drugs and I'm to hand them over to a contact after leaving Harwich. I'll call you again tonight when I've got more information about the handover."

"Understood. I'll organise a reception committee."

Chapter 16 – John 1991-5

My call had taken less than half a minute and I'd had time to return to the clothes stall before my companion emerged from the back of the van imitating Mary Quant. She checked I hadn't run off then darted back inside to change again.

When she had finished paying for the minidress and boots, I suggested to my companion we had a coffee at a nearby cafe. As we sat and sipped the scalding liquid, she turned to me and said "Thank you for not causing trouble at the market. My name is Ingrid, by the way."

"I'm John," I replied. "What is the arrangement for when we get to the ferry? There is only one person booked to accompany my car and I've got a cabin reserved for me for tonight and I'm not prepared to give that up so you can keep your eye on me. There is no way I'm going to try to sleep on one of the seats."

"No need to. I think all of the cabins have at least two berths so I will share with you."

Our ferry didn't sail until ten, although boarding would start at around 8. As it was only about an hour's drive, we still had some time to kill before we needed to leave for the Hook, so I told Ingrid I had planned to have a look around the Rijksmuseum which was near the hotel I had used the night before.

"Good, I too would like to see the paintings by Van Gogh."

We stayed in the museum until closing time, then made our way back to my car. I checked my street map for the address from which we were to collect the package and worked out the best way to get there.

The address we needed was in a street with contrasting sides. One the right were new blocks of flats and open spaces with well-kept lawns and flower beds; on the left were semi derelict houses and shops that looked ripe for clearance and rebuilding. Many of the windows were broken, doors had been replaced by corrugated iron and what gardens there had been were now overgrown. Those houses which were still being used looked to be occupied by squatters. The few old shops which remained in business offered second-hand goods, cheap clothes and ethnic foods. Above the shops were a handful of offices. The remnants of the signs on the windows showed they were used by a courier service, a taxi company and an import export agency — plus a few other names which could have concealed any sort of business.

Chapter 16 – John 1991-5

I parked opposite the door to number 124 which was sandwiched between two of the remaining shops. Ingrid crossed the street and disappeared inside. A few minutes later she reappeared and, having checked the road for traffic, returned to my car.

She handed me a note which gave details of the arrangements for the handover in England. I was to take the A120 out of Harwich and stop at the first lay-by after the village of Wix. There I was to go to a telephone box and receive further instructions.

It was about 7.30 when we joined the queue of vehicles waiting to board and I told Ingrid I needed to use the toilets. She said she would come with me. She then waited outside the entrance to the gentlemen's while I was inside.

Once in a cubicle, I took out my portable phone, thankful I had bought the most compact model available, and phoned Carol. She was still at her office, waiting for me to call.

I passed on the instructions I had received and pointed out I would undoubtedly be watched when I made the call at the phone box and might be tailed by the drug gang to ensure I wasn't also being followed by the police or customs. This might make it difficult to pass on further details of the transfer. A great deal would depend on whether or not Ingrid intended to stay with me until after the handover.

Carol told me she would arrange for calls to the phone box to be monitored and, unless the gang sent me to a series of other locations, there would be little problem. In any case, they could arrange for cars to be standing by at both Manningtree and the outskirts of Colchester to provide back up. She was quite insistent I simply obey the instructions I received even if it seemed the transfer might go undetected.

Once on board, I went to the Purser's office to sort out my cabin while Ingrid watched. We then made our way down to one of the lower decks and located the cabin I had been allocated. As Ingrid had predicted, the cabin had twin berths and an en suite shower and toilet.

Ingrid dropped her case onto one of the bunks and immediately went into the toilet — leaving the door ajar to ensure I did not disappear. The poor girl must have been absolutely desperate!

Over dinner in the restaurant, I asked Ingrid where she was from and what she did for a living.

"I'm from Kramfors, on the coast about 300 kilometres north of Stockholm. Do you know Sweden?"

"No, I haven't been to Scandinavia at all. I would certainly like to go there some time, though."

"It is very beautiful, but there is little work. I came to England as an au pair, but there was trouble with the wife because she thought I was sleeping with her husband. So, I then went to Germany."

"What did you do there?"

"I worked as a waitress in a nightclub. The pay was not much, but some gentlemen were very generous with tips."

"So how did you become involved in what you are doing now?"

Ingrid hesitated.

"Sorry," I said, "it's none of my business."

"No, it is not your business and I do not wish to discuss it, nor do I ask how you came to be involved."

After finishing coffee, we visited the duty-free shop where I purchased some perfume for Anne and some cigarettes for a colleague at the agency then, after a drink at the bar we decided to call it a night.

Over breakfast the next morning, I pointed out to Ingrid I would need to call in at the customs office as I had some equipment in the car which was covered by a carnet. I then asked her how much further she would be travelling with me.

"I leave you when you go to your car," she told me.

I finished the last of my coffee and returned to my cabin to collect my case, then made my way to the car deck. Ingrid waited until I started to drive off then disappeared back into the ship.

Having cleared immigration, I drove over to the customs office and took out the carnet document which needed to be cleared. Inside, none of the officers appeared to recognise me or give any indication anything out of the ordinary was happening. Back in my car, however, I found an envelope had been slipped inside the paperwork.

Carol's message told me they had planted a microphone inside the telephone I had been instructed to use and reminded me to do exactly as I was instructed. They would handle everything.

I drove out of Parkstone Quay on the A120 and found the lay-by. I had no doubt I would be under surveillance, although I couldn't see anyone nearby. Nevertheless, as soon as I opened the door to the kiosk, the phone rang.

"Mr Ives?" It was an indistinct voice, male but muffled.

"Yes. Who is that?"

"Never mind who I am. Have you got the package?"

"Yes, I have, what about the photographs and my money?"

"You are to take the A120 to the A12 towards London. Drive at 60 mph. A motorcycle will overtake you and signal you to stop. You are to pull in at the next lay-by. He will then take the package and give you what we promised. You will then go straight home. Is that understood?"

"I think so. I take the A120 to the A12, then the A12 driving at 60. A motorcycle will overtake me and signal me to stop at the next lay-by."

I just hoped Carol had got the message.

"That is correct."

Knowing I was under surveillance, I went straight back to my car and headed west. I thought about trying to call Carol on my portable but I couldn't be certain the car behind me didn't contain members of the gang. As I drove around the Colchester by-pass, I noticed a motorcycle approaching from behind. But he simply drove past and disappeared into the distance. Shortly afterwards, another bike appeared in my rear-view mirror. This time, as he passed, he signalled me to pull into the lay-by about a quarter of a mile ahead.

Having stopped, I waited for the rider to come up to my door. His helmet and tinted visor made it impossible for me to get any idea of what he looked like. All I could tell was he, or it could even have been a she, was about five feet six tall, medium build for a man or heavy for a woman, about a size seven of eight shoe and had long dark brown hair showing below the helmet.

The motorcyclist held out his hand and took the package from me and handed me mine. Then without a single word, returned to the bike and drove up the embankment, through a gap in the fence and onto a road which crossed the A12 at that point. Even if I'd been inclined, there would have been no way in which I could have followed in my car.

I'd taken the bike's number although I was quite certain it would prove to be false. I opened the package I had been given and, to my surprise, found it contained £100 and the photographs. All of them had been taken in the nightclub and were quite innocuous.

As there was nothing more I could do, I started the car and drove on down the A12 until I found a roadside cafe where I stopped for a coffee. I called Carol from the phone box, but she was still out.

I eventually reached home about an hour and a half later and told Anne what had happened. I showed her the photographs which she put on one side ready to add to an album we kept of "Angela's" activities.

That afternoon, Carol phoned.

"Your courier led us to an address that has been suspected for some time. We thought they would use the motorcycle trick, especially when a police patrol car had found the fence cut and held in place with string. The drug squad have arrested five bodies so far and are hoping to get information on others. You might be interested to know one of those arrested was a certain Tim Williams. Seems he's got quite a record now and was out on licence after serving eight out of twelve years for armed robbery."

"Not the one who was Liz's boyfriend?"

"That's right. Small world, isn't it? By the way, why did the gang think they could blackmail you? What WERE you up to in Amsterdam? Don't tell me, let me guess. Cinders up to her old tricks again?"

Carol was the only relative that knew I was a cross-dresser. She and Anne had become very close friends and there was very little they kept secret from each other.

I had to give a statement to the police about my involvement in the drug smuggling but was told there was little likelihood I would be called to provide evidence as those being tried had been caught red handed. I handed over the money I had received from the gang, but was offered the opportunity to apply for a 'community action award' for my assistance in helping the police. I was going to refuse, but then decided to go through with it and donate it to a local charity.

Two days after giving my statement, Carol rang again.

"John, I'm sorry to have to tell you this, but Tim Williams has escaped from custody while being taken to a remand hearing. He recognised me and somehow made the link to you. We don't think he will try anything, he's much more likely to try to get out of the country, but can you take Anne and Samantha away for a few days? Just to be on the safe side."

As soon as Carol had rung off, I called Anne and told her to pack enough for a couple of weeks. I'd just started two weeks holiday with the intention of getting some work done around the house. Instead, I called a travel agent and booked seats on a flight that afternoon to Los Angeles. Anne and I had been promising ourselves a holiday on the west coast of America for some time and this seemed like the perfect excuse.

Chapter 17. Mary — 1991-94

I joined the board of Arthur's holding company Intertrade Developments Inc in 1991 as 'Vice President for the Future,' a grandiose title which gave me responsibility for evaluating potential areas in which ID could invest. I was also responsible for a team of Product Development Managers whose task it was to nurture the new ideas and monitor progress until they were launched. Or until they were discarded.

My deputy, Amos West from Tennessee, was a Harvard Graduate. He'd had to overcome considerable prejudice, due to his colour, to reach his current position and he'd done so by demonstrating he was one of the company's ablest executives. I knew he had hoped for, but had not expected to get, my job and I would need to ensure he didn't resent my appointment.

Prior to my arrival, he had been responsible for overseeing ID's interests in BAME owned businesses. His success rate had been higher than anyone else's. But this was not necessarily the ideal measure of success. It could, just as easily, imply too much caution in selecting projects as an ability to manage them well.

I soon realised he took as many fliers as any of the other managers, but he then spent far more time visiting and helping the projects. It was this commitment and support which drew even more out of the people involved in his projects that generated the success he enjoyed. It was rumoured he also applied emotional blackmail on some of the clients, pointing out every black run project that failed reinforced the view Negros were poor businessmen. Whatever his methods, they worked.

Arthur had already told me he expected Amos to take over my role when I became his deputy later that year, but he had wanted a second opinion in case he had subconsciously been tempted to adopt positive discrimination. After two months, I assured Arthur I totally agreed with his decision.

Just as I was working with Lionel Brown to familiarise myself with his responsibilities, I let Amos grow into my position insisting he make recommendations for action rather than asking for my decisions. It was only on rare occasions I asked him to reconsider his view and suggest other factors which might influence his estimates.

ID's corporate headquarters were in Dallas. A city that had only recently become more famous for Southfork and Ewing Oil than as the site of JFK's assassination. Some might wonder which was worse!

Arthur had invited me to dinner with his wife, Nancy, the day after my arrival. She'd been concerned about a possible personal relationship between Arthur and me and her initial welcome had been tempered by this niggle. Although Arthur and I had certainly become friends, and had spent many nights together in the same hotels, there had never been the slightest suggestion of an affair.

Having met me, Nancy soon realised her doubts had been groundless and we became firm friends. We met regularly for dinner and drinks and she helped me to settle in and introduced me into her own circle. She took me around town and provided valuable information about clothes shops, hairdressers and beauty salons and restaurants. When I had dinner with both her and Arthur, I would usually find an eligible bachelor had been invited as my partner.

It had been a long time since OJ's death, but I still didn't anticipate re-marrying. It wasn't that I had made a conscious decision not to, and I certainly hadn't taken any vows of celibacy. I had gone out with several men friends in England over the past seven years and had had brief affairs with three of them. But none of them kindled the same feelings I had felt for OJ. If Arthur hadn't been happily married, I might have been seriously interested in him, but he was and that was the end of the matter.

As well as those provided as dinner partners by Arthur and Nancy, I inevitably met a wide range of men who asked me out. Most of them fell in to the same category as those I'd been out with at home. I enjoyed their company and was happy to be taken to dinner, the theatre and, if they were particularly attractive, bed. That was until I met Miguel Sanchez.

Miguel was not conventionally handsome. But his charm more than made up for his nose, which was broad and flat and his lips were thick, both suggesting some Negroid blood in his Cuban ancestry. He was balding, but still retained a full beard and moustache he'd adopted in his hippy days. His parents had been born in Cuba but had moved to the USA before he had been born. He was certainly overweight for his height, which was the same as my five feet seven. He was, however, as I said, charming and superb company. Constantly attentive, humorous and not at all pushy.

It was not until our fourth date, in November 1992, two months to the day after I had been officially promoted to Vice President, we ended up in bed together and that had been at my instigation. When Diane and her family came over for Christmas, I introduced them and was teased at first until she realised I was serious about Miguel. Diane was delighted for me. Charles was rather more reticent. I, unjustly, assumed this might be his legal mind considering the inheritance position should Miguel and I marry.

We waited until Easter, then had a small, private, wedding with just the family and very close friends present.

It was only later I heard Charles had had a feeling about Miguel. If he had been female, it would have been considered women's intuition. Perhaps he had seen something in Miguel's eyes when he wasn't looking at me. I don't know. But his sixth sense proved correct. Miguel was a hunter. Having snared his prey, he sought out the next victim for his charms.

I'd been working on some figures one evening using a spreadsheet on the computer I kept at home and I forgot to take the disk with the data file to the office the next morning. I needed it that afternoon and returned to the apartment to collect it and, possibly, have a session with Miguel. If he was up to it!

He certainly was up to it. But not with me. When I entered the flat, I found him in bed entertaining the wife of one of my managers. He'd met her at one of the company's functions and persuaded her he could influence her husband's prospects.

Miguel was nonchalant.

"It is my mixed Spanish and African blood, but they mean nothing to me."

I had two choices, I could accept his infidelity with the certain knowledge he had no intention of stopping or I could leave him. I left. Or, rather, I told him to leave as it was my apartment.

I had been angry and disappointed but I was also scared. Aids had become a serious threat to straights as well as gays and drug users. If Miguel was sleeping around, then he had put us both at risk.

As my work load increased with the ever-expanding range of interests ID Inc. was involved in, I put the Miguel episode behind me. The lawyers sorted out a divorce settlement. Our assets and incomes were similar, so we each kept what we had had before the marriage and I gave my share of items we had bought together to charities. Miguel was in line for promotion and a substantial increase in salary that would accompany it. His lawyer was keen to limit any claim I might make against his future earnings and pointed out as I was currently the higher paid, then there was little to be gained from claiming alimony off each other. I didn't bother to argue and told my lawyers to settle.

Chapter 18. John — 15th September 1994

The police had kept a discreet watch on the house while we were away, but there was no sign of Williams and everyone concluded he had, indeed, gone abroad.

They were wrong.

I went back to work and put him out of my mind. Samantha had started at nursery and Anne was talking about getting a part time job, possibly at a local bank.

On Wednesday 13th September, at 9.30am, a date I'm never likely to forget, just as I was preparing for a meeting, Claire on reception called me.

"John, the Royal Infirmary is on the phone for you."

I was stunned – this couldn't be good news.

"John Ives speaking"

"Mr Ives, this is Sister Hughes at the Royal Infirmary. Can I check, are Anne and Samantha your wife and daughter?"

"Yes, they are. Why, what's happened?"

"I'm sorry to tell you that they have been involved in an incident. I think you should get here as soon as possible."

How? What? The questions span round my head.

"An Incident? What do you mean? What's happened? How are they? Are they hurt?"

What stupid questions. Obviously they are hurt or the hospital wouldn't be phoning me.

"They are both in surgery at the moment. It seems to have been a hit and run. The doctors will be able to give you more information when you get here."

I grabbed my jacket and ran down the stairs, stopping briefly in reception.

"Claire, Anne and Samantha have been involved in an accident. I'm going to the Harlow Royal Infirmary. Can you get Stephanie to cover for my meeting and explain to the client? I'll have my portable phone so she can get me on it if she needs to."

"That's awful, John. I hope they are OK. I'll let Steph know what's happening."

Steph called me as I headed out along the A12. She'd worked with me on the campaign we were due to present.

"John, don't worry. You just focus on Anne and Samantha. We'll deal with everything this end."

"Thanks Samantha. I know you'll be fine. Just give my apologies to the client."

"OK. Now get off the phone and concentrate on your driving, we don't want you to end up in hospital too! And give my love to Anne and Samantha."

I then called Carol and told her what I knew. She said she'd get to the hospital as soon as she could. I asked her to let my parents and Anne's know what was going on.

Chapter 18 – John 15th September 1994

It took me an hour to get to the hospital. I ran from the car park to the A&E department. I grabbed one of the staff and they directed me to the reception desk. I'd just given my name when one of the nursing staff approached me.

"Mr Ives? I'm Sister Hughes. We spoke on the phone. Would you like to come with me?"

"How are my wife and daughter? Will they be OK?"

As I asked the questions, she opened a door and invited me to enter a small consulting room ahead of her.

"Please take a seat, Mr Ives. I'm really sorry to have to inform you that your daughter is very poorly. She's had surgery and is now in intensive care. The next few hours are going to be critical. Your wife is still in surgery."

I slumped in the seat. This couldn't be happening. It was an utter nightmare. All I knew was that it had been a hit and run – but how? Why? Where?

"Can I see Samantha? What are her chances?"

"Yes, I'll have someone take you to the ward in a moment. I can't say what her chances are at this stage. As I said, the next few hours will be critical. The doctors may have more information for you. When you feel up to it, the police would like a word with you."

The police? Why? Presumably because it was a hit and run — but how could I possibly help?

"Ah, Nurse Walker, can you take Mr Ives to Intensive Care?"

"Yes Sister. Would you come this way please Mr Ives?"

I followed her in a daze. We went up two floors in a lift then along a wide corridor. Nurse Walker knocked on an office door and opened it.

"This is Mr Ives to see his daughter Samantha."

"Thank you, Tracy. Take a seat please Mr Ives. I'm Staff Nurse Clarke."

"Can't I just go and see Samantha? What's the problem?"

"I just want to explain that Samantha has a number of tubes and leads attached to her which might seem frightening. But they are all to help us monitor her and give her the fluids and pain relief that she needs."

108

"I see, but she will be OK won't she."

I saw a look of concern flash across her face.

"We are doing all we can but she is very poorly and the next three to four hours will be critical."

"What about my wife? What about her?"

"She is still in theatre. I don't have details of her injuries we only get that information if she comes into Intensive Care. I do know that we have some of the best doctors in the country and they are doing all they possibly can for her. Did you want to come and see Samantha?"

I stood up and followed her through double doors into a side ward with two beds or, rather, one bed and a cot.

"We thought it would be best if we can keep both of them in the one room. You can then see both at the same time and I'm sure your wife would fret if she wasn't with Samantha."

"Thank you, that's very thoughtful."

I stepped over to Samantha's cot. As I'd been warned she had leads to monitors and a drip attached and was swathed in bandages. She looked so vulnerable and I wept when I looked at her. How could we let this happen to her? We had failed her as parents.

"Can I touch her?"

"Yes. You can kiss her if you like and hold her hand." I didn't need any second invitation.

"Samantha, it's daddy. Everything is going to be fine."

Oh God please let that be true. I'll do anything if you let Samantha and Anne recover. I'll give up dressing; we'll start going to church again. I know we've neglected our obligations and drifted away from our faith. But please forgive us. Please let Samantha live. It's not her fault if I've broken your laws. Don't punish her for my sins. Please God. Tears were flowing freely as I sat and looked at the frail, innocent being we'd brought into the world and exposed to danger.

The door opened and a nurse showed Carol into the room. I stood up and she hugged me.

Chapter 18 – John 15th September 1994

"How are they both? Have you any idea what happened?"

"Samantha is very, very poorly — the nurses say the next few hours will be crucial. Anne is still undergoing surgery – she's been in theatre for nearly two hours now. All I know is that it was a hit and run."

"I see — don't worry, John, I'm sure they'll both be OK. I phoned Anne's parents. They are on the way here. They should arrive in the next half hour. I called your parents and Auntie Maureen and Uncle Keith will be here later. I've also told my parents and they send their love."

"Thanks Carol, I don't know what I'd do without you."

She hugged me again and kissed my cheek. "We'll get through it like we always do. Anne and Samantha are in the best possible hands."

Carol was right, of course, but I just sat and stared at Samantha. I felt so helpless.

"Is there anything you need, cuz? Coffee? Something to eat? You' need something to keep your strength up."

"A coffee would be good. Thanks."

"OK, I'll pop along to the machine."

She returned a couple of minutes later and handed me a cup of brown liquid.

"It'll probably taste disgusting — but there you are."

"Mr Ives?" A police officer stood in the door.

"Yes?"

"I appreciate this is a bad time but could I just get some information from you?"

"Yes, I guess so. What do you need to know?"

"From eye-witness reports, it sounds like the car deliberately mounted the pavement to hit your wife and daughter. Can you think of anyone who might have wanted to hurt your family?"

Carol and I looked at each other.

She spoke before I could. "Tim Williams."

Chapter 18 – John 15th September 1994

"Who is Tim Williams?" asked the officer.

"He's someone that has a grudge against John. He was responsible for the death of a friend of ours and was involved in a drug smuggling gang that John helped to expose. I'm a Senior Investigation Officer with Customs and Excise," Carol told him.

"And you think he's capable of carrying out such an attack?"

"Absolutely, he has a record of armed robbery and other violent offences and he threatened John when he was sent down."

Was that the reason that Anne and Samantha were now in hospital? Because I'd helped expose their smuggling operation? Why hadn't I just left well alone? Nothing was worth their lives.

The officer closed his notebook and put it in his pocket.

"Thank you for the information. I hope your wife and daughter recover soon, Sir. We'll be in touch if we have any further information or questions."

As he left, Anne's parents came into the room.

Vivienne immediately went to Samantha's side. "Oh, you poor darling," she said as she gently touched Samantha's cheek. Turning to me she asked "How is she? What have the doctors said?"

"We won't know for a couple of hours yet. If she gets through that she should be OK. It's a case of wait and see. And pray."

"We'll certainly do that," said Clifford, fingering his dog-collar.

Carol had slipped out of the room when Anne's parents arrived but now returned with more cups of coffee.

"It's only from a machine but it's just about drinkable," she told them.

"Bless you, Carol, very thoughtful." Clifford took one cup and passed it to his wife then accepted the second and took a sip. "I've tasted a lot worse at Mothers' Union meetings."

"Could I have a word please Mr Ives?" I heard from the doorway where a doctor in scrubs stood.

Chapter 18 – John 15th September 1994

I went into the corridor with him. I tried to judge from his face how things were going but didn't dare raise my hopes.

"We've done what we can at this stage and your wife is now in the recovery room. We'll bring her down to the ward once she's stabilised after the anaesthetic has worn off. We focussed on the life-threatening aspects first but she will need further surgery in a few days. Do you have any questions?"

"What are their chances? Will there be any long-term effects?"

"I really can't say at this stage. I will say that we are doing everything possible for both of them."

"I see. Thank you, doctor." It hadn't been the answer I really wanted to hear — but I suppose it was as positive as it could be under the circumstances.

He squeezed my shoulder, gave me a wry smile, then turned to leave, walking wearily along the corridor.

Back in the side ward, Clifford was sitting in a chair across from his wife and holding Samantha's hand. His lips were moving silently but I was sure he was praying for his granddaughter. It was strangely comforting to see him doing so. Maybe there was something to be said for having faith — at least it gave you some hope. Vivienne wiped a tear from her cheek then gave me a forced smile.

There was little any of us could say so we sat quietly, the silence interrupted by the beeb-beeb-beeb of the heart monitor and the sound of Samantha's laboured breathing.

I don't know what the others were thinking but my thoughts focussed on why had this happened? Was it punishment from God for my crossdressing? I knew that the bible described it as an abomination but I hadn't taken that seriously — those laws seemed so hopelessly outdated, but maybe they did still apply. How would I tell Anne if Samantha died? How would I cope if Anne died and Samantha lived? Please God. Let them both live. Let them both be well. Please, Please. Please.

My prayer, such as it was, was interrupted by my parents coming into the room. Vivienne and Clifford made room for them to see Samantha.

"What a terrible thing to happen," said my mother.

Chapter 18 – John 15th September 1994

"It is, Maureen. I don't understand how anyone can deliberately run down anyone; but to do it to a young child is just evil," replied Vivienne.

"Can I ask you to leave the room for a few minutes while we bring Mrs Ives in and get her settled?" asked a nurse from the doorway.

"Can I please see her now?" I asked.

"You can stay in the room, Mr Ives, but we do need room to work so I'm afraid the others need to leave for the time being. She is still unconscious. We really shouldn't allow more than four in here at a time in any case — just don't tell Sister."

I stood aside while they transferred Anne from the trolley onto the bed next to Samantha's and connected the various leads and tubes. I knew the nurses were all highly professional but it was, nevertheless, impressive and reassuring to see them going about their work calmly, unhurried, and in a very efficient manner. After just a few minutes one turned to me, smiled and told me I could approach the bed now.

It was horrible standing between the beds where the two people I loved more than anyone else in the world lay; two people I'd have willingly given my own life for, but knowing there was nothing I could personally do for them at this stage; except pray. I took Anne's hand in mine and leant over and kissed her lips. Her head was swathed in bandages as were her arms and as much of her body as I could see.

"Can you tell me what her injuries are?" I asked the doctor.

"She has a number of serious internal injuries as well as a fractured skull and other broken bones. We've dealt with the internal injuries as far as we can and stabilised other areas. We'll keep her sedated for at least 24 hours and see how things go," she said.

"I see, but she will recover, won't she?" I begged.

"God willing; but I must caution you that I can't promise anything at this stage. Her injuries are significant and there is a risk of organ failure."

Vivienne and Clifford came back into the room to see their daughter. I made to get up but Clifford pressed me back into the chair as his wife sat down opposite me.

"Maureen and Keith have gone with Carol for something to eat rather than crowd the room," he said. "When they come back, we'll go — you really should do the same."

"I really couldn't face anything at the moment and really must stay with Anne and Samantha."

"I understand — but you must keep up your strength. You'll need to be fit when they both come home from hospital."

I smiled wryly at his optimism.

We all fell into silence, lost in our own thoughts; well, I was certainly lost in mine and I assumed they were lost in theirs. I remembered the first time I saw Anne, our first date, dressing as 'Lorraine' to fool the neighbours; Samantha's birth, her first steps, her first words. My pride showing her off to my parents and wheeling her in her stroller. I hoped we'd still have a future together as a family. It wouldn't all be smooth sailing of course — no doubt there would be tears over broken friendships and boyfriends, or girlfriends if that was the way it worked out. I wanted to look forward to walking her down the aisle at her wedding and seeing her own children if she wanted any. If she didn't, well that would be fine too. Just as long as we did have a future. Just as long as she recovered from this vicious attack.

Had it been Tim Williams? Had he been seeking revenge?

At about eight o'clock, mum and dad were beginning to flake so I suggested they went with Anne's parents to our house for the night. I took Anne's keys from her handbag and gave them to mum.

"The spare room is made up and there is spare bedding in the airing cupboard for our bed — I'm staying here tonight," I told her. It was almost a relief to be able to deal with practical issues instead of being helpless.

"OK darling, you take care and try to get some rest too. We'll come back in the morning."

Chapter 19. Mary — 1994

Nancy and I continued to meet for "girls only" evenings and, as we sat drinking coffee after dinner in my apartment, she dropped a bombshell.

Chapter 19 – Mary 1994

"You remember when we first met; I'd been worried about a personal relationship between you and Arthur?"

"Yes, I do remember, but there never has been anything more than a good friendship and working relationship."

"I know that now, but I'm almost sorry you and Arthur aren't having an affair. I'd then know he would have someone to turn to when I'm gone."

"Gone? But you're younger than I am, for goodness sake. You've got years ahead of you yet!"

"I'm afraid not. I've got six months at the most."

"God! No! I'm so sorry. I had no idea."

"Nor do most people. Apart from the medics, Arthur and the children you're the only one."

"Is there anything I can do to help?"

She put a hand on my arm looked me in the eyes.

"Yes, Arthur is going to be under a great deal of pressure over the next few months and will certainly need your support with the business. Can you try to take over as much of his work as possible?"

"Of course I will. You know I'll do whatever I can."

"Bless you. I know I could rely on you. You've become my best friend. You know that don't you?"

I leant over and put my arm around her and dragged her into a hug. I felt her sobbing before she pulled away, took out a tissue and wiped her eyes.

"Dammit. I swore I wasn't going to blub," she said with a forced laugh.

"There's something else too."

"What? Anything, you just have to ask."

"I know there's never been anything improper between you and Arthur."

"Absolutely," I started to interject.

"Now hear me out. As I said I know there's never been anything improper but I do know that Arthur really admires you and I know you and he enjoy each other's company. So, I'm not trying to match make, but if things develop between you and Arthur after I've gone, I want you to know you have my blessing."

Nancy continued to have treatments, the best available at any price. They provided relief from some of the pain and retarded the inevitable outcome. But inevitable it was, unless there was a miracle.

No miracle occurred and she died in her sleep at 3.37am on 14th February 1994. It seemed ironic for Arthur to lose his wife on Valentine's Day. But his heartbreak was tempered by the knowledge Nancy's suffering was over. They'd had a full life together and he had no reason to feel guilty.

Chapter 20. John — September 1994

I was stiff after sleeping fitfully in the chair between Anne and Samantha's beds. When I looked at Samantha, her eyes flickered then opened.

"Hello darling."

She stared blankly at me then started to whimper.

"Hurts," she cried.

I called the nurse.

"There isn't anything more we can do as far as pain relief is concerned but it should ease," she assured me.

I took Samantha's hand in mine and tried to absorb some of her pain somehow and feed her some of my strength.

One of the nurses brought me a cup of coffee. "Don't tell Sister, will you? Visitors are supposed to just use the machine."

I had just finished when there was a knock on the door.

"Mr Ives? I'm Detective Constable Crawford. Could I have a quick word with you?"

I went out into the corridor with him.

"The vehicle that hit your wife and daughter has been found abandoned about a mile from the scene near the railway station. We've examined it for fingerprints and can confirm that Tim Williams' have been found on the steering wheel. There is also evidence of him having hit his head and bleeding. We are checking CCTV from the station to see if we can establish if he caught a train. We think it's likely he'll have gone back to London."

"I see. But what if he hasn't gone back to London? What if he tries to finish off what he started here?"

"My DI doesn't think that's likely but I can try to persuade him to have someone on duty here just in case — though we are stretched at present investigating other aspects."

I was about to argue the point when an alarm sounded from the room where Anne and Samantha were. After just a few moments, a doctor strode purposely into the room, picked up Anne's notes and looked at the monitor.

"Get her into theatre as quickly as possible please, Staff. And warn them that we may need several units of blood." She turned to me. "Mr Ives, your wife's blood pressure has dropped which suggests internal bleeding so we are going to take her back into theatre to find the problem and sort it out. This is not unusual after such extensive internal injuries. We'll keep you informed as soon as we have further information."

I couldn't think of anything to say. My mind was just numb so I just mumbled. "Thanks."

She touched my shoulder then turned and left the room.

I was torn. Did I go and wait near the operating theatre or stay with Samantha?

The nurses took the decision out of my hands.

"You can't do anything waiting near the theatre. You're much more use here in case Samantha needs you."

That made sense so I sat down again next to Samantha and took her tiny hand in mine.

"Want mummy," she cried.

"Mummy will be here soon," I assured her and leant over and kissed her forehead.

"Hurts."

"I know, darling, but it will be all right soon, I promise." How easily we make such promises with no means of keeping them. And how readily we'd take their pain on ourselves if we possibly could.

"Where's Anne?" Carol asked as she came into the room with Anne's parents.

I told them what had happened, then left them with Samantha while I went to the toilet to freshen up.

The minutes dragged by as we waited for news of Anne. We assured each other that she was in the best possible hands; but the wait was still agonising. In the end, though, I'd have preferred to keep waiting rather than seeing the look on the doctor's face when she eventually came in to see us. She signalled me to join her in the corridor.

"I'm so sorry Mr Ives but we weren't able to save your wife. The bleeding was just too severe. I really am so desperately sorry."

No. It couldn't be true. She can't be dead. Please God. Let this just be a nightmare that I'll wake up from soon. The tears flowed down my face and my throat closed up as Carol took me in her arms.

"Oh John, I'm so very sorry." She was crying too. My legs were giving way under me as she helped me to reach the chair by Samantha's bed and slump down into it.

Clifford was holding his wife and praying.

What was I going to do now? How would I cope without Anne?

"John," Carol said gently, "I know you're in pain but Samantha needs you now more than ever. You've got to keep going for her sake."

"How?" I asked. "How do I keep going?"

"God will give you the strength you need," said Clifford, "if you let him."

I looked at Samantha who had, thankfully, fallen asleep again. Oh God, how am I going to tell her that her mother has gone?

When my mother and father came into the room, they looked at our faces and didn't need to be told the news. Mum lifted her hand to her mouth and let out a whimper. Dad seemed to shrink several inches before pulling his shoulders back and standing erect once more. Carol quietly explained to them what had happened to Anne.

Samantha woke again and started to cry. "Want mummy, hurts, where mummy?" When I touched her face, she felt hot.

I called the nurse who felt Samantha's face then took her temperature. She looked concerned which worried me.

"What's wrong?"

"Samantha's temperature is higher than we'd like it to be. It may indicate an infection. I'll get a doctor to have a look at her."

The doctor arrived a few minutes later and confirmed the nurse's thoughts. He prescribed some further treatment and sent the nurse off for some antibiotics.

I realised that infections weren't uncommon and could usually be treated — but it didn't stop me fretting about this additional complication.

Carol had to go to her office but promised to return that evening. I stayed with Samantha for the day while her grandparents took turns to join me. I managed to force down a bowl of soup at lunch — knowing that I had to try to keep up my own strength as I'd need it over the coming days and weeks.

Samantha's temperature stayed high in spite of the antibiotics but the nurses assured me that it would take a few hours to fight the infection and her temperature to go down again.

As I sat there, I thought about my life with Anne and how it had seemed so perfect. I remembered our first few dates and sailing together, the adventures at Greenbreaks and how she had supported my crossdressing. I knew then that her death was punishment for my transvestism. I had disregarded what the bible said about it being an abomination and now I was paying the price. Worse, Samantha would also be punished for my sins. Wasn't that what the bible also threatened, the iniquities of the father passing to further generations? I determined to purge all of my female things and give up that evil behaviour. I would speak to Clifford about it and ask for absolution.

That evening, my parents and Anne's had gone back to the house and I was on my own. Having stayed awake most of the previous night, the tiredness caught up with me and I dozed in the chair next to Samantha's bed.

I was woken by the alarm from Samantha's monitor sounding. As I shook off the sleepiness, a nurse came running in. She took one look at the monitor and hit the red alarm button on the wall.

"What's going on?" I asked. I looked at the heart monitor and say that the line was flat and it was making a continuous beep.

"No. NO, NO! Not Samantha too. No," I screamed.

A nurse took me by the arm. "Please leave the room Mr Ives. We need space to work. We'll look after Samantha."

 More nurses and a doctor rushed into Samantha's room. I heard someone call "Clear." Then "Charging." There was then a warbling sound. The sequence was repeated a number of times before I saw the doctor come out of the room looking dejected. I suddenly felt sick. I knew what was coming.

"I'm so sorry, Mr Ives, but Samantha suffered a heart attack and we weren't able to resuscitate her. The infection on top of the other injuries were just too much for her tiny body to cope with. I really am so very sorry."

No. This can't be happening. This is a bad dream. I'm going to wake up from this nightmare. I have to. This isn't real. Please God don't let it be real.

I pushed past them to the bed.

I collapsed across the bed and just wept. My entire life had disintegrated in the last two days.

One of the nurses brought me a cup of tea. I just stared at her. Did she really think that would solve anything? Then I felt guilty, she was only trying to be kind. It certainly wasn't her fault Samantha was dead. The staff had done everything they could to save her.

Chapter 21. Carol — September 1994

As soon as I woke, I checked my phone for messages. There were none. Was that good or bad? Had Samantha's infection been managed? Dear God, I hoped so. There was no answer from John's phone — but that meant nothing as he was bound to have switched it off. I quickly showered and dressed then went downstairs.

Chapter 21 – Carol September 1994

Aunt Maureen was in the kitchen making a pot of tea while Uncle Keith was on the telephone.

I watched as his face paled and he seemed to shrink in height.

"What is it?" I asked — knowing the answer but hoping it wasn't true.

He took a very deep breath and wiped away a tear before answering.

"That was the hospital. It's the worst possible news — Samantha passed away during the night. Her poor little body couldn't cope with the infection."

"No. It can't be," cried Vivienne who had just walked into the room.

Aunt Maureen put her hand to her mouth and sobbed. "Why? Why them? Oh God, why? What did they do to deserve this?"

I grabbed my bag and jacket "I'm going to the hospital now — does anyone want a lift? John's going to be devastated, he's going to need us."

"You go first Carol, you're already dressed. We'll follow on as soon as we can."

The hospital car park was already crowded when I arrived and it took ages to find a free space. I had to queue at the machine to pay — and wait while the person in front of me fumbled in her purse for change. Why couldn't they get a move on? Finally, I took the ticket and ran back to the car to stick it on the windscreen before dashing into the hospital. The lift indicator showed it on the third floor so I took the stairs to the intensive care unit.

I was shocked to find the side ward had already been cleared for other patients but the Staff Nurse on duty told me where I'd find John.

He was just sitting there staring into space. Even when I stood in front of him, he didn't register my presence.

I touched his arm and he finally turned to face me, pulling himself out of the chair wearily.

"Why Carol? Why them? Damn that bastard Williams to hell." He paused and his eyes stared vacantly past me. His mouth turned down at the corners. He blinked as tears formed at the corner of his eyes.

I had no answer that would help. All I could do was hug him close as he wept freely, his body shaking with his sobs. God knows how long we stood there. It might have been seconds — or hours.

Eventually we broke apart and sat down pulling the two chairs together. I held his hand. He lifted his eyes to mine.

"What am I going to do Carol? What's the point of carrying on? They were everything to me. My whole reason for living. What is there now? We had such plans. A brother or sister for Samantha. Now there's nothing. Everything has gone. Why? Why? Why?"

I didn't know what to say. I felt as guilty as him. If I hadn't been a custom's officer, he wouldn't have had anyone to call about the attempt to blackmail him into smuggling the drugs into the country. Then Williams wouldn't have been caught and he wouldn't have had a grudge against John and his family. How could I make-up for John's loss?

We just sat there in silence — lost in memories. I watched as his face reflected different emotions; mainly pained and sad but occasionally the hint smile or brightening of the eyes would indicate a happy memory before being dashed, perhaps by the realisation that they'd never share such times again.

Chapter 22. John — September 1994

Nothing made sense. I just went through the motions, signed what I was asked to sign, agreed to whatever was suggested. What did it matter? The deaths had been reported to the coroner and there would be an inquest. There would be post-mortems – though the causes of death were obvious. OK. Yes. Whatever you say. Their bodies had been mutilated already – post-mortems wouldn't make any difference.

All of a sudden Carol was there. Or had she been with me all morning? I didn't know. It was just a blur. I prayed it was a nightmare I'd wake from – but knew it wasn't.

I prayed that I'd fall asleep and never wake. I prayed for the chance for revenge on Williams – but knew God wouldn't grant that prayer. I prayed for forgiveness for my sins. I cursed God for taking Anne and Samantha.

We must have walked out to Carol's car and driven home but I don't remember any of it. Mum must have been watching for us to return or heard the car as she opened the door as we reached it. I stared at her then she took me in her arms and I wept on her shoulders. I wept with Vivienne as the two grandfathers tried to stay strong for the rest of us. We prayed with Clifford for our losses. And I wept. I wept because I knew this was all my fault.

Looking around the room, everything reminded me of Anne and Samantha from the colour of the paint on the walls – usually Anne's choice; the painting over the fireplace, chosen on a holiday together. The ornaments on the window ledge.

Five faces looked at me. I could see the sorrow in everyone's eyes. Sorrow that I had caused. Sorrow I'd have to live with for the rest of my life. There was also pity. Pity I didn't deserve. It was my fault that Anne and Samantha were dead. I was responsible. And, it had nothing to do with trapping the drug gang or for Williams' actions. He was just the tool to punish me for cross-dressing.

I was to blame. I had allowed my filthy crossdressing to rule my life. I needed to cleanse myself.

Standing up, I announced "I'm going to have a shower then I need to be on my own. I'm sorry but I can't face anyone else at the moment."

I trudged up the stairs; past more souvenirs on the wall Anne and I had chosen together on holidays. At the top of the stairs, the door to Samantha's room stood open, revealing some of her toys waiting for her to come and play. I sat down on her bed and picked up her favourite teddy and hugged it to my face as tears flowed again.

Oh God. How would I get through this?

In our own bedroom, Anne and Angela's make-up and jewellery sat on the dressing table. I opened the wardrobe and stared at their clothes hanging there. Turning, I caught sight of my reflection in the mirror. I looked like shit — which is how I felt. I ran my fingers through my hair. I unbuttoned my shirt and dropped it into the laundry basket then sat down and stripped off my trousers, socks and boxers. Standing, I padded over to the en suite bathroom. More of Anne's cosmetics and beauty treatments stood beside the sink — as did some of my own.

I heard the others moving around downstairs before the shower drowned out their voices as I angrily twisted the control to full and stepped under the spray. Maybe I hoped the water would wash away the pain — but, of course, it didn't. It did remove some of the grime and body odours from the last 36 hours — and the smell of the hospital.

As plodded back downstairs, I could hear Carol in the kitchen.

"I've made some scrambled eggs. We need to eat something," she said.

"I asked you all to leave," I reminded her.

"Not a chance, John. I know you blame yourself because of cross-dressing. Well, if it is, then I'm as guilty as you. I was the one that started it by getting you to take my part in the panto. And, if it wasn't that but the drug bust, then I'm still as responsible as you. If I hadn't work for customs, you wouldn't have reported the gang; you'd have told them to piss off as Anne didn't only know you cross-dressed but encouraged it. So, they could stuff their blackmail attempt."

I played with the food but I did feel a little better having forced it down.

After eating, we sat and reminisced, gradually emptying a bottle of scotch. We spoke about the good times we'd enjoyed and wept together. We played music that Anne loved. Dusk fell but we didn't close the curtains or turn on the lights until much later.

We must have gone to bed at some stage because I woke several times during the night — reaching out to cuddle Anne before the dreadful memory returned. Then I'd toss and turn, wondering what life held for me now. Was there any point going on?

The next morning, I carried out the vow I made in the hospital and packed up my sinful female paraphernalia, gave the clothes to a charity shop, burned the wigs and prosthetics and threw the make-up in the rubbish. Maybe, then, I could get absolution. While I was handing over the bags of clothes, I saw a bible and was about to pay for it when the volunteer said they wouldn't take my money in view of the items I'd just donated.

Back at home, I opened it at Deuteronomy Chapter 22 and read the verse that described my guilt. *"A woman must not wear man's clothing, nor is a man to put on a woman's clothing. For all that do so are abominations to the Lord your God."* There wasn't anything ambiguous there. I'd sinned. Worse, Chapter 5 confirmed *the iniquities of the father would be visited on the children.* It was my fault Samantha had died. I had no excuses. None at all. I now had to live with my guilt and try to atone for my sins – if, indeed, I could. Maybe Clifford could guide me.

Chapter 22 – John September 1994

At night, I'd toss and turn. I thought of asking the GP for sleeping pills but didn't feel I deserved to be able to rest. This was part of my punishment. Days passed in a fog. I had no energy, no purpose, no incentive to do anything.

Once the post-mortems had been completed, Anne and Samantha's bodies were released for burial and I was able to arrange for Clifford to carry out a joint funeral.

Samantha's tiny coffin looked so wretched as it was lowered into the grave to rest on top of her mother's.

Carol was my rock. She was there to support me and listen to my woes. If it hadn't been for her, I'm sure I'd have broken down or turned to drink. She was there holding my arm at the funeral.

"That bastard Williams has a lot to answer for," she said as we turned away from the graveside.

"He certainly does and if I get my hands on him, he will regret ever having lived."

I hadn't noticed Detective Constable Crawford approaching but he heard me.

"I can appreciate how you feel Mr Ives but please leave that to us," he said gently. "In fact, you'll be pleased to know we've arrested him and charged him with murder. With his previous offences he'll almost certainly get a very long sentence. I don't suppose he will have a pleasant time in prison, either, child killers are despised by the other inmates."

Perhaps I shouldn't have been pleased to hear that he was likely to suffer — but I was.

The house just contained too many memories for me and was far bigger than I needed so I put it on the market and bought a flat instead.

Work was as bad. Everyone was so kind but I could see the pity in their eyes. I needed a fresh start. Thankfully I was offered a new role out of the blue with a company and threw myself into the job working fifteen to eighteen hours a day and leaving myself just enough time to eat and sleep.

Chapter 23. Mary — 1994

Whilst 1994 was good for business, it was a tragic year for friends. A few weeks after Nancy's news, I heard John's wife and daughter had been murdered. As I was in the UK at the time, I drove over to see him. I knew what he was going through and realised he needed to keep busy to avoid any tendency to mope.

One of the companies we had financed were about to launch a desk top publishing programme. I explained the situation to their MD and persuaded them to take John on as Advertising Manager to coordinate the operation. He had been reluctant as, frankly, the task didn't need someone of John's calibre full time. Without telling John, I gave the company £5,000 towards his salary; the bonus OJ had wanted to give him, suitably increased in line with inflation. John's contribution to the company was quickly recognised and, within a year, he had been promoted to Marketing Manager.

In 1994, ID Inc.'s income from earlier investments totalled nearly $50 million. Just under 80% of this was reinvested. The projections for the next twelve months were for income to double.

Nancy had left me her shares in the company now worth about $4 million and the dividends plus my salary amounted to more than a quarter of a million dollars in 1994. Whilst I hadn't been destitute when OJ had died, I was now rich and had no concerns about money for the rest of my life.

Each year, Arthur and I visited the UK. The company's key personnel insurance policy prohibited us from flying together, so I flew over first and would spend a couple of weeks with Diane and her family. They also visited me in the States each school holiday. Charles, Diane's husband, was a solicitor and was retained by ID to look after their UK interests. Their retainer provided him with a solid base for his business in exchange for around half of his time.

Charles was a fan of American Football and as Arthur had an interest in the Dallas Cowboys, they spent much of the Christmas visit attending matches.

Chapter 24. John — March 1995

I was putting fresh flowers and tidying up the grave on Anne's birthday, 30th March when I realised that Clifford had come up to me.

"How are you John? You promised to keep in touch but we haven't seen or heard from you since the funeral."

"Yes, I'm sorry about that. I've been so busy." It was a feeble excuse and I knew it — and I knew Clifford knew it too. The truth was, I hadn't wanted to be reminded of Anne and Samantha; nor did I want to be reminded that it was my fault that Clifford and Vivienne had lost their daughter and granddaughter.

"Well come on over to the rectory for a drink when you've finished. Vivienne would love to see you." With that, he walked away and pretended to be sorting out the notices on the board by the entrance. There would be no escaping him today.

"We knew you'd be here today, John, as it's Anne's birthday," said Vivienne as she poured me a cup of tea. "How have you been?"

"Oh, you know, getting by. Keeping busy to avoid having time to think. How about you and Clifford?"

"It's been hard, I have to confess. It's challenged my faith at times. I kept asking why God had taken Anne and Samantha. What was his purpose? And I can't find the answer."

I put the cup back on the saucer and stared at it.

"It was to punish me," I said; my eyes unable to meet hers or Clifford's.

"What do you mean?" asked Clifford.

"I broke God's law. Taking Anne and Samantha was my punishment."

"Why would you think that, John?"

"I was a cross-dresser and the Bible says that's an abomination."

"Ah," Clifford nodded. "Deuteronomy?"

"Yes."

"I think we really need to talk. John."

And talk we did.

For several hours.

Clifford took me into his study and he assured me the God he worshipped was loving and would not have punished me by taking Anne and Samantha and explained the current interpretations of the passage that had convinced me that

I was evil and had been made to pay. He showed me various commentaries on the chapter and verse from the dozens of theological tomes on his book shelves.

As the afternoon turned into evening, my mood was lightened by a greater understanding of the words that had caused my guilt and the cup of tea was replaced by a glass of wine.

I was amazed at Clifford's compassion — though I don't know why I was surprised.

Vivienne then opened the study door and announced "Dinner is on the table."

I looked at my watch and discovered it was eight o'clock.

"I really ought to be on my way," I protested.

"Nonsense, judging by the state of that wine bottle, you're in no fit state to drive. I've made up the bed in the spare room John so no argument. You stay the night."

Over dinner, I told both of them the full story of how I'd started to dress — and even how I'd dressed to get in their house without rousing the curiosity of the neighbours.

"I'm not sure whether we should be grateful for avoiding embarrassing us or annoyed because of the deception," said Clifford, at that revelation. The twinkle in his eye suggested his stern voice was a front.

"I often wondered who Mrs T was talking about when she said Anne had had a female friend to visit," remarked Vivienne.

I took some books that Clifford had given me to read and studied them over the next few weeks.

They initially convinced me that his God, the one I'd been brought up to believe in, would not have punished me by taking Anne and Samantha.

Yet, according to the bible, God had inflicted plagues, floods and pestilence and had destroyed whole cities. Wasn't that a contradiction? And look at the way religion is used to justify discrimination and murder and has been for centuries — it really is appalling.

The more I read, the more contradictions I found.

Chapter 24 – John March 1995

Was the bible really the word of God? Could it be? It had only been written four thousand years ago — yet mankind has existed for nearly two million years. So, what happened? How did the bible get written?

Were the first five books written by Moses as some claimed or had it been handed down by word of mouth?

If it was inspired by God, then what about current evangelists? They also claimed to be speaking for God — but they spout hatred more than love. How were they different from the biblical prophets? Were the Old Testament prophets, with their predictions of fire and brimstone, more reliable because they'd been recorded in a book that we'd been taught to believe in?

Ok, it makes sense that the Old Testament is basically the history of the Jews — combined with rules on behaviour and effectively using superhuman explanations for anything that couldn't be explained at the time. Even the promise of rewards after death — or punishment for misdeeds made sense in that context. That I could understand.

It kept the masses in line — and maybe that's the real reason religions developed.

How did All Things Bright and Beautiful go? '*The rich man in his castle, the poor man at his gate, God made them high and lowly and ordered their estate*'.

So, should we take the bible literally? How can we? The first few verses describe the earth being created first but we know that's not how it happened.

It makes much more sense that the bible and other religious beliefs were created to explain the inexplicable. Some men claimed supernatural powers and the ability to speak with the forces that caused natural events that threatened or benefited. They then acquired power and took advantage of it. Oh, I know a lot of religious people, such as Clifford, are good. But do we need to believe in any religion to be a decent person? I don't think so.

It felt strange concluding that there was no proof of the existence of a God — let alone one that would punish me for an entirely natural drive that didn't hurt anyone else. At least I was convinced that I hadn't been punished for cross dressing and that was important.

Chapter 25. John - June 1995 Trial

I t took an eternity for Williams to come to trial. After a brief appearance at the Magistrates' Court where he hadn't entered a plea, he'd been committed to Crown Court for trial. In the meantime, he was remanded in custody — his solicitor's application for bail having been dismissed out of hand by the magistrate.

Detective Sergeant Mike Crawford (he'd been promoted since the attack) did his best to keep me aware of what was going on but it seemed the case was bogged down.

"We need to ensure that we present a water tight case," he explained. "He's refused to say anything in interviews — which he's entitled to do. If he'd been arrested after 10th April, there's a new caution that warns that if a suspect fails to mention something they later rely on in court it may harm their defence. Unfortunately, that can't apply in this case. Galling, I know. So, we need to anticipate any possible defence he might offer at the trial."

"What can he say?" I asked.

"Well, he might try and claim that it was an accident. Or that he only intended to scare them. That's the problem. We don't know what he'll say. We are doing our damnedest to cover everything we can think of. Believe me, we want this bastard almost as much as you do."

"Accident? How the hell can he claim it was an accident? He drove straight at them on the pavement!"

"I know — but we need to be able to show intent. That he wasn't distracted by something; or avoiding a dog in the road. We both know it was deliberate but we need to prove it beyond reasonable doubt. And it takes time to collate statements from witnesses and put it all together. Believe me, we aren't dragging our feet."

"I know you aren't, Mike, and I do appreciate that you're doing your best. It's just so fucking frustrating and it's hanging over me — and Anne's and my parents and Carol."

"Well, Williams isn't enjoying prison I can assure you. The other cons don't like child killers and the screws are tending to look the other way when they deal out their own retribution. He's been in the prison hospital twice with broken ribs he got from falling down some stairs – well that's what the report says; lost teeth through falling against some railings and a black eye walking into a door frame."

Chapter 25 – John June 1995

It didn't make up for what he'd done to Anne and Samantha — but I got some satisfaction from hearing about his injuries.

Eventually, Mike Crawford rang to tell me that a date had been set for the trial.

Carol and I had been listed as witnesses as to his attitude towards me to demonstrate likely intent. We sat where we could watch Williams. He'd already done what he could to hurt me so he couldn't intimidate me anymore. The CPS's be-wigged barristers in their black robes introduced themselves before taking their places on the bench behind piles of documents. Near them, Williams own solicitor and barristers sat with their papers.

"All stand," called the clerk of the court as a door opened and the judge entered. As briefed, we bowed as did everyone else in the court. Everyone, that is, except Williams who stood in the dock accompanied by a Prison Officer. I wasn't unhappy to see that his nose bore signs of having been broken and he still had traces of a black eye. He was still having a rough time inside it seemed.

We sat and the court began selecting the jury.

The charges were read and Williams asked how he pleaded.

"Guilty,"

I was stunned. I looked at Carol then at DS Crawford and realised that we'd all been shaken by the plea. It was an anti-climax. We'd expected a fight and have to relive our experiences on that awful day and the time leading up to it. But it wasn't needed.

The case was adjourned for sentencing and the jury, who'd hardly had time to settle in their seats, was dismissed.

A week later, we were back in court. My own parents and Anne's were with Carol and myself this time.

The judge entered and took his place. He looked over at Williams, glanced at his notes then said: "You have pleaded guilty to the charges laid before you but you waited until the last moment to do so. You cannot, therefore, expect any reduction in the sentence as a consequence. This was a calculated, cold-blooded and deliberately spiteful act. You took the lives of two innocent individuals, one of them a child, in a deliberate act of revenge and in a manner that endangered the lives of others nearby. Further, you have previously served sentences for other violent crimes. You are clearly a serious danger to the public and I see no mitigating circumstances for your actions. The mandatory sentence in this case is life imprisonment. You will serve a minimum of twenty-five years in custody. Take him down."

Six of us went for lunch after sentencing. I should have felt satisfaction knowing that Williams would be locked away for much of his adult life. But it didn't bring Anne or Samantha back — it was just a waste of three lives; four, if you included Liz who had taken her own life because of him.

Chapter 26. John — September 1996

It had been two years since the tragedy and fifteen months since William's trial. I'd moved on from the Desk Top Publishing company which simply couldn't compete with PageMaker and Quark's offerings and was now involved in one offering complete CAD systems aimed at design engineers.

We were organising a series of exhibitions around the country and had plans to move into Europe the following year. We'd commissioned the conversion of a coach as a display unit from an exhibition company and I was visiting some potential venues in the north to finalise where we would hold some open days to demonstrate the systems.

My schedule was fairly flexible. I'd driven up to Leeds that morning and had checked out the Post House near the airport. I'd made myself known to the manager and had been shown the facilities. I then visited another couple of other potential sites in that area including a pleasant country hotel set in its own grounds just north of the city — where I was stopping for the night. This had promise, but somewhere south of the city offered better road communications.

The next morning, I'd be heading over the Pennines to Manchester. I wanted to have a look at the G-Mex centre where we were involved in an exhibition the following year. As I planned my route, I saw it took me down Bury New Road to the city centre. Why did that ring a bell? Then I realised there was a cross-dresser shop on Bury New Road. Or was it Bury Old Road? I'd also heard that Manchester had a celebrated gay scene. Were these signals for me?

Once I'd purged all of my feminine clothes and accessories after Anne and Samantha had been killed, I thought all that was behind me. Recently, however, I had found myself looking at ladies clothing and touching the underwear as I shopped in Marks and Spencer's and knew I missed the pleasure of dressing and the feel of silky fabrics against my skin.

Disposing of everything that reminded me of Anne and Samantha had been as part of my reaction to their pointless deaths. Deaths that had strengthened my hatred of drug addiction and those who encouraged youngsters to experiment and then preyed on their habit.

But drugs and the deaths of those I had loved had nothing to do with my transvestism. So why did I resist the temptation to start dressing as a woman again?

I lit a cigarette, a habit I'd started after Anne and Samantha's murder, and made a cup of coffee from the supplies in my room and started to make a list of what I would need IF I was to start dressing again.

I made a deal with myself. IF I could afford everything I'd need from what I had in my wallet and what I could draw from a cashpoint and IF I could find the shop, then it would be a sign from the universe that I should start dressing again. But finding the shop might be the problem. Then I remembered, they advertised regularly in Exchange and Mart.

Having made my list, I totalled it up. I checked my wallet — with what I had in it and what I could draw from a cashpoint, I would have more than enough. Ok, so can I find the shop?

I grabbed my car keys and headed for a newsagent. I picked up a copy of the publication and glanced at the pages towards the back. Yes. There was the advert. Bury Old Road. I hadn't been far off. I saw some packets of blue tack and, remembering an old trick I'd used, grabbed one of those.

There was a café near the newsagents so I popped it and bought a coffee. I lit a cigarette while I thought through my plans for Manchester. What would I need to get and where? I glanced at a woman sitting at one of the other tables and felt the anticipation of looking like her in a few hours. It had been too long. Far too long.

I knew I could pass once dressed — providing I could remember the techniques I'd learned, but I still didn't fancy walking into a shop dressed as a male and trying on female clothes. I didn't want to cause a riot in the changing rooms. I lit another cigarette and pondered the problem. It didn't take me long to work out a solution.

As I came out of the café, I could see the familiar fascia of Boots. Great! I could get the false nails I wanted and a few other bits and pieces there. There was also a bank nearby so I withdrew my maximum just in case I needed cash for some of my purchases.

Back at the hotel, I took out the box of false nails, I selected the best fitting ones for my fingers and put them in hot water in the sink. While they softened, I turned the lid upside down and stuck ten blobs of blue tack to it. Having moulded the false nails to my own, I stuck them on the Blue tack while I applied nail varnish. It was one of the tricks I'd learned. Too often in the past, false nails had pinged their way across the room because they weren't fitting properly. Let these try that! While the first coat of varnish dried, I applied Immac cream to my legs, smoked a cigarette while it worked then scraped it off along with any hairs. By then, the nails were ready for a second coat of the deep plum varnish.

The next morning, I had an early breakfast and was on the road by eight. I realised it was Friday 13th and hoped that wasn't an omen for the day.

An hour later, I drove down Bury Old Road, found the shop I wanted, parked round the corner and went in. It didn't take long to complete my purchases of a light brown highlighted, shoulder length wig and some false breasts which had cost an arm and a leg; fair exchange I thought. I hadn't bought items which were readily available elsewhere mainly because of the prices. I certainly wasn't prepared to pay £50 for a pair of high heels when I could get them elsewhere for less than half that price.

It took another half hour to get to G-Mex. I wanted to get an impression of its ambience, principal traffic flows and dead spots so I would have an idea of which stand to apply for. Having checked this out, I found my hotel and dropped my company Cavalier in the car park.

In Marks and Spencer's, temporarily located in Lewis' department store due to the Arndale bomb earlier that year, I picked up a basket then proceeded to select some underwear, a pair of ski pants and a sweatshirt, a nightdress and negligee and a bathrobe. I took them over to the checkout and offered my credit card. I wondered if the cashier would comment on my purchases — not that I cared if she did.

Chapter 26 – John September 1996

My next port of call was the beauty department where I asked one of the girls to help me select some make-up, telling her it was for me as I wanted to ensure I got the right shades. My confidence was returning and I felt quite comfortable discussing the shades with her.

As I paid for them, the assistant told me to let me know if I needed a hand with doing the make-up.

It was then nearly half past two, I decided to go back to my hotel and register before putting the next part of my plan into action.

Once in my room, I put on my new underwear, tights, ski pants and sweatshirt. It felt so right to be dressed again. After doing my make-up and fitting my wig in place, I slipped my feet into the trainers and looked in the mirror. The vision that looked back at me seemed so right. Even if I said so myself, it was a reasonably attractive female. "Welcome back, Angela," I whispered, blowing myself a kiss. I then realised I'd forgotten to buy a handbag or purse so had to slip my wallet and keys into my pocket.

Carefully opening the door, I glanced up and down the corridor, checking that no-one else would see me leaving my room. The passage was empty apart from a cleaner's trolley at the far end so I pulled the door behind me and walked towards the lift. Just as I approached the last bedroom, the door opened and an overweight guy strode out nearly colliding with me.

"Sorry, darling," he said, as he stepped back out of my way.

I gave him a smile and walked on towards the lift. He followed and stood on the opposite side of the doors as they opened and an elderly couple got out. He then waited for me to enter first.

"Ground floor?" He asked, his finger hovering over the buttons.

"Yes, please."

As the doors hissed closed and the lift dropped, he looked at me quizzically. Had he spotted something?

"Do you know Manchester?"

"Sorry, no, I don't. I'm just visiting," I replied.

"Ah. You wouldn't know how to get to Old Trafford, I suppose?"

"I'm afraid not. I'm sure reception will be able to help though."

"I guess. Well, enjoy your day." Once again, he stood aside for me to exit first.

What had that been about? Had it been innocent? Or had he been trying to chat me up? That possibility, as ridiculous as it was, sent a frisson through my stomach.

Once out of the hotel, my first stop was for shoes. I was fortunate as I took an eight; on the large size for women but still stocked by most shops. There would be time enough another day to look for special shoes to go with specific outfits; today I just wanted some basics.

There was a good selection at around a third of the price charged by the TV shop in the first outlet I went in. Several times when trying them on and looking in the mirror, I found myself turning to ask Anne for her opinion. She may not have been there in person, but I felt her presence and her encouragement to 'go for it'. I could have spent half the day in there just trying on the different styles and colours; but I had a lot to do so I controlled my excitement and settled on a pair of black courts with slim, not quite stiletto, three-inch heels and a pair of taupe driving loafers. I added a handbag and purse to my purchases.

I wandered up and down the road deciding which dress shop to go in first. Then I saw a fabulous silver jersey dress with long sleeves in one of the windows. Would they have it in my size? Would it fit? How would it look on? There was only one way to find out. I pushed the door open and went in. Once inside, I found the dress from the window in my size — the material felt so sensual and I knew I had to have it. It wasn't exactly something to wear during the day though — so I'd need some other items as well.

My original holiday plan had just been to tour the Lake District; do some walking and generally relax. As John, I could spend evenings in the pub or hotel bar in casual clothes. As Angela it would be much more fun to dress up for dinner. But that would mean even more outfits — I could hardly wear the same things two consecutive evenings. What a shame!

Fortunately, there was plenty of choice and I was well laden when I asked to use the changing cubicle.

The silver dress was gorgeous and fitted like a dream falling just on my knees. I also found a sleeveless, midnight blue dress with maroon trim and dark blue sequins that shimmered as I moved. A couple of skirts and tops and a lightweight raincoat joined the pile that I planned to buy.

I kept a skirt and blouse on and carried the rest to the till. I'd worn the high heels while trying on the dresses and, as anticipated, I felt them pulling my calves taut as I carried my purchases to the till.

"Is that everything?" the assistant asked.

"For now," I replied and handed her my credit card, remembering at the last moment that it was in my male name. Oh well, what could she do? I needn't have worried; she rang up the total, filled in the slip, passed it to me to sign, compared my signature with the one on the back of the card, put the slip and card into the machine — then handed me my receipts.

Laden down by all my packages, I struggled to open the door and was relieved when a couple approached and the guy held the it open for me. "After you, love," he said. I smiled and thanked him. I was quite certain I wouldn't have been shown the same courtesy as 'John'. I did, however, need to deal with carrying all my purchases — and those I still planned to buy.

Fortunately, a few doors up was a luggage shop where I added a dusty-pink wheeled suitcase to my next credit card bill. Having paid, I put all of my packages into the case. Now it was back to Lewis'. As I walked in through the doors, I was enveloped by the fragrances from the perfume department. I picked up a basket and wandered between the counters trying out the testers; quickly running out of places to spray as the scents started to mingle.

"Would you like some testing strips?" an assistant asked.

"No thanks, I've decided on the Rive Gauche. Do you have matching talc, body lotion and bath gel?"

"Certainly, did you want it in a gift set or as individual items?"

"Is there any difference in price? It's for me."

She glanced around. "I shouldn't really say this, but the individual items are much better value but the store makes more profit on the gift set."

"I'll take the individual ones then, please."

As she registered the sale, I sprayed my wrist and neck with the tester. A shiver went down my spine as I inhaled the lovely aroma.

I had a number of other purchases to make. A silk scarf, some designer sunglasses, a couple of necklaces, bracelets, earrings and three dress rings and a watch; an evening bag and a couple of cosmetic bags. I hadn't had so much fun for months, well, since the tragedy. I really had missed it. I just kept wishing that Anne was still with me to share the pleasure. Having completed my list, I deliberately sought out the assistant who had helped me to select the make-up.

"Remember me?" I asked, as I handed her my purchases.

"No, I'm afraid not. Oh, wait a minute, yes, of course. You look great — but you could do with some shading around the chin line, and your eyes are a bit dated. I hope you don't mind me mentioning that. I like the skirt and top, where did you get them?"

"At Allan's, just down the road. You said you might be prepared to help me with the make-up, are you doing anything this evening?"

"Nothing that can't be put off. My shift finishes at 6 but it's usually another half hour before I get away. Do you want to pick me up or are you staying in a hotel?"

"I'm at the Piccadilly. Room 554. Just across the road."

"Yes, I know the Piccadilly, I'll come over to you, then. It's probably better that way. We aren't exactly encouraged to make dates with customers. What time should I come?"

"As soon as you like."

"OK, it will probably be just about 6.30."

"Thanks, I'll see you later then."

My original estimate had been well short of the final total but, then, I had bought rather more than I'd planned. Not that it mattered. I'd not exactly spent much on myself since the funeral.

Back in my room, I laid out my purchases. The clothes on the bed, the cosmetics, facial treatments and 'smellies' on the dressing table.

I made myself a coffee, lit a cigarette and found the earrings I had bought. I then went to try them on and found my lobes had healed over. I checked the time. If I was lucky, I'd be able to get back to the beauty salon in the department store and get them pierced again. It was that or a sharp needle — and I didn't fancy the latter!

Half an hour later, I was back in my room. I cleaned off my make-up while I ran a bath adding loads of Rive Gauche gel to the water.

I applied a face pack and then enjoyed a relaxing half hour letting the perfumed bath ease away my cares, before dragging myself out of the water and slipping into my towelling bath robe. Once I'd cleaned off the face pack, I cleansed and toned my skin, still hairless after electrolysis, and applied some body lotion and talc to the rest of my body.

I checked my watch, 6.20, the girl from the make-up counter would be here soon. I realised I didn't even know her name!

Which dress should I wear this evening? Perhaps I would ask the beautician. In the meantime, I had better make myself decent and put on some underwear. Just as I finished putting on the slip, there was a knock at the door.

"Hi, hope I'm not too early for you."

"Not at all, please come in," I told her. "Would you like a drink?"

"Thanks, I'll have a vodka and tonic, please. By the way, I'm Joy."

"I'm Angela, when I'm dressed like this."

"Fine, Angela. You certainly seem to have all of the gear. Have you dressed much in the past? I can't believe it's your first time, yet you needed a complete set of cosmetics."

"I used to dress a lot but I stopped for a while." I didn't want to explain why and Joy didn't pry.

"Well, you certainly aren't alone in giving up and starting again. We see quite a few TVs in Manchester, there's quite a good scene for them."

"You mean the gay village? I've heard about it. Is it as good as they say?"

"Absolutely. I often go there myself. It's a lot of fun and I don't have to constantly fight off guys trying to hit on me."

"I'll have to check it out for myself. Where's the best place to eat."

"Well, there are plenty of places. My favourite is Taurus at the top of Canal Street — I'm going there once we've finished. Why don't you join me? I can show you round some of the clubs afterwards if you like."

I considered her offer. How did I feel about going out with another woman? It would be the first time I'd been out with anyone since Anne died. Not that it was a date — just someone being friendly. On the other hand, I really should repay her kindness.

"That would be great. But only if you let me pay for your meal."

"OK, I won't argue. Right, let's see what we've got here. I also brought a few extra bits and pieces with me in case we need them." The 'few extras' was a display case full of cosmetics. "I also work with photographers and film and television companies as a make-up artist," Joy explained.

She asked me to sit down and put a band around my head to keep my hair away from my face.

"What sort of look are you after? Normal day make-up or a more glam for evenings?"

"You said I needed to shade my chin line and my eyeshadow was a bit dated, can you show me what you meant? Then, perhaps, if you've got time, you could do my face with something suitable for going out?"

"No problem. We can cover both in an hour or so."

My hair wasn't as long as it used to be, certainly not enough to make a pony tail as I used to do. But it still covered my ears and, with a bit of back combing and gel, could be transformed into a feminine style.

"It could do with a setting and some slight trimming, but do you see what I mean?" Joy asked. "You could even have a complete perm though they are a bit 1980s. Now, let's have a look at your face. It's lovely and smooth, you've obviously had electrolysis, haven't you? And you've looked after it well with proper cleansers and moisturiser. Yes?"

"Yes, I have 'though not for a couple of years. I expected to see some re-growth by now."

"Well, there are a few hairs, but nothing worth mentioning. You don't have any shadow area which would need concealing before we start with foundation.

140

In fact, to be honest, you don't need much shading around the chin, either. But let me give you some suggestions for doing your eyelids. The style you are using is a bit harsher than today's fashion."

She demonstrated how she suggested I should apply my eyeshadow, using much more subdued tones than I had used before. And much finer eyeliners in shades that toned in with the eyeshadow, rather than the dark blue I'd traditionally used — explaining every step so I could recreate the look in the future. It took me back to when Anne first showed me how to do it. God, I missed her — and Samantha.

"Now, for evening, you can go for a rather more striking look. Especially for the clubs we'll visit tonight. What are you planning to wear?"

"I wasn't sure." I picked up the two dresses that I'd laid on the bed. "I've got this dark blue one with sequins or this silver jersey dress. Which do you think?"

"Either would be fine."

I decided on the blue sequined dress and Joy redid my make-up emphasising my cheek bones with an intense blusher then using purples and mauves on my eyelids, extending the liner and shadow beyond the eyebrows and using much more mascara than I would normally go for— making my eyes 'pop'.

Once, she'd finished, I pulled on the dress and looked in the mirror. Wow. What a difference she'd made.

"Happy?" she asked.

"It's brilliant," I told her.

"Ok, then. Ready for this?"

"Absolutely!"

We drained our glasses and I put on my coat and scarf and picked up my handbag. On the way down in the lift, Joy told me the restaurant she had in mind wasn't far.

"This is the famous Canal Street" she told me as we turned a corner. "The restaurant is just here on the right."

"Good evening ladies, table for two?"

We followed the tall waitress to a table near the window. "Can I get you a drink while you decide what you want?" I realised from her voice that she and I had something in common.

"Glass of white wine for me. What about you Joy?"

"I'll have the same please."

"Well, let's order a bottle then."

"Cheers," I said holding my glass towards her; she clinked hers against mine. "Cheers."

"How long are you staying in Manchester?" she asked offering me a cigarette. I took it and offered her a light.

"I'd only planned the one night, then go on to the Lake District for a holiday but I might stop over tomorrow night as well. It'll give me chance to do a bit more shopping tomorrow and another night out."

"Sounds lovely, I wish I was coming with you."

After dinner, we visited a number of the clubs around the area. Joy was obviously no stranger to the scene as she was constantly introducing me to some of the other TVs and men and women we met.

"I sometimes do make-up demos for one of the trans support group," she explained, "so I've met a few of the girls."

Just wandering the streets from club to club was incredible. I'd been to the group in London and to drag and trans balls and one or two other clubs but it had always been a case of minimising the risk of exposure — dashing from car or cab into the venue and avoiding mixing with 'normal' people. When I had been dressed in public, I'd always been concerned about people seeing through my disguise. But here in the village, it didn't matter. Everyone was accepted for who they were and it didn't matter how you dressed or how you looked. It was incredibly liberating.

As we danced together in one of the clubs, I realised my libido was responding. Whether it was being dressed again, my perfume, Joy's body being held close to mine, or just being totally relaxed, I wasn't sure. But, for the first time in more than two years, I was aroused. Was I betraying Anne's memory? Was this what I'd subconsciously been looking for when I sought Joy out and asked for help with my make-up? Had I been fooling myself when I said it wasn't a real date? What would Anne have said? I knew she wouldn't have wanted me to remain celibate for the rest of my life any more that I would have wanted her to, if the positions had been reversed. Our ethos had been that life was for living.

Joy was also aware of my erection. She could hardly miss it pressing against her. She turned her head towards me and offered her lips for a kiss. I fondled her and felt her hands caressing my bottom. We kissed again and I probed between her lips with my tongue. By the end of the dance, I had a flagpole which needed to be restrained and I made my way to the toilets to sort myself out. While buying a round of drinks, I picked up some free condoms from a dispenser on the bar and slipped them into my handbag.

Joy and I sat out a couple of dances and had a drink, a cigarette and a cuddle, before making our way back onto the crowded floor. Nobody took the slightest notice of our embraces. And I didn't care whether they thought we were lesbians or realised I was a TV.

At about 2am, we walked back over to my hotel. Once in my room, I took Joy into my arms and, as our tongues entwined, felt behind her and unzipped her dress. I felt her doing the same to mine. Leaving our dresses where they had fallen, we shuffled across to the bed and collapsed onto it.

Chapter 27. Mary — 1996-7

Towards the end of 1996, ID invested in SeaCon to enable them to develop a new range of yachting instruments. As we didn't interfere with the day-to-day management of well-run companies, we had no inkling of their plans to appoint a new advertising agency.

During the family's visit in 1997, Charles reported SeaCon had commissioned Halls to prepare the launch material for the OceanMaster Range and handle existing products. He also advised us Peter Judge, SeaCon's owner, was thinking of retiring at the end of the year and had asked Charles to investigate possible buyers.

One of Arthur's other interests at that time was an American company which was also involved in the sailing industry and had their own, limited, range of instruments which they needed to expand.

Chapter 27 – Mary 1996-7

I saw this as an opportunity to get my revenge on Hall. I could raise the two million Peter was asking for without disposing of my shares in ID Inc. if the forecast results materialised and ID's dividends were on the same scale as the previous year. It certainly wasn't a wise investment. There was little prospect of the two million providing anything like the same returns as my investments were currently earning. But that wasn't important.

Arthur was aware of my previous involvement with Nigel Hall. "Looks like he has it coming to him and I want to help."

"I suggest the first step should be to express and interest in principle, if that's what you want. In the meantime, I'll have SeaCon checked out — especially any contacts of Nigel Hall's," replied Charles.

The reports filtered in. It was fairly obvious that Collins was living beyond his salary and, as no other legitimate sources of income had been identified, there was little doubt he was on the take. We also learned Collins was gambling heavily and was having an affair with his secretary, unbeknown to his wife.

The dossier gradually grew. We had investigators observe Collins and Hall when they visited casinos where they watched Collins pick up chips that belonged to Hall. We also investigated Hall and obtained evidence of payments to some other clients. How these were obtained, I neither knew nor cared.

I was looking forward to renewing Hall's acquaintance, short lived as it would be.

In the July, I met Peter Judge and gave him a banker's draft for the option to buy his shares as agreed. The actual purchase would take effect in the December.

On 16th November, I flew from Dallas Fort Worth into Heathrow where Charles met me. He had relocated his practice some years earlier when ID Inc. had first retained his services.

Charles, Diane and their two children Olivia and Richard, now lived in a delightful part of Surrey near Guildford where Charles' offices were located. Driving from Heathrow to their home could take anything from about 20 minutes to well over an hour depending on traffic on the M25.

Being a Sunday, our journey was relatively quick and I was soon assaulted by Olivia and Richard demanding to know if I'd bought them any presents and was it true I was staying in England for good this time.

Chapter 27 – Mary 1996-7

I promised them I was back for a long time, if not ever. And, yes, there were presents.

The next morning, Charles and I met Peter Judge to finalise the details for the purchase of his company. Our meeting was in a hotel as we were determined it should remain secret as long as possible. Peter shared our wishes if not our reasons. He was concerned his staff should not be faced with uncertainty in the run up to Christmas.

I assured him that with one immediate exception, if his staff were competent, they would be retained for at least six months. Beyond that, it was totally impossible to give firm commitments no matter how well intentioned they might be.

Charles gave Peter details of what we had discovered about Collins and I explained my personal involvement and the proposed solution.

"You must do what you consider appropriate, Mary. Frankly, I suppose I realised something was going on, but I had become complacent and, I must admit, weary. I left too much of the day-to-day operation to characters like Collins."

I had asked Peter to bring samples of all of the publicity work done by Halls together with invoices, contact reports and media schedules and any other documentation.

On Tuesday, I took this material down to Penny and Paul in Southampton. The 2 Peas had been hit, as had many others, during the recession, but their strategy of providing core services and contracting specialist work from freelancers to whom they provided desk space had paid off. They were, of course fortunate to have had a landlady who had not imposed swingeing rent increases over the past eight years. I'd been content to see the value of the premises rise year by year and even doubling their rent would not have affected my personal circumstances significantly. The secretarial bureau had also developed, in spite of the recession and now also provided a desk top publishing service for both outside clients and the agency and its freelancer artists and designers.

Penny and Paul started to examine the documents I had brought with me. Whilst detailed evaluation of the costs would take some time, and involve contacting the printers and publications used, they were both immediately critical of the creative approach and the finished quality of much of the work. They promised to let me have their report by the end of the week.

In the meantime, I had other work to do. Charles had made an office available to me in his premises and had installed at my expense, the equipment I would need to prepare my next steps.

On the Friday, Penny arrived with "The 2 Peas" report on SeaCon's promotional campaign.

When talking to magazines, they'd said they were pitching for an undisclosed potential client. Each magazine had offered appropriate series discounts and hinted bigger discounts might be negotiable if necessary. On that basis, Halls had overcharged by at least 10% on advertising spaces.

The printing showed a similar story. Paul had identified the printers used by Halls and had requested quotations based on the precise specifications of the SeaCon brochures. Halls had marked up the costs by nearly 70%. The creative work was, similarly, between twice and three times the appropriate rate.

If the work had been superb and the results had been sales, then that might have been acceptable. High, but acceptable. But the work was poorly conceived and even more poorly executed. Even the corporate logo was in the wrong shade.

I had the evidence I needed.

Chapter 28. George — 21st November 1997.

Before the company stopped work for the weekend, Peter Judge called the staff together for a meeting. He announced Intertrade Developments Incorporated, who had provided finance for the development of the OceanMaster range, was providing a further injection of capital in the company. As part of the deal, Mary Sanchez would be joining as Marketing Director effective as of Monday.

I viewed the news with mixed feeling. It put somebody else over my head but, equally, it demonstrated a commitment to marketing and could lead to a bigger budget. I had little doubt I would be able to charm Mrs Sanchez even if she was from the States where they seemed to breed forceful business women.

I considered cancelling my trip to Le Touquet with Nigel Hall, but needed to relax for a few days. I'd also been unlucky recently at the tables and needed to pick up some money.

Chapter 28 – George 21st November 1997

There was a yacht race from Chichester to Dieppe and we were then hiring a car. Nigel would be covering all the costs, of course.

The Monday evening found us enjoying a delicious meal in the hotel just over the road from the golf course. A meal made even more palatable by the company of two extremely attractive girls. Kristina was sitting on my left and constantly leant forward to listen to the conversation, giving me tantalising glimpses of her breasts, which were barely restrained by the long red dress she was wearing. As the dress was also slit from ankle to well above the knees, I had also been treated to frequent sights of her well-tanned thighs.

After dinner, we went on to the casino, where Nigel gave the girls a batch of chips. I cashed a cheque I couldn't really afford for a thousand francs worth myself and took Kristina over to the roulette table.

I had a simple system which usually meant I came out ahead, even if it wasn't likely to result in a fortune. I waited until red or black or odd or even had come up three times in a row, then bet on the other. I also kept track of the individual numbers that came up and bet on groups that had not recently occurred — gradually reducing the numbers I was covering until I might be on one or two single numbers. If I lost, I would double my bets until I did win.

Scientifically, I'm told the odds on each roll are identical and no one number is more likely than any other to occur regardless of what has happened before. I prefer to believe that over the course of an evening, every number should have an equal chance of coming up and if it hasn't occurred recently, then the odds are in my favour. Providing the table isn't fixed.

My method demands an almost photographic memory. But I've always been good with numbers. Give me a phone number once and I'll remember it for years. Faces and names are another matter. They just don't register. Or, maybe I'm just not interested enough to bother.

Betting this way, my initial stake remained fairly constant for the first half hour while I took stock of the individual numbers which were coming up. I then started to play some of the groups. Luck, obviously, also plays a part and I was fortunate one of four numbers I'd covered with a 100-franc bet came up on the second attempt. I now had nearly double my initial investment. But this didn't stop me picking up a stack of chips Nigel placed next to me.

Kristina had been duly impressed by my winnings and linked her arm into mine.

Neither Nigel nor I were particularly interested in staying too long in the casino. We both had other ideas in mind for entertaining the girls.

Back at the hotel, I retrieved my room key and put my arm around Kristina as we walked along the corridor to my room. I fondled her gorgeous bottom, but could feel no trace of any panties. As soon as I closed the door behind us, Kristina slipped her arms around my neck. As I fastened my lips to hers, she pressed herself against my erection. I reached behind her and found the fastening for her halter neck. Her dress fell to the floor and she stepped out of it. I had been correct, apart from a tiny thong, a necklace and her perfume, she was naked. She reached for my waist and undid my belt and top button then unzipped my trousers. Her long-nailed fingers slipped inside my pants and pulled them down.

"Oh chéri, c'est magnifique! Your prick, it is so big! Come, feed my pussy with it."

I needed no further invitation. I kicked off my shoes and trousers, stripped off my shirt and pants and joined her on the bed. Her body was perfect. It went in and out exactly where it should, her complexion was flawless and there was now no doubt her long blond hair was natural. As I pulled her to me, she pressed me down onto my back, the straddled me and rubbed her breasts up and down my chest. She offered me each nipple in turn to kiss and suck then her tongue traced a sensuous path from my neck, over my chest and stomach to my prick. It flickered over the tip, driving me wild. She licked under my balls, then took the entire length of my cock into her mouth. I'm not given to boasting, but I'm well endowed. As she sucked, I thought I would come there and then, but she controlled me. She lifted her head and leant forward to offer me her tits once more so I could flick the nipples with my tongue. She shuffled up, rubbing her slit where her tongue had passed before. Eventually, she pulled my arms out to the side and knelt on them, preventing me from moving at all. She lowered her slit down onto my face and I greedily sucked and licked away. She moaned and writhed as my tongue forced its way into her slit.

Then she rolled onto her back and pulled me on top. My penis slid easily into her soaking cunt and she wrapped her legs around me.

"Fuck me chéri. Fuck me hard, as hard as you can."

Chapter 28 – George 21st November 1997

As I did as I was asked, she continued to moan and match my thrusts with her own.

"Plus fort, chéri. Mon dieu, c'est fantastique. C'est si grand, Encore, chéri, plus vite, faster, harder, plus fort. N'arrête pas, encore, encore . Oh aah, aaah, tu es le meilleur, the plus meilleur. Ohh! Ahhh! Ahhhhh!" Kristina convulsed as I finally shot my spunk into her.

"Chéri. That was terrific," she assured me. "Your prick, it is so big! So long. You are hell of a stud. Other women are always after you. Yes? Now I will lick you clean, then you can do the same for me. Ça va?"

The next day, the two girls caddied for us while we played golf. Frankly, I would just as soon not have bothered. There was a bitter wind blowing off the channel. In fact, we decided to call it a day after the first nine holes. I'm not a golfer. I can generally reach the green within the expected number of shots, but then take 3 or 4 more putts to sink the ball.

But too much business is done on the golf course for me to let my opinion become too obvious. When we had first started playing together, Nigel had tried to let me win. I told him not to bother — he would just get frustrated. So, now, on the rare occasions when we do go for a round, I satisfy myself with getting within five feet of the pin and call it a day rather than hold up others following us.

That evening, we returned to the casino. My previous evening luck had deserted me and it was all I could do to hold on to my initial stake. In fact, I lost a few hundred francs before were returned to the hotel.

Kristina and Yvonne swopped places. Yvonne lacked Kristina's animal passion, but she knew plenty of other, more subtle, ways of arousing the senses. On our final evening, Nigel asked which of the two girls I would prefer — or did I want both?

"Do they perform on each other?" I asked.

"They'll do whatever we ask them to do," he replied.

I took advantage of his offer. After Kristina and Yvonne had given us a very private show, Nigel left us to it and I joined the girls on the bed.

The next morning, we drove back to the yacht and had a leisurely sail back to the Hamble.

Chapter 28 – George 21st November 1997

On the Friday morning, I arrived at the office a few minutes after nine to be met by my secretary.

"Good morning Miss Kirby, and how are you today?"

Joan looked worried, or angry. She had been one of a series of temps we had used until I'd suggested a full-time position might be possible in exchange for certain favours. After a dinner that evening, we had returned to her flat. At first, it had been clear she was only obliging me for the sake of getting a job. Later, she confessed she enjoyed my large prick, and had even come to like me. God knows why! If she had learned about the girls in France, my life wouldn't be worth living. It was bad enough already. She had started to get a bit possessive and had started dropping hints about me getting a divorce and marrying her. That was not even a remote possibility.

Gail, my wife, was a nag. But she stood to inherit a packet when an old aunt of hers died. The aunt was terminally ill and not expected to see out the winter. Her death and the inheritance would solve all of my immediate financial problems. But if Joan caused trouble, and finding out about France might give her an excuse, then God knows what I would do.

"What's up?" I asked.

"Mrs Sanchez wants to see you as soon as you arrive."

"Well, I'm sure she can wait until I've taken my coat off."

So that was all. Well, it was hardly surprising she would want to see me as I was, presumably, her deputy.

"Which office is she in?"

"She's using the boardroom at present. By the way, she's asked me to be her secretary."

"Has she now? Well, it's probably not a bad idea. You can keep me informed of what's going on, can't you?"

Joan didn't answer me and wouldn't look at me either. Typical bloody women, I thought. Always moody for no reason. Probably time of the month. Bit of a relief that, I was shagged out after France!

Chapter 29. Mary — 28th November 1997

As far as SeaCon staff were concerned, I was joining the company as part of a deal involving a significant injection of capital. Whilst changes were inevitable, Peter Judge had advised everyone there would be no redundancies for at least six months.

I would join SeaCon as Marketing Director and use that title until I officially took over the company on 1st January. This would give me a month to get to know people and obtain opinions not coloured by the fact they were talking to their new boss.

It was in this role I sent for George Collins as soon as he returned from his golfing trip to Le Touquet with Hall.

"Come in Mr Collins, please close the door and sit down."

"Thank you, Mary. It's all right for me to call you Mary, I hope. We don't tend to stand on ceremony in SeaCon. Congratulations on your appointment, I'm sure we are going to work well together."

"As it happens, yes, I do mind you calling me Mary. And there are going to be a number of changes around here. Changes that directly concern you."

Collins' face went pale.

"What is your relationship with Nigel Hall?"

"Nigel's the owner of our advertising agency. They've been handling our promotional work since earlier this year and, in my opinion, are doing a fine job now some earlier problems have been overcome."

"I don't share your opinion and I have to say I suspect, no, I have proof, concrete proof, you have been accepting bribes from Hall."

"That's ridiculous. I demand to know who's made such unfounded allegations and I'll instruct my solicitor to take appropriate action over those lies."

Collins started to stand up.

"Sit down! I've been assessing the campaigns run for us by Halls and obtained independent advice. They're appalling, their costs are unjustified and we've been paying author's corrections for errors that were down to them. I know for a fact Halls negotiated substantial series discounts which were not passed on to SeaCon. I also have evidence of gambling chips, being passed to you by Hall. The conclusions are inevitable. Either you're totally incompetent or you're guilty of gross professional misconduct. In either case, there's no place for you with SeaCon."

Collins seemed to shrink into the chair.

"Well, at least you are not adding lying to your crimes. You have two options. You can resign citing whatever reason you wish as the excuse for your departure, perhaps resentment at having someone brought in above you, or I'll sack you. If you resign, we'll pay you until the end of the month as well as any other benefits which may be due. If you choose not to resign, we will summarily dismiss you with no compensation for lack of notice. There is, however, one condition to allowing you to resign. It's that you will not communicate with Hall by any means until after 12 noon. Do you understand?"

"Yes, I understand. But it isn't how it looks. Yes, Nigel gave me the odd chip when we visited casinos and I know we had some teething problems when he first took over the account, but I genuinely believe his agency do a good job for us. I was aware his charges were higher than some other agencies, but you get what you pay for and it's difficult to put a price on creativity."

"What you say may be correct. But the fact remains Halls did not pass on discounts to which we were entitled and it was your job to monitor such matters. Their mark up on print was far higher than it should have been and, again, you should — and I believe did — realise that. I don't think you are incompetent. I believe you were greedy and anxious to accept the gifts Hall offered. Faced with the choice of taking Hall to task over his charges and giving up those bribes or accepting both, you chose to do nothing. That was totally unacceptable."

"What happens now?"

"You'll return to your office. A security officer will accompany you and allow you to remove your personal possessions but nothing else. You'll then drive home and he'll collect any company equipment you may have there. You'll clear your car of any private belongings and give him the keys. He will remain with you until 12 noon during which time you will make no telephone calls nor attempt to make any other contact with anyone. After that, you may do as you please."

Collins had been a fool. But I knew how Hall operated and how easily it was for those responsible for major budgets to be fêted by their suppliers. Most accepted entertainment, but declined anything which could be interpreted as bribery. Collins had stepped way beyond the line.

Now it was Hall's turn.

Chapter 30. George — 28th November 1997 mid-day

I was in the shit. Out on my ear with little to show for years of loyal service. My prospects were grim. There was little chance of getting a job with Nigel's outfit as it seemed highly likely he'd be losing the SeaCon account. That'll put a hole in his cash flow. Fuck, I'm not likely to pick up any more bonuses from him, nor trips, nor girls. Shit.

The security guard accompanied me to my office. Joan was nowhere in sight. He watched as I sorted out my personal belongings and packed them into a box. The bastard even had the nerve to ask who'd paid for things like my calculator! I'd had to admit it had gone down on expenses.

"Then it's not your property. Is it, sir?" he'd said smarmingly.

The house was empty as Gail was staying with her aunt until the end of next week. The computer and printer were taken out to the car. While he was loading them in the boot, I picked up the phone. My guard reminded me of the restrictions on me calling anyone until after twelve.

"It's damned near twelve now. Look, it's five to, what difference is five minutes going to make?"

"I would guess about three thousand pounds, sir. That's about the value of your final pay cheque I believe. Use the phone and I have instructions to hand you this envelope. Do as you're told and you receive the other. Which is it to be?"

I turned on my heels and went into the kitchen and made some coffee. As I poured myself a cup, the security guy said "Don't bother to make me a cup, sir. I'll be leaving in two minutes."

I'd had no bloody intention of making him a coffee in any case, which he had, of course, realised. But I felt I'd come off far worse in the exchange.

I'd had a good run at SeaCon. But that was now over. The chances of finding another job looked dire. I put the coffee cup down and poured myself a large scotch instead.

Chapter 31. Nigel — 28th November 1997 evening

Nicky had helped me to relax and I left the office in a slightly more buoyant mood to drive to the Albion Lodge and my meeting with Peter Judge. In spite of Mary Jones or Sanchez's decision to fire us, I was confident I'd be able to persuade Peter to allow us to complete the launch of the OceanMaster range. Surely, he'd realise they couldn't appoint and brief a new agency in time.

Regardless of what happened after that, I knew there were ways in which I'd be able to justify additional costs and pad out the invoices. We also owned the copyright on the work we produced. If SeaCon wanted to reprint any of the material or continue using our designs, they would have to pay heavily. On balance, therefore, I felt I would be able to salvage something from the mess even if we did ultimately lose the account.

When I arrived at the hotel bar, Peter and another man were sitting in lounge chairs either side of a coffee table I wondered who that might be. I'd heard that SeaCon had had an injection of capital — maybe he was something to do with that. As I walked over to them, Peter gestured towards me with his head and the other person looked over at me. I greeted Peter. Neither of them attempted to get up from their seats to shake hands. Was that significant?

"Good evening Nigel. This is Arthur Wilkes. President of InterTrade Developments. Arthur, Nigel Hall."

"Pleased to meet you, Arthur. Can I get you both a drink?" I asked.

"We're fine, Nigel."

I ordered myself a scotch at the bar, walked back over to them and sat down. Taking a sip of my drink I looked at the two of them. Solid businessmen; used to dealing in facts and figures and acting logically — not letting emotions get in the way. Men I knew I could deal with because we thought the same way. I was confident they'd recognise Mary bloody Sanchez was being typically female, letting her personal feelings get in the way of business. Yes, we should be OK after all.

"I've been trying to get hold of you, Peter, because Mary Sanchez informed me, she was terminating our contract with SeaCon. I thought we ought to at least discuss it."

"The fact is Nigel, I've sold my shares in SeaCon to InterTrade Developments, so you'd better direct your remarks to Arthur."

That was a blow I hadn't expected. But Arthur Wilkes looked to be a typical hard-headed fifty something American tycoon — traditional suit, plain shirt and tie, his short, grey hair well groomed, his eyes hiding any emotions he may feel. He was sure to see things my way.

"Well, Arthur, I don't know how much you know about the background, but we were appointed to handle the SeaCon account earlier this year. I'll be the first to admit there were teething problems, there always are, but those are now behind us and we have been working flat out on the launch of the OceanMaster range. In view of the time scale, I'm amazed Mary has terminated our contract. You may or may not be aware we've known each other for nearly twenty years. Her first husband and I were partners. Unfortunately, he and I split up and he was later killed in a boating accident."

I took another sip of my scotch before continuing. Arthur's face was dead-pan, I couldn't read what he was thinking.

"Mary blamed me for Oliver's death. Absolute rubbish, of course. He'd run into trouble with a client and, I gather, had taken his boat out for a last sail before selling it. But Mary can't accept this had nothing to do with me. She claims if I hadn't pushed OJ out of the partnership, he wouldn't have set up on his own and failed. Then he wouldn't have taken his boat out on that particular day and wouldn't have been killed. Well, I ask you. Is that reasonable?"

As neither Peter nor Arthur made any comment, I felt they were tacitly agreeing with me so I continued.

"I'm afraid Mary's decision to terminate our contract has nothing to do with business. It's entirely personal. Pure vindictiveness. Nothing more. And she certainly can't have thought through the consequences of her actions. If you fire Halls now, there's no way in which the OceanMaster literature can be ready for the launch. Can I make a suggestion? Let us complete the launch material for SeaCon. Judge us on our performance, then decide whether to retain us or not? Surely that's in your interest as much as ours?"

"What about the bribes to Collins?" asked Arthur, taking a sip of his whiskey — from his accent with a southern drawl, I'd bet on it being Bourbon.

"There were no bribes. Look. I know Mary claims George received payments from me. OK. He did, sometimes, borrow cash when we were away and hadn't had time to get to a bank. Maybe he didn't always pay me back — but it was nothing worth bothering with. And I could hardly refuse to lend him the money, could I?"

"So, it was Collins who instigated the bribery, was it?" Calling it bribery sounded judgemental. I needed to play down that idea — or it could rebound on me.

"As I said, it wasn't bribery, just a few loans. But, yes, it was George who asked if I could help him out. I didn't offer him any money. We certainly got together a fair bit for sailing and other things. But, then, I also took Peter sailing sometimes. Didn't I, Peter?"

Peter tilted his head in acknowledgement of the fact.

"There was nothing underhand about it. Just entertaining a couple of very good clients whose company I enjoyed. Mary has blown things out of all proportion. Frankly, as I said before, she's just being vindictive. And, like most women, she's over-reacting. I didn't kill OJ. It's totally ridiculous to claim his death was my fault. How can I be blamed if he was a lousy businessman? Yes, I competed with him and I won clients which he wanted. But that's business. Look, Arthur. You're a successful businessman. You know life is tough in the real world. OJ just couldn't take it."

"Nigel, I hear what you're saying. Sure, it's a tough world. And life sure as hell isn't fair. Sometimes the good guys get walked on simply because they don't have the killer instinct. I guess OJ was one of those. Right?"

I knew he'd understand. Now Mary Sanchez needed to watch out.

"That's exactly it, Arthur. But you and I are realists. You need to launch the OceanMaster Range and I don't want to lose your account. Why don't you do as I suggested and let us complete the material for the launch? You can judge our performance for yourself and decide then whether to keep using us or not. If you decide not to, then I'll accept your decision and tear up the contract. Is that fair?"

"Well Nigel. The fact is we're not under any pressure to launch the OceanMaster range as originally planned. We have an American company which also produces instruments for boats and we plan to merge the two lines. That rationalisation is going to affect the literature substantially so everything is on hold in any case. That kind of eliminates any reason to keep using your outfit to avoid delays, doesn't it?"

That was a shock. But there was still the actual contract we had with SeaCon.

"That does put a different light on the matter, certainly, Arthur. But you'll still need to launch the range and there are very few agencies with our personal experience of the market. And we do still have a contract with SeaCon which has six months to run."

As I finished reminding Arthur about our contract with SeaCon, Mary joined us, sitting down next to Arthur.

"Nigel. You're full of shit," declared Arthur. "Mary has worked with me for about ten years and I respect her judgement completely. I've heard your side of the story and I've heard hers. No prizes for guessing which I believe."

He paused to light a cigar.

"There is no way in which you will continue to work for SeaCon. I believe it's essential to trust your advertising agency and we don't trust you. The evidence of bribery is conclusive and not just of George Collins, but other clients too. You could try to sue us over the contract, go ahead and try; see where it gets you."

He pulled on his cigar, then blew the smoke towards the ceiling before continuing.

"In any case, even if I wanted to, I can't override Mary's decision. She's the new Managing Director of SeaCon and the majority shareholder, not me." He put his hand on Mary's. "I might also point out we're getting married next month."

That did it. I had to accept that I was beaten. But Mary then turned the screws tighter still.

"Face it, Nigel. You're finished. You're up to your eyes in debt. You've lost your largest client. The bank is pressing you to repay your overdraft. Take any action against us and we will certainly enter the evidence of your corruption and details of everyone involved as part of our defence."

I left them to gloat, got in my car and found a pub. Totally dejected, I got thoroughly pissed. As I started to stagger outside, Nicky came up to me.

"God, what happened, Nigel? I've been looking for you all over the place. I've been in every bar in the area."

Somehow, she got me into her car and took me back to her flat. I slumped onto the settee and must have passed out because the next thing I knew, it was morning. Nicky had, presumably, undressed me, lifted my legs onto the sofa and covered me with a quilt. I'd certainly been in no fit state to do it myself the previous night.

My head ached and my mouth felt like hell. I struggled into the kitchen and filled the kettle to make some coffee. As I poured the water into the cup, Nicky wandered in.

"I assume you didn't manage to persuade Peter to keep using us."

"No. I didn't. He's sold out to Mary Sanchez and an American."

"So, what happens now? Where does that leave me?"

"I honestly don't know Nicky. I'll have to make cutbacks, obviously. Maybe that'll save us, maybe it won't. I just don't know at the moment."

The coffee revived me and I put my arm around Nicky and pulled her to me. As I kissed her, she pulled away.

"God, Nigel, your breath is foul, and you stink. Come and have a shower."

We showered together, then went back to bed.

After fucking and another coffee, I perked up. Although it was Saturday, I needed to go into the office and work on some figures to try to rescue something from the mess. I checked what was owing to the agency; just enough to cover the overdraft and salaries. The overdraft was secured by a charge against book debts and my house. If I closed the company now, it would be cleared by the outstanding debtors. It meant all of the other creditors would get nothing, but that wasn't my problem.

I called Bill and Jerry and asked them to come in to the office. Bill's wife wasn't too happy, as she'd expected him to take her Christmas shopping, but both of them arrived about half an hour later. I told them what had happened and outlined my plans.

"I'd like you both to stay with me in your present roles. You'll be getting significant redundancy payments which will compensate for the lost bonuses. But, if you do decide to come in with me, I'll need you both to inject some capital, and to co-guarantee any bank overdraft with me.

Jerry was first to reply. "I'll have to discuss it with Sally, but, in principle, I'm interested."

"Same here," agreed Bill.

"OK. Let me have your decisions on Monday. It's going to be a bloody day. I'll have to go and see the accountants and get the liquidation under way and get a new company set up. So, I'm afraid you two will have to see the staff and give them the bad news. Not the best of times to be fired, but we don't have any choice."

Chapter 32. George — 28th November 1997

After the security guy had left in my Carlton, I phoned Nigel. He was as devastated as I was about the day's events. I felt it was his fault I'd been fired; I'd just been a pawn in Mary Sanchez's plan and I made this clear in no uncertain terms. He accepted there was a lot of truth in my argument, but said he was in no position to help me. Frankly, I don't think he'd have helped in any case as I was no longer in any position to help him. Bastard.

I wasn't about to mope around the house all evening, so I called Joan and invited her for a drink. She told me Mary Sanchez knew we were having an affair and had given her an ultimatum. Stop seeing me or quit SeaCon. If she stayed, she'd be promoted as she was familiar with the company's publicity work.

"Sorry, George, it was great while it lasted but I'm sure you appreciate my position." Bitch.

Gail had taken the train to her aunts rather than drive all the way to Inverness and her Fiesta was in the garage. I found the keys and went to the bank to pay in my cheque. The payoff would have to last me some time. But I drew two hundred in cash and decided to go to the club in Brighton where Nigel and I often played the tables. I deserved some relaxation after the day I'd had and two hundred wasn't going to make a significant difference.

The club didn't open until nine so I stopped en route and had a meal at a steakhouse.

Suitably refreshed, I sat and enjoyed a coffee and cigar and reflected on the day. I'd lost my job, my girlfriend and the source of extra cash. That was the set of three luck comes in, so I was due for a change.

At the casino one of the hostesses welcomed me and brought me a drink while I changed my cash for some chips — the house refused to accept cheques from me after a misunderstanding with the bank. I looked around the plush bar area; everyone was smartly dressed; casual wear was discouraged and trainers, baseball caps or t-shirts or jeans were certain to get you barred. There was money here and respectability, at least on the surface.

I took the drink from her and went over to a table to watch how the ball was rolling. I adopted my usual system and watched the pile of chips in front of me gradually grow. My luck *had* changed. But how far could I push it? I decided to take a flier and put £100 on eighteen. Against the odds, it came up. I took my winnings and put the original stake on twelve and won again. I was nearly seven thousand ahead for the night.

After a couple of hours, I checked my pile of chips. I had more than ten thousand pounds. It was time to take a break. I ordered another drink and lit another cigar.

One of the girls brought my drink over to me. I was tempted to push my luck and ask her to join me for a nightcap, but knew the casino discouraged familiarity with clients. It wasn't morals that resulted in this attitude. According to rumour, Frank, the owner, had other interests which would cover virtually any sort of sexual companion you could imagine.

"Mr Fielding wants to see you," said the girl as she set my drink down on the table next to me. "You know where his office is, don't you?"

I did. I'd had a couple of earlier meetings with Frank Fielding to discuss my credit limit and how I anticipated repaying my debt. No doubt this was another such meeting. I sighed, finished my drink in one gulp, such a waste of scotch, even if it wasn't Glen Garioch, and walked down the corridor to Frank's office.

The door was open. Frank sat in a high-backed, cream leather reclining executive chair behind a light oak desk with an inset leather panel that matched his chair. A beige computer sat on the return extension to his left. His suit was probably from Saville Row; his shirt, from Jermyn Street, was striped with a white collar and the stripes on his tie were, I'd been told, the colours of his old school; it was coincidental that the colours were the same as a more famous establishment.

"Come in George. Glad to see you've managed to recoup some of your losses. Understand you've taken us for about ten grand tonight. So that would only leave about another ten to find. Right?"

Chapter 32 – George 28th November 1997

My credit limit was twenty thousand and I'd been at that level for nearly a month.

"The problem, George, is I can't see how you're going to be able to clear the balance. You were lucky tonight, but luck changes and I can't rely on that as a source of income. When we gave you your limit, it was on the basis of you earning thirty-five K per year. But I hear you've lost that job and you don't stand much chance of picking up another. Is that right?"

Shit, who had told him? I remembered Nigel saying that Mary bloody Sanchez had told his bank about him losing SeaCon's business — maybe she'd informed Frank.

"Oh. I'll get another job soon enough. Or I'll set up as a consultant. Plenty of work around if you're prepared to look for it." I hoped I looked more positive than I felt.

"I'm glad to hear you're so confident. But I'm afraid we can't wait for ever for the money. In fact, my partners have been quite critical of my leniency in allowing your debt to stay as high as it is for so long. They don't know you personally, of course. They don't know you can be trusted to pay up. But you see my position, don't you? As long as you had a good job, I could keep their feathers smooth. But now you're out of work, they're going to ask how I expect you to pay. And they aren't patient people. They don't like having clients who can't pay their debts. They think it encourages others not to pay theirs. Then where would we be?"

Frank's amiability was false. I knew it and he knew I knew it. There were no partners. There didn't need to be. Frank was as hard as they come. Born in Peckham he had fought his way up from the gutter and it was only lack of proof of involvement in crime allowed him to obtain a gaming licence at all. The police knew he was behind a great deal of South London's illegal activities.

"Well? Can you pay? Or at least give me some indication of how you're going to be able to pay?"

"I need time, Frank, you know I'll settle as soon as I can."

"Do I? You had a cheque today for a substantial sum, I understand. But I don't hear you offering to pay me any of it."

"I'll need it to see me through until I get another job or I'll set up as a consultant. It shouldn't take long. A couple of months, three at the most."

"I don't see how we can wait that long, George. No. I'm sorry, but it looks like we will have to talk to your wife. I gather she has a bit stashed away. Unfortunately, she isn't going to be too happy to hear of the company you've kept here, is she?"

I was in the shit. And I knew it. What I couldn't understand was why Frank was playing with me. He knew I stood little chance of getting another job and setting up my own consultancy wasn't going to produce any serious income for at least six or nine months by the time the work had been done and the invoices paid. He had to have something up his sleeve. The question was, what?

"There is another option, George. Something that could be right up your street. If you're interested, it would get you off the hook and you could earn some real money."

Whatever was coming wasn't likely to be legal. But I had little option.

"What have you got in mind?"

"My partners and I have recently acquired a company which imports yachting accessories — your sort of line I believe."

"Yes."

"I thought so. Now the original owner put the business up as security against a loan he's been unable to repay. Sad case. He had a heart attack three months ago. We need someone to run it for us. Someone who's clean. Are you interested?"

"Yes, of course. But what's the point?"

"If I tell you any more, you're committed. Doesn't matter what you do or where you go, if you try to back out, you'll regret it. Do I make myself clear?"

"Very clear. I assume you want me to run the business as a front for other activities?"

"You're very astute," Frank replied, sarcastically. "As far as you're concerned, you run the company legitimately. Some of the consignments that arrive will be collected separately. All you have to do is store them for a couple of days."

I had little doubt the consignments would be drugs.

"What happens if the police find out and I'm arrested?"

"As far as you're aware, it's a consignment of special paint. All you know is the shipment comes over from a factory in France, it's collected, you invoice a client, the invoice is paid each month and you pay the supplier. Other than that, you keep your mouth shut. If things go wrong and you get sent down, then that's tough luck. But you'll have had no reason to question the contents of the cans and just took over an existing arrangement. The fact you're clean might convince the judge you were an innocent bystander."

Frank looked at me as he lit a cigar. Then he continued.

"The previous owner wants to retire and isn't likely to live long in any case so won't be around to be questioned by the police. We've already entered some extra invoices into their system so they predate your arrival. You'll find there's a substantial mark up on each consignment which will cover basic overheads. What you do about the rest of the business is down to you. You can take out of it whatever you make. We'll also cancel your debt after three months and we'll overlook interest in the meantime. One word of warning. If you ever attempt to track the shipment in either direction, or cooperate with the police to help them to follow the trail, you'll wish you were dead long before you are. Do I make myself clear?"

He had. I didn't like the idea of being involved in drugs, if that's what it was; but I liked the idea of being maimed or even just beaten up even less. And I didn't *know* it was drugs. It might not be. Who was I kidding? Of course, it had to be drugs; but what choice did I have? At least I wouldn't have to explain to Gail about losing my job. I could now make it look as though I'd left because of this opportunity. She wouldn't have the excuse to belittle me like so often before. Hell, I might even make enough from the deal to leave her.

I went to look over the company the following Monday morning. It was in a side street in Clapham, near the common; a rundown area with little to recommend it. The sign proclaiming Horrell Marine Ltd was faded and all the window and door frames needed repainting. The warehouse itself was on several floors with an ancient lift that struggled to cope with the lightest loads. The staff comprised a teenage secretary, more concerned with the appearance of her nails than the letters she produced on an ancient electric typewriter; a pimply young lad who probably spent half the day bonking the secretary in one of the multitude of hidden corners in the rambling building or, more likely, wanking off in the toilet dreaming of what he'd like to do with the secretary; and a "foreman" who looked as though he ought to have retired ten years ago.

The young ones didn't know or care about what was going on. The secretary hadn't got a clue about the filing system, invoices or delivery notes. The youth wasn't interested in what happened to the products once he'd packed them and less about the paperwork. The old man was different. He'd been with the company for years and remembered better days. He also knew his stock inside out; where everything was and which retailers ordered what.

I went to see Frank again that afternoon. I told him it would be wise to pension the old guy off and move the operation to another site, losing the other two in the process. This would make it far more difficult for the police to establish the shipments had only started when I joined.

Frank agreed, "OK. It doesn't really matter where the firm is located. Your comment about being nearer to the south coast marinas probably makes sense. But you'll have to finance everything yourself."

Frank was being affable because he needed me almost as much as I needed his goodwill.

"Fair enough," I said. I decided to push my luck — what was the worst that could happen? "The books show a consignment was collected and an invoice raised for five thousand last month. The scheme is only going to work if the books stay straight and that means a payment needs to be made to cover the invoice."

Frank laughed. "I like your nerve, George. You're facing a possible kneecapping, or worse. You owe me ten grand and now you're trying to put the bite on me for another five. Unbelievable. But you're right. You'll have the cheque before you leave. OK?"

I let out the breath I'd been holding. "That's fine. I'll start looking around at some premises. And sort out some cash flow projections."

"OK. But don't bother me with the details. By the way, there is a company car which is at the previous owner's place. He knows it's being picked up some time. Here's the address."

I picked up the paper and found the address in the London A-Z. The address was in Wimbledon. I now had a problem of a different sort. Two cars, instead of one.

I drove back to Eastleigh that afternoon and left Gail's car in the garage. I called a taxi and took the train to Clapham Junction where I took another taxi to the address I'd been given.

I was met by Samuel Horrell, the previous owner of the company, who invited me inside. He offered me a drink then told me about the problems he'd had with the business.

"It's basically sound. But we had a major bad debt which caused the cash flow problem. I borrowed to cover the loss, but the interest payments crippled us. I'm glad to see the back of it. It's given me nothing but stress for the last year or so and led to a heart attack three months ago. Fortunately, I had insurance against being unable to work and, as I'm 65 next year, my pension will see me right."

I took the car keys from him and wished him well as he showed me to the car, a two-year-old Volvo 740 estate.

The first thing I needed was a decent computer to get things sorted out and drove to a dealer I had seen advertised in PC User.

The assistant showed me what was available and recommended an IBM clone.

"This is a Pentium 200 with 4 gigabyte hard disk and 32 megabytes of RAM. We can supply software, naturally, and if you are planning to use a spreadsheet, database and word processing I'd suggest either Lotus SmartSuite or Office 97 integrated packages. There's not an awful lot to choose between them and either will do the sort of work you've outlined. You also say you want a stock control and accounts package. I'd suggest Sage. You'll also need a printer."

Megabytes and rams meant little to me, but I took his advice and asked if he could have the software preloaded and everything ready for collection the next day.

"Certainly, if you can give us until about 10.30 or 11. How will you be paying? We can accept credit cards or bankers' drafts but we need five days to clear company cheques."

"I'll pay by credit card," I told him. I'd paid off some of my balance with the money Frank had returned.

"That's fine sir. May I just take the details now so we can get clearance beforehand?"

I gave him the card and watched and listened as he telephoned for clearance.

"That's fine sir. Thank you. I'll see you again tomorrow."

It took me half an hour to make my way back to the old warehouse in Clapham.

I considered telling the three members of staff I planned to move the company as soon as possible, but decided they'd be likely to leave before the move and create more problems I really didn't need at that time.

I started to go through the paperwork. Most sales seemed to be repeat orders with little, if any, new business generated over the past year or so. But Horrell had been correct. Even on this basis, the company had been viable without the interest and loan repayments. That's what had killed it.

Frank had said the income from the special consignments would cover the basic operating costs and my initial calculations showed this was about right. Moving the firm to new premises would, however, add to those costs. Even so, I felt certain there was considerable room to expand sales. With overheads subsidised, I'd be able to review costings and implement some sales or publicity campaigns to increase the turnover.

I decided to call on Frank and try to establish some sort of agreement for the future. I pointed out if the size of his consignments increased, the appropriate invoices would also have to increase to ensure the cover remained intact. He accepted this was reasonable. I also pointed out I would have to pay off the existing staff as part of the move and this, again, was to maintain a credible cover. He eventually agreed to return the ten thousand I'd won at the tables the other night and I'd then invest this in the company.

If it hadn't been for the fact the whole operation was a cover for drugs importation, I'd have felt on top of the world. As it was, I was still rather pleased with myself. Hell, if I hadn't agreed to do it someone else would and I'd have been crippled or worse.

The couple of weeks, over Christmas and New Year, I split my time between finding new premises and planning the marketing for the business. The shares had been transferred into my name for a nominal amount and I registered myself as Company Director. Gail had accepted my explanation about leaving Seacon because of the opportunity to run my own business — and she'd even put some money into it.

The premises were relatively easy to resolve. There were trading estates all along the South coast and it was only a matter of selecting a location that was convenient and negotiating the right price. I eventually found one where the local council who owned it were prepared to rebate any rates due in the first two years and allow six months' rent free. That would help the bottom line significantly.

Finding staff was also little problem. And for the same money that had been paid in London, I was able to hire an attractive secretary who could actually use the word processor and two storemen, one of whom would act as driver for the van I had decided to lease.

I visited customers and introduced myself, then offered them some very special prices on existing stocks to avoid the necessity to transport them to the new warehouse. We halved the stocks within a month as a result. I also discussed their other product needs and identified some lines we could probably market profitably. My visits and our new, more convenient, location also generated an immediate boost in orders in spite of the recession.

Things were beginning to look up.

One of the ideas I had considered when I had examined the business was the possibility of setting up a mail order business. I had to be careful not to be seen to compete directly with existing chandlers, but that could be overcome by setting up a separate company apparently operating from its own premises. All it would take would be a mailing address and a telephone line. The actual orders could easily be redirected to the main offices.

It was important to promote the business before the sailing season got under way and time was already tight. I called Nigel Hall and arranged to brief him on what I needed. The budget of around £60,000 wasn't in the same class as SeaCon's, but Nigel was happy to pick up any new business at this time.

When Nigel came to see me, I ran through my plans and pointed out I couldn't afford to pay anything like the production rates he had charged SeaCon. I also offered him a flat fee for planning the campaign and a share of the turnover generated by the mail order side if he would pass on the agency discount allowed by the publications.

Chapter 32 – George 28th November 1997

After sorting out the details, Nigel and I shook hands on the deal. Our relationship had been strained as a result of Mary Sanchez's actions but that was now behind us.

Part Four. Spring 1998

Chapter 33. Nigel — February 1998

I had been surprised to hear from George again and even more surprised to hear he was now running his own company and wanted to discuss some advertising.

The new agency was still struggling to find its feet. Not all clients had remained with us and turnover was well down on what it had been at the same time last year. But we were picking up some smaller accounts and were nearly covering our much-reduced costs.

Jerry had remained with me, but Bill's wife had stubbornly refused to let him invest his redundancy money in the new company. She had persuaded him to go freelance instead. He had even managed to poach some of the clients we'd previously worked for.

Nicky was still with me and I'd made her a director when she had offered to contribute five thousand into the business. She was now using her feminine charms to good effect and it had been her efforts, almost as much as mine, which had brought in some of the new clients. She'd shown a talent for the PR side of the business which had widened our offering.

The creditors' meeting for Hall Advertising had been bloody, to say the least. Mary Sanchez had told some of our suppliers Hall's had lost the account because of corruption. Whilst nobody had dared repeat the allegations out loud, this led to some barbed questioning. In the end, however, the meeting had to accept that without the SeaCon account, I'd had no option but to go into voluntary liquidation.

I drove over to George's new premises between Chichester and Arundel. They were located on a modern industrial estate, just off the A27 about forty minutes from our offices on the edge of Southampton.

George showed me around his operation then took me to his office.

"As you can see, Nigel, we distribute a range of yachting accessories. Ninety percent is sold to chandlers. They are our main target audience and I think direct mail needs to be our main medium. However, I'm thinking of offering some dealer support advertising for them to promote our ranges. I also want to do some PR. And I've been thinking about offering a mail order service. That would be under a different name. I don't want the trade to think we are competing directly with them."

"What sort of budget are we looking at?" I asked.

"I'm thinking in terms of around fifty thousand, all in. That's media, production, printing, postage and PR."

"It's not a lot for what you want to do, George."

"I realise that, but it's all we can afford at present. It should be enough, but I'm going to need you to keep your costs to a minimum and I'm going to want you to rebate any agency commission on the mail order adverts and produce them free of charge. Instead, I'll pay you a percentage of the turnover."

I wasn't sure I liked the idea of that, but needed to know more about the potential figures.

"What turnover do you anticipate and what percentage are you thinking about?"

"It's impossible to say at this stage. But we would be looking at a budget for mail order of around twenty K. That's only going to bring you in two thousand a year in commission and say another two on production. To break even, we need to turn over around forty thousand. I'll pay you ten percent of turnover instead of your commission. We both break even then at forty thousand and are on the gravy train above that level. If you can do deals on space and increase our coverage, sales should go up and you'll earn more."

It was an interesting idea. It would also concentrate our minds on ensuring the adverts really did sell the products. George had been a damned sight easier to deal with when he'd been working for someone else. Even so, it wasn't a bad deal. We'd still make money on the trade publicity.

"OK, you're on. Now, have you got time for a spot of lunch?"

"Of course. There's a very pleasant pub in a village the other side of the A27. The beer is excellent and their steak and kidney puddings are out of this world."

George was right. Both the beer and the food were superb.

Over lunch, I reminded George the Cowes to Ouistreham yacht race was scheduled for the Easter weekend. Prior to Christmas, we'd planned to take part but, as we hadn't seen each other since, I wasn't sure if he was still interested.

"You've still got the Sadler then?" he asked. "I thought the bank might have repossessed it."

"Oh yes. I've still got it. Actually, I didn't come out too badly. I picked up a fair bit of redundancy, the bank overdraft was covered by book debts and I persuaded Jerry and Nicky to inject capital into the new company."

"Nicky is still with you then? Still giving her one as well, I expect, you randy bastard! God. Do you remember those two girls in Le Touquet? Christ, could they fuck. Knew every trick in the book. I'll have to get in touch with them again sometime. Have you still got their number?"

"I have, but if you want them, it will cost you an arm and a leg and you'll need to book them at least six months ahead. I take it you're still on for Easter then?"

"Too true. I need to blow some cobwebs away. Could be a cold trip. If you need any more gear, let me know. I'll do you a good price. Fancy a satellite navigation system? Plots your position to within ten metres. Linked to a computer, it can even take account of tides and currents, wind conditions and weather forecasts to give you the optimum course to sail. The only problem is, the data is still being digitised for Europe and, of course, it's only as accurate as the forecast."

"Sounds interesting. Is it expensive?"

"About two thousand. But a lot of that is the portable computer you need to link it with. It needs to be thoroughly waterproof. You then need to buy the data disks for the area you're sailing in and they are likely to be another thousand each. Mind you, one disk will cover the entire Channel."

"I think I'll pass at the moment, but perhaps we can give it a trial sometime when the data is available."

"Good idea. I reckon by continually giving the best course to steer, it should reduce the track made good by anything up to five, perhaps even ten percent. On the Ouistreham trip that could save at least an hour, possibly two. Who else is coming with us, by the way?"

"A bloke called John and a mate of his. They've both got a bit of coastal experience but not cross channel. John's a potential client."

Chapter 34. John — Easter 1998

Ian and I had been invited to crew on a Sadler 32 for a race from Cowes to Ouistreham and back. We'd sailed together in dinghies and had shared a 5-0-5 until a move forced by Ian's job had made it impractical for him to get up to the club where we'd kept the boat.

I'd met the boat's owner, Nigel, at a conference a couple of months before and had already been out with him for cruise around the Solent. Nigel ran his own advertising agency and I was under no illusions he was interested in handling the account for which I was responsible and this, rather than my sailing experience, was the main reason for the invitation to join him on this trip.

Still, I wasn't complaining. I had my own reasons for allowing him to present proposals for a forthcoming review of the account which had been forced on us by our existing agency winning a major slice of business from a division of a group which included one of our competitors. It's a crazy world in advertising, the account they'd won didn't compete directly with any of our products — but other products manufactured by the same group competed with those produced by other divisions of our parent company.

So, I had to look for a new agency — and Nigel had been quick to drop a few hints about the personal benefits could come my way should his company be appointed. Nothing could be interpreted as a direct bribe, naturally. More along the lines of it was a pity this race only allowed an overnight stop in Ouistreham before the return leg. If we'd had longer, it might have been pleasant to drive down to Paris for a few days. Perhaps some other time?

He might have thought I could be attracted by such invitations. But he was wrong. I enjoyed my job too much to appoint a second-rate agency to handle the advertising. I'd discussed the trip with my boss, a policy I'd adopted since I'd started receiving such invitations. I had also told him something Nigel Hall had not realised — our paths had crossed before when I worked for OJ Associates.

Whether OJ's death could be directly blamed on Hall was debatable. Mary, his widow, had no doubt it was Hall's actions which had led to OJ's business problems. OJ had certainly taken his Wayfarer out for a final sail that afternoon before selling it to help pay off his company's debts.

And there could be no doubt Hall had picked up the Plasglaze account after OJ's death and had profited from OJ's misfortunes. I couldn't bring OJ back, nor could I recompense Mary for the financial losses OJ had suffered at Hall's hand. I could, however, ensure Hall also lost money producing proposals for the Desktech account. Proposals which would never be accepted.

Frankly, even if Hall came up with some brilliant creative work, there would be ample reasons not to appoint his company. As far as I was concerned it is absolutely vital to trust your agency; and I wouldn't trust Hall an inch. My boss hadn't approved of my reasons for stringing Hall along, but he hadn't vetoed the idea either. He realised I was bloody good at my job and if he had ordered me to drop my plans, then I might have resigned.

I would lead Hall on, letting him invest time and money in creative concepts, dropping hints and wait for him to offer me an incentive to place the work with him. Then, and only then, would I remind him of OJ.

In the meantime, I would be amicable. I'd let him entertain me and I'd hide my contempt.

Although Ian and I were experienced dinghy sailors and had both done the occasional coastal trip on larger boats, this was our first cross channel trip and we were both a little apprehensive. The forecast was for winds to increase to force 6, possibly 7. Neither of us knew whether we'd end up being seasick, but the opportunity was too good to miss.

I'd stayed with Ian the night before at his house near Winchester and we were now driving down the country lanes leading to Hamble Point marina.

"What are we doing here?" I asked, watching the nearby trees bending in the wind.

"God knows."

"According to the map, we turn left here then it's another 3 miles or so."

"This looks like it — we want berth J14."

We parked the car, took out our kit and walked down the quay. We soon found the berth and were welcomed by Nigel.

"I suggest we have a spot of lunch first then get stowed away. Our start is at 6 so if we aim to leave at about 4.30, we should be in plenty of time. George Collins will be joining us later."

Ian and I dropped our gear in the cabin and the three of us walked over to Nigel's Range Rover. Fifteen minutes later we were sitting outside the pub enjoying a drink while our lunch was prepared.

"I like to work a 4 hour on, 4 off, watch system and suggest Ian and George take one watch and you and I take the other," said Nigel.

"Suits me," I replied.

"Fine," agreed Ian.

"How long do you expect the trip to take, Nigel?" asked Ian.

"Obviously depends on the weather. Under ideal conditions, we ought to be able to do it in about 20 hours but it could take a lot longer if the wind is on the nose or we have to shorten sail if it picks up too much. Some of the others will probably do it in little more than half our time — we've got company from some of the Admiral's Cup team. The latest forecast is for a westerly 6, veering west-northwest and increasing to 7 which would be ideal. But there is a possibility the low will come south of the predicted track and we could be faced with a beat most of the way across with the wind increasing to 8 or 9. Great, here's our lunch, tuck in, we've got some prepacked meals for the trip — but this is likely to be the best you'll get until we reach France."

"I gather you've known each other some time," Nigel remarked to Ian.

"Certainly have — our fathers were stationed just outside Brussels in the 70's and we went to school together."

"Really, so you both speak French, presumably."

"I don't. What little I learned, I've forgotten. "

"So, when did you two start sailing?"

"I guess we both started with our fathers, Ian in Cyprus and me in Hong Kong I was about four. But we got together when Ian and I both lived near London and we sailed a 5-0-5 for about a year. Unfortunately, Ian had to move to Winchester and it was a bit far to go each Sunday."

By now we'd all finished our lunches and, as time was running on, we decided to head back to the boat.

Chapter 34 – John Easter 1998

Nigel told us where we could stow our gear. The forward cabin would be used for the spare sails during the trip, so we'd all be using main saloon for sleeping. Before changing into our sea going kit, we all made use of the toilets on shore — I don't know how anyone manages to use the heads on a cruising yacht at sea, especially when wearing waterproofs! It's difficult enough when tied up to a jetty — but when the boat is heeling and crashing into waves every few seconds, you need at least two pairs of hands to hold on, keep the seat up, your clothing out of the line of fire and aim for the bowl! As for sitting down, the least said about that in the cramped space the better!

Under Nigel's instructions, we uncovered the mainsail and bent on the jib before we left our berth under power. As we headed down the Hamble, we hoisted the jib and main and sheeted in and cut the engine. The wind was westerly which gave us a broad reach down Southampton Water and we used the opportunity to check the spinnaker. We were making a respectable 8.5 knots as we left Calshot to starboard and headed across the Solent to Cowes.

With our dinghy sailing experience, Ian and I were well used to spinnaker work — although the pole was far thicker than our mast had been on the five-oh. We suggested Nigel try a few gybes so we could get used to handling the larger spinnaker, before turning back into the wind for the run up to our start.

George had rigged the spray canvas bearing our number and the Red Ensign had been taken down and our racing pennant hoisted.

Nigel expected there to be at least 3 other Sadlers in the race, but we could only see two as the 10-minute gun went.

"Fairly typical," he remarked, "One is based over in Chichester and is always late for the start."

The five-minute gun found us just behind the start line — so we bore away on a timed run aimed at getting us to the line at top speed as the start gun went. It didn't quite work out that way as we had to take avoiding action as a power boat cut across our bows just as we were tacking for our final approach. Even so, we were only 30 seconds late crossing the line and the other 2 Sadlers were later still.

The first leg took us out past the Needles before heading for the French Coast.

With the tide against us, we tacked down the Solent towards Yarmouth a distance of about 10 miles. We were making about 5 knots over the ground, so it took us about 2 hours before we reached the race off Hurst Castle — a nasty stretch of water, particularly when the wind and tide are opposed. Off to starboard, the coast receded towards Christchurch and Bournemouth — off our port bow lay the Needles, the first mark of our course.

The fleet was already spreading out. The faster boats having taken little more than half our time to reach this point, some slower ones and some late starters were still astern. We had gradually pulled out a lead on the other two Sadlers by going further inshore on each leg and taking advantage of the reduced effect of the tide.

Having rounded the Needles, we hoisted the spinnaker and furled the jib. The main was eased and Clippa started to increase speed until we were averaging around 8 knots in a steady force 5.

Night was already beginning to fall and George offered to go below and prepare dinner. Ian and I checked all the sheets and halyards were neatly coiled and ensured we knew what each one controlled in case there were any emergencies during the hours of darkness. We also checked out the spare sails and ensured the storm jib was handy and the spinnaker bag was easily accessible. If the winds dropped, there would be ample time to increase sail, but if it strengthened, it might be necessary to react rather more quickly.

By the time we'd completed our checks, George had warmed up some ready to heat meals and we tucked in to lasagne. Once dinner was out of the way and the dishes washed, Nigel suggested George and Ian turn in. We would call them if their help was needed, otherwise they could take over from us at 2 o' clock.

St Katherine's light on the southern tip of the Isle of Wight was still visible to the north as we prepared to cross the shipping lanes.

By next morning, we were closer to France than England and approaching the lee of the Cherbourg peninsular. The wind had dropped overnight to around a force 5 and had veered slightly to the west north west. The spinnaker and main were still driving us along on a broad reach at about 8 knots.

By the time George and Ian were ready to take the watch again, the coast of France was visible. We were heading for a mark off Le Havre before turning westwards for Ouistreham.

Chapter 34 – John Easter 1998

As we would be needed on deck to drop the spinnaker and bend on the genoa, the large foresail, before rounding the mark for the final leg and expected to finish in about three to four hours, Nigel and I decided to stay on deck rather than go below for another sleep.

The wind gradually faded as we approached the coast. The final leg required a course of 240° and, as the wind was westerly, we would be unable to sail directly to the finish, but would need to put in at least a couple of tacks. Each tack involved releasing the big genoa as the bow went through the wind, then sheeting it in hard with the winch. As one of the crew turned the winch handle, the other 'tailed' the sheet to prevent any snarl ups.

We radioed the committee boat when we were about 6 miles from the finish and gave our ETA as 13.30. They acknowledged our call and informed us we were the first of the Sadlers to check in and two of the other boats in the race had encountered problems overnight and one had returned to England.

Ian was first to spot the committee boat as we approached the finish. Twenty minutes later, we took the gun and a shouted welcome from the commodore of the local yacht club.

Entering the estuary of the River Orne, we dropped the sails and motored past the cross-channel Caen to Portsmouth ferry moored at its berth on the west bank and joined the queue waiting for the lock.

The bridges across the River Orne had been one of the principal objectives on D-Day and had been attacked by gliders. It had been renamed Pegasus Bridge after the emblem of the paratroopers. I had just finished reading a book about the event and had learned a couple of interesting facts which I mentioned to the others.

"Apparently, when they were making the film "The Longest Day," the producer wanted to show Germans jumping out of the window of a local cafe, but the owners had absolutely refused to allow it as they said no Germans had been or ever would be permitted in their cafe."

"Is that right?" asked George. "I'm not surprised. That was a good film. One of my all-time favourites. Wasn't it Richard Todd who played the commander of the glider assault?"

"Yes. And, as it happens, he was involved in the actual invasion. He was with the group that relieved the paratroopers apparently, according to the book."

The lock gates were opening and we motored in between the towering walls. Ian and I finished packing the genoa and spinnaker into their bags and covered the furled main with the boom cover as the incoming water lifted us up to the level of the river proper. We checked the rigging and gear for any damage that might have been incurred during the night but found none.

The yacht club moorings were on the east side of the river and we entered the basin and tied up on the outside of another boat. We soon completed sorting out the boat and took the spare sails on deck to leave the forward cabin free for Ian and I to use.

With the boat tidied up, it was time to sort ourselves out. We collected our washing gear together and made our way across the deck of the inboard boat in our raft to the jetty. Stepping onto shore after more than 24 hours afloat, it felt as though the land was moving.

After living in thermal underwear for the last day and night, and in waterproof wet weather gear for most of that time, a shower was very welcome. It was a relief to be able to strip off and have a damned good scratch! It was also a relief to be able to sit on the toilet!

The prize giving reception was scheduled for 7.30 that evening, so, as it was only about 5 by the time we had finished washing, shaving, scratching and changing, amongst other things, we wandered into the town for a drink.

The reception itself was in the upper bar of the yacht club and they had done the visitors proud, with an extensive buffet and, as you would expect from the French, ample wine. The race results were posted in the bar and I saw we had won our class and had been seventh overall on handicap out of a fleet of nearly twenty. Nigel received a cut glass trophy for the class win. It was the first time he had actually won his class and his highest overall placing.

"Dinner is on me this evening. Well done crew."

Chapter 35. George — Easter 1998.

Three months into running the new company, things were looking quite promising. The mail order side had taken off and was generating a reasonable return and the company bank balance was firmly in the black.

Chapter 35 – George Easter 1998

We had now received four special consignments for Frank Fielding but I was aware these were restricted in size by the volume of paint he could justify using. If he was to increase the imports, it just might attract undue attention. He had asked me to keep my eyes open for alternative opportunities to bring in additional supplies of drugs.

The trip across from Cowes had been one of our fastest to date, John and Ian certainly knew boat handling and had contributed to the first place in our class. Nigel had been particularly pleased. The return leg should be equally interesting.

After the presentation, we walked into the town and found a restaurant. It was virtually packed with other crews but we managed to find a table.

Having ordered our main courses, we turned to the wine list. As usual in France, there are very few foreign wines offered, which is a pity as I prefer a white wine and find most of the French wines either too dry or, like the Sauterne, far too sweet.

Nigel isn't too bothered as he likes reds in any case. But even he doesn't consider most of the French wines to be the best in their class any longer.

"The new world wines are hitting the French in overseas markets and quite rightly too. There are some superb products being produced all over the place now and it's only snobbery keeps the French at the top of the pricing structure. People just don't appreciate what else is available. Not just from California, but Australia, New Zealand, Chile. They've all got a lot to offer," he claimed.

"That's absolutely right," agreed Ian. "But people are reluctant to risk buying unknown wines. I know some off licences offer tasting sessions for their customers, but the chains and supermarkets don't bother and that's where most people shop these days."

"Perhaps someone should launch a sampling service. Charge a subscription and send them small bottles of different wines each month," suggested Ian.

"That's not a bad idea. You might even find the importers would provide the samples free of charge, or even pay to be included," added John.

"And it's not just wines you could use for that sort of offer. You could do the same with perfumes, cheeses, liqueurs, whiskies anything with a large range of products where customers are generally reluctant to experiment because of the cost," remarked Ian.

I thought about what they were suggesting. It made sense. But would the costs stand up. How much would people be prepared to pay for the subscriptions. Twenty-five pounds a year? Thirty? Fifty? What would it cost to handle, pack and distribute the products? How much advertising would be needed to generate the orders? Probably too much.

"You could possibly offer subscriptions as Reader Offers in various magazines; they're always looking for new ideas to boost circulations. You might have to pay them commission on orders generated, say fifteen percent." John must have been reading my mind.

"I reckon the biggest cost would be distribution. A box of say three bottles would probably cost around a pound or so for postage, and say another fifty pence for packaging and twenty or so for labour to pack the sets up. That's what? One seventy per month excluding the cost of contents. Say twenty pounds a year. If you charged thirty pounds a year for the subscriptions, paid the publications fifteen percent and allowed VAT on the subscription, you'd be looking at about one pound fifty profit per subscription. Make the subscriptions fifty quid and you'd be looking at about sixteen pounds profit on each one. The question is whether anyone would pay fifty and whether you could get the samples free of charge."

"You'd need someone to coordinate the offers and produce artwork." Trust Nigel to spot an opportunity. But he was right. On the other hand, he might be persuaded to take a cut of the turnover again.

"You're into computers, John. What would you need to handle an operation of that sort?" I asked.

"Depends on the response and the number of orders received. But if you reckoned on a hundred thousand for each type of product, you could be facing a total database of half a million names and addresses. That's not a major problem in itself, but you'd need to be able to enter the data quickly. To cover fifty thousand names and addresses each month, you might need half a dozen terminals working eight hours a day."

"So, what would you recommend?"

"Probably something like a reasonably powerful server with a large fast hard disk array, possibly around five gigabytes each, plenty of RAM, a back-up device and maybe half a dozen basic machines for data entry all linked to a network. Then you'd need a fast printer to produce labels etc."

"What would that cost?"

"You should get away with well under twenty thousand for the lot."

"Could be worth looking into. Half a million sixteen pounds is a nice bit of money."

"There's no guarantee you'd get that level of response, though."

"True, but I always reckon you can sell any idea to at least a quarter of one percent of the population. With over twenty million households, that's fifty thousand. And even at that level you'd be looking at four million profit."

"Maybe we should work on some figures and talk about it back in England, George," said Nigel.

"Couldn't agree with you more. What about you two. Would you be interested in coming in on such a project?"

"Depends what sort of investment you'd be looking at," said Ian.

"I think I'd have to pass," replied John. "The figures sound good when we've had a good meal and a few bottles of wine, but I suspect there would be rather more problems to overcome and, frankly, I'm not particularly interested in making millions. If you need any help with the computer system, though, let me know."

"I'll certainly do that," I assured him. To be honest, I hadn't really wanted anyone else involved. I could raise all the finance I needed from my own resources and, if necessary, from Frank. That way it didn't matter whether or not the level of orders we'd played around with came in. We could certainly use the importation of the products to cover additional drug shipments. OK, so Nigel could handle liaising with the publications in exchange for a commission on orders. But I didn't need anyone else.

We finished our liqueurs and went for a walk along the quay. The Portsmouth ferry was loading with holiday makers, many of them probably veterans of the Normandy invasion who had been touring the area. If they'd been visiting any other part of France, they would probably have taken an alternative route

"Have you visited this area before," I asked Ian and John.

"Yes, back in the 70s. We camped at Arromanches while our parents were based at SHAPE – that's the main NATO military headquarters in Europe, but I haven't been back since. It's probably changed out of all recognition by now," Ian replied.

After I'd bought some English cigarettes in the ferry terminal, and John and Ian had posted cards back to the UK, we returned to the boat, taking care not to disturb anyone already asleep as we crossed the inside yacht. The re-start was scheduled for 8.30 the next morning and we needed to get a good night's sleep ready for the return trip.

The forecast was not very promising. Another low was tracking in and threatening gales on the nose as we crossed the Channel.

Chapter 36. Nigel — Easter 1998

As I lay in my berth, I considered George's idea for 'products of the month' clubs. The figures we had used were totally arbitrary, but I could see they weren't entirely unrealistic. If I could persuade him to pay us even two percent of turnover, we could be looking at a potential quarter of a million income. And that was nothing to be sneezed at. On the other hand, if I could persuade him to pay us a flat fee that would cover the time involved in liaising with the publications and a percentage, we'd be even better off. I'd have to work on him.

It was time for me to separate Nicky's part of the business from my own. So far, she'd contributed just under half of income but whichever option George went for, that work would be worth a lot more than Nicky's PR side.

The next morning, we woke to find the wind had picked up as forecast. Another couple of boats had joined our raft since we had arrived and we waited until they had cast off before we did the same. As we joined the queue for the lock, Ian and John bent on the genoa and uncovered the main ready for hoisting. I had considered using the smaller jib, but decided to wait until we saw what conditions were like before reducing sail.

As we motored out to the start, George prepared breakfast of bacon sandwiches in chunks of crispy baguettes smothered with Normandy butter and large mugs of coffee. The grab box was still well stocked with Mars bars and other nibbles, plus an ample supply of canned drinks.

All being well, we should reach the finish by lunchtime on Monday. But it would depend on what the low chose to do. At present, it was centred over Ireland and the wind was from the north north-west. The chances were it would move north-easterly and the wind would move round onto our nose and gradually drop. If it came south of track, we could expect stronger winds but with an increasingly easterly component.

Time would tell.

As we left the river, we encountered a nasty chop as the near gales drove the sea onto the shelving sea bed. My choice of genoa might have been optimistic so I asked Ian and John to replace it with a smaller jib. Ian went forward and knelt by the forestay. We were all wearing safety harnesses clipped to lines which ran along each side of the deck.

As Ian unshackled the genoa, the waves burst over the bows in a flood of green water. Ian shrugged off the impact and continued to replace the foresail. The bow was rising and falling eight or ten feet as the waves lifted it then passed under the boat. Every fifth wave, larger than the others, crashed over the bow, rather than just lifting it. John passed Ian the jib and packed the genoa into its bag. Between them, they timed the incoming waves and thrust the genoa down into the forward cabin, closing the hatch cover before another flood hit them. They then came back to the mast, wrapped the halyard around the winch and hoisted the jib, one of them pulling the halyard out from the mast then releasing it as the other took the strain by pulling it around the winch. As the jib rose to its full extent, they had to resort to using the winch handle to tighten it the last couple of feet.

With the jib up, they turned to the main and repeated the process. I decided we should take in a couple of reefs rather than be overpowered.

There was still about fifteen minutes to go before the gun so we had an opportunity to look around us and work out if there was a favoured end to the start line.

If it had been a single class race, we might have opted for a port tack start from western end. But with substantially faster boats also jockeying for position, that was a very risky manoeuvre. It would mean we would have to give way to all boats approaching from the other end of the line and even if we timed the start to perfection, the superior speed of some of the other yachts would place us on a collision course. We would have to play it safe.

As the five-minute gun went, it was obvious several of the larger and faster boats had also identified the port end to be favoured, but they had the performance to take the gamble. The other boats in our class were holding back slightly, anxious not to be over the line when the race started. John and Ian were trimming the main and jib as I manoeuvred the boat towards the line. George was counting down.

"One minute."

We were about the right place for our run. There was another boat to leeward of us, but far enough away to be of little threat if he decided to try to block our way to the mark.

"Thirty seconds"

The leeward yacht had had to bear away as they were in danger of reaching the line too early. But there was another yacht to port of them and they had too little room to manoeuvre. They eased their sails and their speed dropped off dramatically as they ploughed into a wave.

"Fifteen seconds"

We were approaching the stern of the committee boat. The yacht which might have posed a threat to our start had lost ground and was now astern. This had left us a gap of about ten yards to the next boat off our port. They were already sailing as close to the wind as they could and, unless we'd misread the timings, we would hit the line at full speed as the gun went.

"Ten seconds...... five, four, three, two, one."

Crash. The committee boat's gun fired. There was no recall, so everyone had made a clean start.

Now the faster boats were approaching our port side. If they could pass clear ahead of us, they would be able to maintain their course, but if we touched, or had to alter course to avoid them, they'd be disqualified.

It was time for some bluffing. We had made an excellent start crossing the line exactly as the gun had gone and at top speed. The others crossing our path had also made good starts, but that's what you would expect of competitors at their level. They also had faster boats than ours, but even so, they would need around four or five seconds to clear our path and they were not yet that far ahead of us.

"Starboard! Crusader! Starboard!"

I yelled at the top of my voice at the leader of the trio. Warning him I had right of way. The helmsman had already seen us and had obviously been calculating the closing angles in his head. He might still clear us. Or he might not. Should he risk it? If he held his course and we collided, he would be out of the race seconds after the start. Even if he didn't hit us and I took avoiding action, he might still be disqualified if the jury considered I had reasonable grounds to think a collision was likely.

He couldn't take the risk. Disqualification would severely damage his chances of selection for the Admiral's Cup team.

He then had two choices, to tack or to sail under our stern. He chose the latter.

As he altered course, the second of the larger boats saw us approaching. They'd started just a couple of seconds after Crusader, but the extra distance we had to cover before reaching them had given them the time to clear our course.

"Hold your course Sadler," came the cry from the helmsman. He had acknowledged he had seen us and he thought there was enough room. He was right, their stern was no closer than five feet from our bows as we passed.

The third of the trio of Admiral's Cup contenders had been unsighted by the second. They had made the worst of the starts and were now faced with the ignominy of a cruising yacht forcing their racing thoroughbred to tack to avoid a costly collision. My entire yacht, even new, had probably cost less than some of their sails. There was a fury of activity on the other yacht as they tacked.

"Bit of excitement for a change. Eh George?"

"Yes. Not a bad start at all. Now all we have to do is finish ahead of them."

We were already being caught by some of the other larger boats had started on the same tack as us. It's a factor of displacement boat design the maximum speed is dependent on the length. The longer the waterline, the faster a boat can sail. And we were now being overtaken by forty- and fifty-foot boats. The only way to overcome this limit is to skim over the surface rather than drive through the water.

We settled down into a routine. Four hours on, four hours off, even if we just rested below during the day rather than actually sleeping. We gradually tacked our way north out of the bay formed by the Cherbourg peninsular. The wind remained from the north and was too strong for us to shake out the reefs or swop the jib for a genoa.

The grab box was raided for refreshments, cups of coffee, soup and hot chocolate were brewed; and a further supply of bacon fried for more sandwiches.

As night fell, we were still struggling clear of the French coast. At least the rain had stopped and the skies had begun to clear. Not that it stopped us getting soaked. The bows were still crashing into the waves and spray was still washing over us.

We had swopped the watch arrangement around for the return trip and Ian and I were together for the 6 to 10 duty.

"What do you think of George's idea for this 'product of the month' club?" I asked him as Clippa headed northwest, with the Pole Star over her starboard bow.

"If you can get the response he's after and the samples for nothing, it should be very profitable. But those are the big questions."

"That's what I thought. But it's certainly worth a try, don't you think?"

"I certainly agree it's worth contacting various distributors in the UK to see if they'd be prepared to contribute. I doubt if they'd be prepared to pay to have their products included in the packs, though."

"You're probably right. Would you be interested in putting money into the scheme?"

"That would depend on how much would be involved. Why?"

"Well, as I see it, it was your idea, not George's, so why don't you do it yourself. I could handle the promotional side."

"I though you and George were mates. I'm surprised to hear you thinking about cutting him out."

"Business is business. What line are you in by the way?"

"I'm an accountant with the County Council. Which means I wouldn't be in a position to run such a venture without giving up my job and I wouldn't be prepared to do that."

"Fair enough, but you'll keep this conversation to yourself, won't you?

"It's no skin off my nose, so sure."

John and George took over from us at ten and we went below for a sleep.

When we returned on deck at 2am, we were well out into the Channel and crossing the shipping lanes. We kept well clear of the container ships and tankers that were making their way to Rotterdam and other ports.

By just before 6, dawn had broken and were alone in the vastness of the sea. George handed me a coffee as he came up on deck.

"John's got yours, Ian. Any problems Nigel?"

"None at all. The wind has dropped a bit so we might think of shaking out one of the reefs if you're happy."

"OK, why not. But I don't think we'll change the foresail just yet."

"Fine, it's your decision. John, Ian, can you take one reef out of the main when you're ready?"

Leaving them to deal with the main, I went below to listen to the shipping forecast. The low was tracking away as expected and the winds were forecast to drop to around force three by late morning. After logging the forecast, I stripped off my waterproofs and climbed into my sleeping bag. As I dozed off, I heard Ian coming below and doing the same.

As we dressed and went on deck again four hours later, the Isle of Wight was about ten miles off our port side and we could just about make out Shanklin. The race finished at Gilkicker point, south of Gosport and virtually opposite Ryde.

After clearing Bembridge, we tacked and started to head into the Solent. As forecast, the winds had dropped away and George and John had replaced the jib with the bigger genoa and had shaken out the second reef from the main while Ian and I had slept.

It took us another three hours to reach the finish, passing between the two forts which protect the entrance to the Navy's principal base.

By mid-afternoon, Clippa was tied up at her berth on the Hamble and we were able to head for the showers.

It was still a bit early for dinner, so Ian and John headed off back to Winchester and George and I went for a drink.

Chapter 37. George Easter 1998

On the Tuesday after the race, I went into my office and started to work on some figures. If we were to offer, say, quarter bottles of wines as samples, and had just 10,000 subscribers, we would be looking at importing one thousand seven hundred and fifty litres of each wine. With, say, four different varieties per month, it ought to be possible to conceal at least a hundred kilos in each batch.

The perfumes would be much smaller samples as would the liqueurs, but would also provide cover for forty to fifty kilos per month and miniature cheeses could probably be made with small quantities of drugs in their centres. In all, I calculated the operation could easily cover approaching three hundred kilos per month.

I called Frank and arranged to meet him at a pub near Shoreham that evening.

"You've got some excellent ideas here, George. I like them. Especially the cheeses. By making the cheese around the drugs, there would be no join to give the game away of they were examined and we could use particularly strong-smelling ones to cover any smell. Bloody good idea. How much do you need to get it off the ground?"

Twenty-five grand would be more than enough for the computer system we'd need to handle the legitimate side and pay Nigel Hall to set up some deals. With another twenty a week, we could actually do some advertising rather than have to wait for approval of Reader's Offers. But we'll also have to look at additional premises. Say another ten to fifteen to make it look genuine. Say a hundred in total?"

"That's peanuts. We're looking at a potential million pounds a month cover here. And the legitimate side of it would provide cover for laundering some of the cash generated. What are you looking for as your cut?"

"How would you feel about thirty pounds a kilo and the profits from the legitimate side of the business? The scheme depends on being able to obtain samples apparently free of charge. Some of the suppliers might not agree to provide the quantities we want without charge. But if I offer them cash which can't be traced, I think most of them would be prepared to do a deal."

"OK. I'll go for that. But you'll have to cover the set-up costs. I'll lend you the money, that way it looks legit. You can pay it back over three years. And if you come up with any other ideas, I'll pay you the same. Fair enough?"

Considering I had been facing the distinct possibility of a painful death at his hands just four months earlier, I felt it was a perfectly reasonable offer. We shook hands on the deal.

The next day, my secretary faxed details of my plans to nearly two hundred vineyards around the Europe while I located the numbers. By five that evening eight had agreed to provide samples of their wines free and four others had said they would supply it at a substantial discount.

Once the first four had accepted, I called Nigel and told him I wanted to discuss advertising to launch the project and suggested we meet for dinner. In the meantime, I asked him to identify publications we could get into as quickly as possible.

"You don't waste any time, do you?" he said as we shook hands that evening.

"None to waste!" I told him.

We discussed his ideas and the options we had for advertising. Magazines were basically out due to the lead times involved, but we could get in some of the national press. We would, however, have to apply for MOPS clearance. I reminded him we already had clearance from the Mail Order Protection Scheme for our existing business and we could use that to cover the clubs.

Nigel had already prepared some initial ideas for advertising which looked reasonable. We mapped out a basic campaign of three columns by twenty-centimetre ads in the Observer, Mail on Sunday, Sunday Express, Sunday Telegraph and the Sunday Times with three insertions in each.

"That's around sixty thousand, George. Have you got that sort of money?"

"It will be nearer fifty-two when you take off your commission, Nigel. I'll pay you five percent of turnover as discussed on the boat. But, yes. The money is available. Now, when can we get in the papers?"

"It's just possible we could make it this week with some of them if I have copy tomorrow. But next week for certain."

"You won't have copy tomorrow, so let's leave it until next week. I don't want to waste time, but it's got to be right. Now when can you start working on the Reader's Offers?"

"Look, I don't mind booking these spaces on spec, but we are looking at a hell of a lot of potential effort to organise the offers and I'll need a guaranteed payment for that time. How about a thousand a month as a retainer and four percent of turnover?"

"If you're not prepared to put your money where your mouth is, Nigel, I might be prepared to go for a thousand a month and one percent, but four is far too much."

"Let's split the difference. A thousand and two and a half percent?"

"I'll go to two percent, but no more. Take it or leave it."

He took it.

Over the next week, I contacted more potential suppliers spreading the net wider and wider until we had faxed hundreds of vineyards. I'd had no idea there were so many. As we only needed forty-eight for the first year's operations, we had little difficulty in filling the quota. I asked each of the suppliers to provide fifty thousand quarter bottles, or the equivalent in bulk. There had been no problem finding a bottling plant which could provide and fill smaller bottles for us and it was an essential part of the scheme for at least some of the wine to arrive in bulk.

The local council were more than willing to rent us the unit next to our existing premises for assembling the packs and cartons and protective packaging were easily obtained.

Nigel produced some literature to accompany the wines and provide information about each together with details of the UK distributor who would then provide information on local outlets.

All in all, the project was coming together nicely. I had also called John to remind him about the computer system I would need. He agreed to come over and discuss it and work out the precise details of the network we would need.

When the advertising appeared, I was pleasantly surprised by the response. The first week produced just over five hundred subscriptions, more than covering the advertising costs. Based on our experience with the yachting mail order, I was confident we would see this increase to about five times that level after five or six insertions, then remain there for three to four insertions before starting to tail off. By increasing the reach of the advertising, we could probably more than achieve my initial objective of fifty thousand subscribers within about three months. I decided to hold off on the reader's offers idea for the time being. They might be useful to keep topping up the scheme, but we could control matters more effectively by using direct advertising.

If the other products were to go as well as the wine had, I would be looking at clearing at least two hundred thousand a year from the legitimate earnings alone. The bonuses from Frank could go into an offshore account, Switzerland, Luxembourg or the Bahamas, just in case things went wrong at some stage. And that was a possibility I had to face.

Part Five. 1998-9

Chapter 38. George — May 1998.

I was always nervous meeting Frank, in spite of the fact that he seemed pleased with the way the Wine Club was covering his own imports. I was still uncomfortable being part of the drugs trade — but what choice had I had? If I'd refused to cooperate, one of Frank's boys would have hurt me badly. And, I have to admit, I enjoyed the money I was now making — so that's what I concentrated on. I told myself that no-one forced the users to take the drugs.

The door to Frank's office was already open but he was on the phone so I waited. He then signalled me to come in and take a seat.

"Sorry about that, George," he said as he put the receiver down. "Coffee, or something stronger?" he asked.

"Coffee please, I'm driving."

"So, my friend, business looks good. Seems you were the right choice for the job. But there's a limit to how much product we can cover through your Wine Club, we need to find other options as well. You're a sailor, there must be a way of bringing in supplies. Customs can hardly search every boat."

This was bringing it closer to home than I liked.

"They can't. A one-off might be possible, maybe even a couple of runs, but if you tried too many times, I'm sure they'd start taking an interest."

"There must be a way. Look into it."

"OK, Frank. Though I do have another idea. We've taken on a new navigation system for yachts. I won't bore you with the details, but it uses satellites to locate a boat's position then calculates the best course to the next point."

"How does that help us?"

"The designer reckons it could be developed for used for vehicles. The big obstacle, he says, is the mapping that would be needed — but that's just a matter of man hours. Now, John, the guy who provided the IT system we needed for the Wine Club, told me his outfit uses a couple of coaches to demonstrate their products throughout Europe. They're constantly travelling back and forth."

I'd obviously grabbed Frank's attention as his coffee cup was paused halfway to his mouth. He put it back on the saucer.

"I see where you're coming from. We could use demonstration trips to bring in the product. How much do you think you could conceal on each trip?"

"I don't know — but a lot."

"OK — check it out and get back to me."

As I drove home, I was relieved that Frank was happy.

On the other hand, Nigel wasn't.

We'd originally negotiated the fees for his work based on profits. He'd thought he was taking advantage of me but I'd reinvested most of the income so he'd been making a lot less than if he'd kept to the usual agency commission. I'd recently allowed him to renegotiate — but he hadn't allowed for me cutting back on advertising spend as we approached saturation point. He'd always had the upper hand in our relationship before and I enjoyed beating him at his own game.

The following day, I rang John to talk about the equipment needed to digitise the maps for the navigation system. When I told him my idea, he suggested this could be very big business. "It could make your wine club look very small beer," he'd joked.

"Too true, so, what kit will we need? I'm happy to use your company's products as long as you match others on price. By the way, did you say you had an exhibition coach?"

"We have two as it happens. They are always off touring somewhere. We keep one on the continent and one in the UK."

"Where did you get them?"

"We used an outfit called Ravens."

"What did it cost for each coach; if you don't mind me asking?"

"They worked out around sixty or seventy thousand each." That would be peanuts compared with the value of a single load.

"Have you got Raven's phone number with you? I'll give them a call."

Once we'd completed our business, we headed to my favourite watering hole. We sat down and took a draft of our drinks.

"Cheers."

Our conversation then turned to the sailing trip we had planned on Nigel's boat.

"Roll on next weekend. I've been so involved in getting the club up and running and sorting out the navigation system I haven't been afloat since Easter," I said.

"It'll certainly be good to blow a few cobwebs away."

"Did I tell you I'm thinking of buying my own boat later this year?"

"No, you didn't. What are you thinking of getting?"

"I've heard one of the old Admiral's Cup boats is going to be put on the market. It would need a bit of handling and, on handicap, I suspect I'd tend to be down the finishing order, but it could be good fun. Be nice to be up with some of the leaders; getting into port over the other side in time to relax and look around. Take the Ouistreham race, for example. It was late afternoon before we had finished and moored up. The boat I've got in mind would have been there by mid-morning. Much more civilised. Admittedly it's more spartan below, but if you're averaging just one night per trip at sea. I reckon that's a small price to pay. Not that it's cheap. I gather the asking price is likely to be well over two hundred thousand."

John let out a whistle. "That's a fair bit of money."

"Well, yes, it is and my wife isn't overjoyed about me buying it but she's about to inherit a bundle from an aunt of hers that died recently. She's paying off the mortgage from that, so we aren't short of a bob or two. The business is also going well at the moment and it could be good advertising. In any case, she has her toys, in her case it's a keep fit instructor from the gym she belongs to. Not that I care. We each have our own interests!"

I took a long draught of my pint of real ale and leant back in my seat.

******

I wasted no time in contacting Raven Exhibitions after taking to John. We went to see Desktech's UK based coach which was visiting a potential client in Eastbourne. This was convenient for me, if rather less so for Tony who had to come over from Bristol.

Chapter 38 – George - May 1998

Even a quick glance told me what I wanted to know. The coach would be ideal for demonstrating the navigation system. More importantly, it had tons of storage space behind the display panels. Frank was going to wet himself!

I told Tony it might be necessary to change the display panels for alternative language versions and asked if this would be a problem; I also explained we might need extra space behind the panels to contain the backs of some of the instrumentation.

Tony didn't seem too surprised at my questions and said neither request would present any difficulty. The more we discussed the project, the more I realised this was an ideal method of importing substantial amounts of drugs. There was no doubt in my mind there would be space for the two thousand kilos I had hoped for. It would nearly double Frank's import capacity at a stroke. And, if one coach could work, there was no reason why more than one couldn't be used.

Maybe it would also stop Frank trying to get me to use the boat. Sailing gave time to unwind and the thought of having a ton of cocaine on board each time when returning to the UK would be far from relaxing.

I told Tony to go ahead and obtain a suitable coach for conversion and to start planning the layout along the lines of John's vehicles.

"The total cost of the project is likely to be around seventy thousand pounds. We usually expect at least fifty percent in advance, especially when we have to acquire a coach and convert it," Tony informed me.

I'd anticipated this after talking to John and Frank had already transferred the necessary funds into the account. I took out my business cheque book and wrote out a cheque for thirty-five thousand. I'd never written such a large cheque before and tried to look nonchalant as I handed it over.

"I trust that's acceptable?" I asked. "Now, how long before I can see some ideas for the interior, the graphics etc and how long to do the conversion?"

"I would say we are looking at something around two months or so from the time we get the basic vehicle. That's about a month to finalise the designs and a further month to fit out the coach. Some of the materials we need can be on long lead times. The paint shop is likely to want at least a week to prepare and spray the exterior."

"That takes us to the early August. Frankly, there's not much point trying to do anything in France in August, but I want the unit ready to go by September. Is that OK?"

"Provided you don't delay any approval of proposals, or require late changes. That's fine. I'll work out detailed costings once I know what coach we can acquire. I'm assuming you don't want to buy a new chassis?"

"Not this time, but we may well want additional units later. I'm convinced this system will make millions." It certainly would — but more from what wasn't seen than what was.

Having completed our discussions, I left Tony and drove up to London to see Frank and give him the news.

As expected, Frank was delighted.

Driving back home, I realised there was a hell of a lot of work to do with the navigation system to make the trip credible. But that was just a matter of man hours.

As the quote from a popular television programme went, 'I just love it when a plan comes together'; I tapped the ash off the end of my cigar.

Chapter 39. John — June 1998

John? It's Tony. I just called to thank you for recommending us to George Collins. He's decided to commission a display coach from us."

"I'm glad to hear it, but a word of caution. He seems to be paying his bills, certainly as far as we're concerned, but I'd be reluctant to extend him substantial credit on products we couldn't shift elsewhere. In our case, that's not too much of a problem, but a display coach might be hard to sell to someone else."

"He's already paid a substantial deposit and has agreed to pay the balance in instalments as the work progresses. The most we would lose would be our profit. Not that I really ought to tell you our client's business, I suppose."

"As he's also our client, all we're doing is exchanging credit information, nothing wrong with that. But I'm frankly surprised he has been able to pay such a substantial deposit. As far as I was aware, he was broke when he left SeaCon just before Christmas, yet, five months later, he's paying out money right left and centre."

"Perhaps he's got a fairy godmother? Or some other source of finance. Come to think about it, he was rather interested in storage space on board the coach — and about being able to get behind the display panels. Do you think he's up to something?"

"What, like smuggling? Always possible, I suppose. But we're adding two and two together and probably making fools of ourselves!"

"Perhaps, John. Just because we don't know where his money is coming from, it doesn't necessarily mean he's involved in smuggling drugs. Does it?"

"You're right. I'm just fantasising. But it would certainly be a good cover — I've thought before that the coaches would be ideal for it. Mind you, I thought they had sniffer dogs that can detect even the faintest smell of drugs. So, if he was up to something, he'd have to solve that problem as well. Anyway, how are things going with the Paris and Munich shows?"

"Paris is coming along nicely. I've got some designs for the French graphics to show you next week. As Munich isn't until late October, we haven't done anything on that as yet, other than ensure the actual space has been reserved and the hotels booked."

"Glad to know you've got your priorities straight."

As I put the telephone down, I considered the evidence against George.

The data I'd scanned when upgrading his computer system hadn't appeared out of the ordinary. There seemed to be a reasonable number of customers for the yachting mail order business, but nothing spectacular. The wholesale side had also seemed realistic. Most of the names and addresses had been chandleries along the south coast, with a few others inland, but there was nothing untoward in that. The Laser I'd had years ago had been built almost as far from the coast as you can get in England.

The wine club had also obviously started well. Nearly twelve thousand subscriptions in a couple of months. At fifty quid a shot, that amounted to six hundred thousand. But he had been spending a hell of a lot on advertising; let alone the computer system.

He could, of course, have simply had a very understanding bank manager. Or he could be gambling on the response to his ads continuing to increase and was using the subscriptions and delaying payment of the media bills.

Could there be something going on? If so, I certainly wanted nothing to do with it. Especially if it was related to drugs.

I'd arranged to meet Carol that lunchtime as she was passing through the area. She was still based at Harwich with Customs and I mentioned my concerns about George to her.

"From what you are saying, it's might be worth looking into discretely. There probably nothing in it, but we're always looking for opportunities to catch not just the couriers, but those behind the gangs," she told me, as we finished our lunch. "Do you have any other information about Collins that might give us some leads?"

"I know he used to gamble a fair bit at a club in Brighton. The Flamingo, I think it was called," I told her.

"Look, can you keep in touch with Collins to see what else you can pick up without taking any chances?"

"I don't see why not. I'm sailing with him and Nigel Hall over the bank holiday and he also wants to discuss what he needs for digitising the maps for his navigation system. I'll see what I can dig up for you."

"Fine, but don't take any risks. Just keep your eyes and ears open. That's all. OK?"

"Don't worry. I'm not about to look for trouble."

Chapter 40. Carol — July 1998.

I hadn't mentioned to John we had already had some information about the Flamingo Club and its owner Frank Fielding. If George Collins was involved with Fielding, then there was a good chance it was far from innocent. And, in view of the other information John had given me, drugs could well be the explanation for Collins's easy access to finance.

Back at my office the next morning, I started investigating. A call to colleagues in the VAT department resulted in faxed copies of Collins's returns arriving on my desk within half an hour. The marine side of the business seemed to be operating rather more profitably than it had been before Collins's took over — nothing suspicious there though. His VATable outputs were substantially up, while inputs were only slightly higher than they had been. He was obviously making a higher average profit margin — again, not unreasonable.

Chapter 40 – Carol - July 1998

I arranged for the local VAT office to give Collins a visit. All businesses receive such routine checks and the officers would be able to demand to see all paperwork related to the accounts. I considered going with them, but decided against it. I had another idea in mind.

Companies House records and other databases accessed through my computer provided other information I wanted.

Having set the wheels in motion, I gathered up my files and went up to see Brian Halliday, my boss.

"What have you got Carol?" he asked.

I showed Brian what I'd collated.

"It certainly warrants further investigation. What have you got in mind?"

"I think it might be possible for me to get closer to this George Collins. I know the guy at the exhibition company producing the coach and I'd like to persuade him to take me on as his assistant to liaise with Collins. By all accounts, Collins is a womaniser so I'll see what I can wheedle out of him. If they're planning to use the coach to smuggle drugs, I'll see if I can't persuade him to use me as the driver. Of course, it may be a total blow out. Collins may well prove completely innocent and unconnected with Fielding other than as a member of the Flamingo Club."

"But you don't think so, do you?"

"No, I don't. This whole set up looks too perfect. Call it a hunch, but I just have a feeling about it. We've had our suspicions about Fielding for some time. But we've never been able to link him to anything concrete. If our suspicions are correct, there is every possibility a load of this size would mean he'll want to be around when the coach arrives. That way we might be lucky and catch the heads of the organisation as well as the pushers."

"I agree. I'm not keen on the idea of you driving the coach, but I'll consider it. In the meantime, I agree you should try to make contact and keep your eye on developments. I assume your cousin can be trusted to keep his mouth shut?"

"Absolutely. He helped us once before, back in 94, before you were transferred here. His wife and daughter were murdered by one of the gang involved in that case."

"Christ. I remember that case now. Your cousin's John Ives, isn't he? The killers name was Williams, Tim Williams if I remember correctly."

"That's right. In fact, we had both known Williams before. He was also responsible for the death of a friend of ours. He's still in prison as far as I know."

"OK, Carol. Set something up with John." I was excited by the possibility of a substantial case to get my teeth into and pleased that Brian trusted me to run the investigation.

The information that filtered through was inconclusive. There were certainly anomalies, but that, in itself didn't prove anything. In fact, if there hadn't been, it might have been even more suspicious.

But, in spite of the absence of any hard facts, the case smelt right to me. The evidence might be tenuous. It might be circumstantial. But it was there.

I called John after he had returned from a sailing trip with Hall and Collins and arranged to see him.

"Two visits in a month after a gap of nearly a year? What's going on?" he demanded. "Anything to do with our previous discussion?"

"Could be, John. But I don't want to talk on the phone."

"OK, come over for dinner. I'll throw some more meat and veg in the casserole I was having. It should be ready by the time you get here."

"Great. I'll pick up a bottle on the way. See you about 8."

Brian had given me permission to explain to John why we were suspicious about Collins and what we wanted to do. I didn't tell John I intended to try to persuade Collins to use me as the driver, only that I wanted to get closer to Collins and see what I could find out.

John agreed to talk to Tony and help persuade him to take me on as his assistant.

Two weeks later, I was working out of Tony's office. The word had been put around I was John's cousin and John had put pressure on Tony to give me a job. We explained that I'd been bumming around the world and now wanted to settle down.

George certainly raised no objections to me acting as liaison on his account. At first, he seemed to assume I would be available for personal services as well as business. I made it clear these were not in my job description, but also hinted I didn't find him totally unattractive and, well, we could wait and see what developed, couldn't we?

Chapter 41. George — July 1998

G ood morning, George, don't tell me you want more money for the demonstration coach," Frank said as he answered my call.

"Not at all. Though if you're offering, I wouldn't say no."

"Eff off," he said — but good-humouredly; a huge change from the polite but menacing tone used during the original conversation we'd had about the money I'd owed him. "I was just calling to let you know everything is on track. We're still good to go in September. How are the arrangements for the other side?"

"They're fine too. I'll have the address for the switchover in a few days."

"Great. I'll talk to you again soon then."

As I put the phone down, I looked at my watch. Time to call it a night. I was meeting Nigel for dinner. On me this time. Well, he'd been helpful in the past and his contributions to the 'Keep George Liquid Fund' had been more than useful, so I felt I owed the guy. Not that I hadn't repaid him with work. Even so, we shared a lot of interests and enjoyed each other's company — most of the time.

As we enjoyed our brandy and cigars, I could see Nigel wanted to say something.

"Out with it, mate, something's bothering you."

He took another pull on his cigar and blew the smoke towards the ceiling.

"I'm impressed with how far you've come in the last few months, George. You've done well." He raised his glass in a toast. "When you started up, we agreed a profit share deal — which sounded OK at the time. What I hadn't anticipated was you reinvesting everything so the actual profit was a lot lower. It hasn't left much for me."

It was a discussion we'd had before.

"To be honest," he continued, "I really need to revert back to the usual agency arrangement. It's not as though you can't afford to pay a bit more for your advertising and you've got to admit that it's been effective."

I swirled my Rémy Martin in the glass before taking a sip. I looked at him and pretended to consider his comment. I took another pull on my cigar before nodding my head and answering.

"Fair point, Nigel. If you're sure that's how you want to play it. Just make sure you keep production costs in check — it's me paying the bill now, not SeaCon."

I used to think he was a shrewd businessman — but he was slipping. We'd now hit the target for the wine club and advertising for the yachting business would effectively stop after the pre-Christmas campaign — he'd have been better staying with the profit share. Oh well, his loss.

My attention was then taken by two very attractive young women, one blonde the other brunette, who'd entered the club. They headed for the bar where they ordered drinks, lit cigarettes, sat back on their barstools and looked around. As the blonde scanned the room, our eyes locked. A hint of a smile appeared on her face as she lifted an eyebrow. I glanced at the spaces on the banquette at our table and returned her smile and winked. She turned to her friend and bobbed her head in our direction. The friend looked over at us as well and nodded her agreement. They stubbed out their cigarettes, slid off their stools, picked up their drinks and sashayed across the dance floor towards us.

As they approached, Nigel and I stood up.

"Good evening ladies, care to join us?" I invited.

They introduced themselves as Virginia (the blonde) and Charlotte (brunette). I was under no illusion that it was our handsome features or potentially sparking conversation that had attracted them. Virginia's perfume wafted over me as she took her place on the seat and I slid in next to her.

The waiter miraculously appeared as we took our places.

"What are you drinking ladies?" I asked. "Champagne?"

I turned to the waiter.

"Dom Perignon. A magnum please."

Chapter 41 – George - July 1998

As the waiter went off to fetch our order, I lit Virginia's cigarette. The four of us chatted about inconsequential matters for a few minutes until the waiter returned and we clinked glasses and started on the champagne.

Nigel and Charlotte put down their glasses, slipped out from behind the table and strolled hand in hand to the dance floor.

"Shall we join them?" I suggested to Virginia.

She snuggled into me as we danced and I could feel my erection growing as she rubbed against it. When she offered her lips to be kissed, I needed no second invitation. Her tongue probed between my lips and entwined with mine. I squeezed her bum and held her close.

Back at the table, she asked me for a cigar. Before putting it to a flame, she touched the end with her tongue and flicked it; then slid it in and out of her mouth suggestively. Her thigh was pressed against mine and her other hand was resting on my crotch and fondling my penis.

I dropped my hand to her leg and slid it under the thigh-high slit of her dress.

She moaned. "Oh, that feels so good."

She could see that I was staring at her breasts; breasts that were barely restrained by her dress.

"Like what you see?" she asked.

"Very much," I told her.

"We don't come cheap, darling — but worth every penny. A thousand for both of us. Interested?"

I was and I didn't need to ask if Nigel was.

Back at the hotel, Charlotte asked us if we had any coke. I unscrewed the base of a perfume bottle and passed her the vial that had been concealed inside. Nigel's eyebrows were raised at the amount it contained.

"What do you boys like?" asked Virginia.

"We do a very exciting show together, if you're interested," added Charlotte, slipping her arm around Virginia. "I take it you can get some music on the radio?"

"Sounds good to me," said Nigel.

"Why not? Just let us know when you need a hand," I told them.

As the music played, the girls slowly stripped each other, fondling and kissing as each new area of their bodies was exposed. Nigel and I sat and watched, drinking in the sensuosity of their performance along with our champagne. From the way he had to adjust his trousers, I knew he was getting as turned on as I was.

Charlotte and Virginia then turned their attentions on us and soon removed our clothes. We sat on the two settees and fondled each other, drank, smoked and snorted some more of the coke.

The champagne disappeared and I called down to room service for a couple more bottles and some caviar.

The girls were as eager as we were and we eventually disappeared into two bedrooms. Charlotte and I were enjoying a post coital cigarette when Virginia walked in. "Any more of the coke?" she asked.

"Help yourself," I told her. "There's plenty more where that came from."

Virginia sat on the bed next to Charlotte shared the coke with her. She then leant across and, cupping Charlotte's left tit, kissed her gently on the lips. I could see their tongues sliding in and out of each other's mouths. Charlotte had placed her hand inside Virginia's thighs and was fingering her.

Nigel came looking for Virginia and, when he saw what they were doing, sat down on a chair to watch the second part of the show.

The two girls caressed each other. Their tits rubbing together as Virginia joined Charlotte and me on the bed. I fondled both of them as their bodies intertwined. As I reached between Virginia's legs, they rolled onto their sides and shuffled into the centre of the bed. I nestled into Virginia's back, my penis pressing against her bum cheeks, my right hand fondling both of their breasts. Nigel joined us and lay behind Charlotte.

As we all lay together afterwards, thoroughly sated, Virginia turned to me and asked if I could let them both have some more coke to take with them. I gave each of them one of the bottles of perfume with the false base.

I suppose it was a combination of feeling magnanimous, the afterglow of the sex and several bottles of champagne that had made me less cautious than I should have been with Nigel around.

After the girls left, he questioned me about the coke.

"Got your own importer, have you?" he asked.

"Better than that," I told him.

"Shit, of course, you are the importer. That's why you weren't too concerned about the cost of launching the clubs. They were a cover."

I'd started to sober up by then and realised I'd said too much already.

"I'm not saying any more and, if you know what's good for you, you'll forget this conversation."

"Don't worry, George. Your secret is safe with me. You can bet your life on it."

"It's not *my* life I'd be thinking about."

Chapter 42. Carol — July 1998.

Hi Brian, nothing much to report — George has been around to check on progress but no further evidence to confirm any plans for smuggling."

"Well, I guess that's to be expected. I don't suppose there will be any developments until it's actually on tour. These things always take time."

"Isn't that a good reason to let me act as driver? We'll need someone on the spot."

"I realise that, Carol, but I'm really uncomfortable with the idea. It could be very risky."

This was so frustrating. If I had been a man, there would have been no hesitation in letting me take on the job but, in spite of the theoretical equality between the sexes, there was still considerable reluctance to put women in dangerous situations. There wasn't any point pushing Brian at this stage though.

"Well, it may not prove necessary. I do have one bit of news though. John and I have been invited to join George and Nigel on George's new yacht during Cowes Week."

"OK, no harm in that I suppose. Maybe George will let something slip; who knows."

I was stopping with John the night before. and, over dinner, he asked how the investigation was going.

"I'm convinced something is going on and their existing operations are providing a cover. But we don't want to move in at this stage as we would probably not be able to tie Collins into Fielding. What we really want to try to do is roll up the complete network in one go. At the moment, all we'd get is the import side. We also need to know where and how the drugs are being distributed."

John looked thoughtful for a moment. "How many distributors would you expect Fielding to have?"

"Difficult to say. Probably at least forty or fifty. Why?"

"While I was upgrading Collin's computer system, we had to transfer several databases. One of them seemed to be a bit odd at the time. It had under a hundred names and addresses; all receiving regular orders. I couldn't work out why it had been kept separate. Frankly, though, I didn't give it much more thought at the time."

"It'd be interesting to see what the names and addresses were. I don't suppose you can get hold of them somehow?"

"I already have them. I kept the tape we used to map the data. It should be in my study. Let's have a look."

John switched on his computer and restored the data from the tape to the main hard disk. Within a few moments, we were able to browse through the list of names and addresses.

"I'd have expected any normal list of customers to be much larger than this file; and for names and addresses to be fairly random. Certainly with at least a couple in most major towns and cities. But at first glance, there don't seem to be any duplicated locations," he said. "Let me sort the file on postcode order."

It took few seconds for the computer to sort the addresses and we were soon able to scan through the database again.

"No duplication even in places like Birmingham and the names are individuals, rather than companies. Bit strange don't you think?" John asked.

"I agree. It may be worth investigating these people," I replied. "Can you give me a print out?"

"Of course. It'll take a few minutes while I create a report."

John's laser printer soon churned out the details I needed for my boss.

"Can you also do a similar report for the other databases?" I asked.

"If you like. Although I'm pretty certain the others are genuine customers. With that number of names and addresses, it'll take a couple of hours to print off and you'll owe me a box of paper."

"This really is a potential break through. Can I use your phone? I'll call Brian and arrange to meet. I'd better avoid the office from now on in case they start to follow me."

"Help yourself. Tell him to come here if you like."

Fortunately, Brian was at home. I explained what we had discovered and he agreed to come straight over. It wasn't going to please his wife, but she was used to his urgent trips.

The computer was just finishing printing off the final few names and addresses from the other three databases as Brian rang the doorbell. John made some more coffee as I briefed Brian and showed him the lists that had been printed out.

"What do you think?" I asked.

"They could be innocent customers, but I agree it looks unlikely. The question is what to do about it. I'll give Bruce French a visit in Ipswich tomorrow morning. See if he has any information about the three names on his patch."

"With this information surely it's more important than ever to have someone on the coach. And I am the only one Collins is likely to trust," I told him.

"I don't like the idea at all. You'll be very exposed and we won't dare arrange any local cover on the continent in case of leaks. If this thing starts to come apart, you could get hurt."

"Is there any realistic option? We can hardly trail the coach all around Europe, can we? And if they decided to use the first trip as a dry run, we'd never know. Then we'd either have to take the thing apart and blow everything or let it through. We have to know whether or not the coach has been loaded somewhere along the route. And that means we have to have someone with it. I'm the only one with a realistic chance of getting the job without it looking like a set up."

"I'm aware of that. But I still don't like it. There would be hell to pay if you were hurt. The media would have a field day about customs using a woman on a dangerous undercover mission."

"Damn it, Brian. If I were a man, there'd be no question. I've earned this assignment and I want it. I'm not intending to get hurt. But if it does happen, then that's the risk I took when joining the department. In any case, George might not want to use me as the driver. In which case, this whole conversation is academic. But I'm still the best chance we've got of getting close to the shipment. So, let me at least try!"

Brian shook his head in resignation.

"I don't suppose we really have any choice, do we? OK. Talk to Collins, but don't push too hard. If he accepts your offer, then fine. If not, then back off. Understood?"

"Understood."

John had kept well out of the way while we'd been talking, but had returned with the coffee when he had heard our voices return to normal.

After Brian had left, I turned to John.

"Well?" I asked.

"Well, what?"

"Aren't you going to argue against me taking the risk of driving George's coach?"

"Is there any point? But promise me you'll let me know if I can help in any way."

"You already have. And don't worry. We're probably taking a bigger chance tomorrow sailing Osprey with George!"

He laughed. "You could well be right. Which reminds me, we'd better get some sleep. We need to be up at six and it's already one o'clock."

Chapter 42 – Carol - July 1998

The next morning, we drove down to Lymington, where Osprey was berthed. For longer trips, Osprey would need a crew of at least eight; but, today, we would be mooring overnight near Cowes so the four of us would be able to handle her.

The day passed pleasantly enough with the mêlée of yachts chasing around the Solent and out into Chichester Bay in what seemed to casual spectators to be random directions. Having identified the marks of the course, this apparently aimless manoeuvring started to make sense. As the yachts beat into wind, they would heel over with the crew sitting over the windward side to provide ballast. Every so often the crew would race to their allotted positions as the boats tacked through the wind to zigzag up to the mark. The big genoas would be released, then sheeted in on the other side as the boom swung across the cockpit to set the mainsail.

With Osprey's performance, we were easily able to keep in touch with the leaders of the race — and could have won if we had been competing.

It was late afternoon when we motored up the Cowes River to find a mooring. We then changed and took a river taxi to a restaurant for dinner. As we sat drinking coffee afterwards, I raised the question of who would be driving the coach.

"Why? are you interested? I thought you had a job with Ravens," George replied.

"I have, but I'd still be interested. It sounds fascinating. Touring the continent, seeing all those places. I was a courier with a tour company for one summer, the only trouble with that one was the clients! You'd always get at least one man who thought he was God's gift to women and who thought he was doing you a favour by chatting you up."

"Can you drive a coach? It's a bit different to a car."

"I took a course on driving one, just in case the driver became ill. I also speak French and German fluently and can just about get by in Italian."

"It's a pity I didn't know this earlier. I've only just organised a driver for the first trip. Mind you, he isn't as attractive as you. Maybe we can discuss future tours."

George had placed his hand on my knee as he made this remark.

"Have you organised interpreters for your meetings? Perhaps I could act as a sort of hostess?"

"Now that's not a bad idea. Trouble is, the coach only has one sleeping berth, doesn't it?"

"True, but there are bound to be hotels in most of the places and, if not, I could use the lounge area in an emergency."

"Let me think about it, darling. I hadn't planned to pay for two people to go with the coach, but I would be saving on interpreters, so maybe we can work something out."

Chapter 43. Carol — August Bank Holiday 1998

It hadn't taken much effort to persuade George to invite me on the race from Cowes to Cherbourg. He'd obviously thought the trip would give him a chance to get closer to me; a lot closer — and maybe I hadn't discouraged that idea.

George had organised the watches so he and I were on together — quelle surprise!

He made it quite clear he hoped we would see more of each other while in port. Fortunately, wet weather gear is not conducive to sexual advances and there's little privacy in any case on a racing yacht, so I didn't have to ward off any advances during the crossing.

It was mid-morning when we reached Cherbourg. We spent the rest of the morning clearing up the yacht and getting ourselves sorted out — then went into the port for lunch.

There was a reception and presentation of prizes at the Yacht Club that evening — which left us the afternoon free. I broke away from the others on the pretext of having my hair done for the evening. Before heading for the beauty salon, I telephoned Brian Halliday at his home to update him on progress. I told him I planned to spend the next week with George in the Loire Valley visiting his distributors. He wasn't exactly overjoyed but accepted my assurance I was a big girl and could take care of myself.

It was a real pleasure to be able to take a sauna at the beauty salon and feel the tackiness from wearing wet weather gear and thermals being sweated out! A massage and facial followed before I dressed again to go into the hairdressing area. A manicure and French polish to my nails and a makeover completed the treatment. I don't often indulge in such luxuries but, with a bit of gentle persuasion, I might be able to swing the cost onto expenses — I was, after all, working! Then I was ready to face the world again!

"Wow! " said George as I returned to the yacht just before six o'clock. "You look fabulous! "

Compliments never did any girl any harm — even if they are from a lecherous old man! Well, to be fair, George wasn't *that* old and if I hadn't known his background, I might well have enjoyed his salesman's patter.

"Here's to us all," he said, handing me a glass of wine.

"Our performance coming over has already impressed a lot of the other yachts and tonight they're going to be even more impressed when they see you, Carol," he added.

"Thanks George. Maybe I can do the same for your customers with the exhibition coach," I replied.

"No question at all about that. We will certainly have to have a serious chat about it next week. In the meantime, I'll just finish this glass — then get over to the club house for a shower and start to get ready for the reception," George remarked.

With my hair and make-up already done, it wouldn't take me long to change, so I sat in the cockpit and slowly sipped my wine.

There were still a number of competitors straggling in. The wind had dropped to almost nothing during the afternoon and they'd been struggling to make the final 20 miles or so.

My daydream was interrupted by John asking if I wanted another glass of wine. He'd been below sorting out his gear so he could catch the night ferry back after the reception.

"I think I'll pass, thanks — may need to keep a clear head with George later," I told him.

"Just be very careful with him, please. I'm beginning to regret telling you about my suspicions — I didn't expect you to be actively involved in following them up. I assumed your people would put someone else on the job," he replied.

"A man, you mean? " I asked.

"Ok — yes, a man," he admitted.

"Typical male attitude. Women should be attractive, wear short skirts and, if allowed out to work at all, they're just good enough to do the typing and make the tea! Any possible risk and they have to be protected," I retorted.

"Oh, come on, Carol! You know that's not what I meant. But, if something were to happen to you, I'd never forgive myself."

I took his hand in mine.

"I know, but I face that attitude all the time from my colleagues. It really pisses me off. They think women can't handle risky assignments; they forget some of the best agents Britain sent to France during the war were women. Don't worry I'm not looking to put myself in danger — all I'm doing at the moment is trying to get close enough to George to get information about his activities."

At the prize giving, George was delighted to receive a silver platter for first place in our class and even happier to hear we had come fifth overall on handicap. As anticipated, top honours went to two of the British Admiral's Cup contenders plus a French boat and an American. It was the best result George had ever achieved. In Nigel's Sadler, they'd occasionally won their class but had rarely even been in the top twenty overall.

His good mood remained for the following week — in spite of me fending off his advances using the oldest excuse in the book and convincing him I was as disappointed as he was. By the end of our stay in the Loire, I'd persuaded George to take me on as 'hostess' for his exhibition coach tour. He'd even offered me a full-time position as his PA.

The clincher had been when I'd let slip at having used my foreign languages for some 'interesting work' in Hamburg after quitting my job as a courier with a coach tour operator. Pretending to be tipsy, I'd let him draw out of me the work had been for pornographic magazines. I'd insisted I hadn't been involved in any of the photographic sessions — but made it clear I wasn't averse to bending, if not breaking, the law if it suited me.

George had more business to take care of on the continent so he dropped me off at Charles de Gaulle airport for my flight home.

He then asked me if I would take a package back with me.

"What's in it? " I asked. Squeezing the bubble pack envelop, I could feel some hard edges; but it could be anything.

"Just some samples we're thinking of importing," he replied.

"So long as that's all they are, fine. I don't want to find I've been suckered into carrying illegal drugs without knowing about it. You hear of too many people being caught like that," I replied. "Doesn't give the courier any opportunity to take precautions — or ask for suitable payment to cover the risk."

"Don't worry — it's nothing to get you into any trouble," he assured me.

I gave him a look to say I wasn't convinced but I accepted his word.

I wasn't concerned about its contents. It was too small for any significant quantity of drugs and allowing a small amount to reach the streets was a small price to pay for stopping a much larger volume getting through. Being stopped coming through customs might resulted in a few problems — but nothing I couldn't solve by getting them to call Brian.

"Just make sure you play fair with me — that's all I ask," I told him.

At Heathrow, I collected my bags, found a trolley and walked straight through the green channel unchallenged.

Sailing kit is bulky and heavy and I also had a folding suitcase so, rather than struggle with it on public transport and be faced with a half mile walk from the station to my flat in Streatham, I took a cab.

Trying to check whether or not I was being followed was impossible on the M4. As far as I was aware, nobody from my flight had been in the queue for the taxis — but I couldn't be certain. In any case, if I'd been George and had wanted to keep a watch on me, I'd probably have arranged for someone I wouldn't recognise to be waiting for me at Heathrow. It could be anyone.

As we turned down Streatham High Street from the South Circular, none of the cars which I could recall having been with us for a significant part of the trip followed. The absence of a tail was confirmed as we finally turned in to Mount Nod Road and, apart from the usual weekly bin collection, could see no one else in the road as the cab pulled up outside my flat.

Once inside, I glanced at the mail that had been waiting for me. The usual collection of circulars would go straight in the rubbish bin, a couple of bills could wait; as could my bank statement. I filled the filter machine and unpacked my bags while the coffee brewed. I sorted out the laundry and started the first wash before sitting down with a cup of coffee. I opened my bank statement and was surprised to see a significantly higher balance than I had expected. The explanation was a £500 cash credit made three days earlier. Was it a mistake or something more sinister? Was I being set up by George? Had he made the payment to look as though I'd been paid for bringing his package in through customs?

It seemed a rather crude way of doing it if it was George. What if I'd declined to carry his package? What on earth was he playing at?

What, for that matter, was actually in his package?

I went over to the side table, picked up the package and examined it.

It appeared innocuous.

I lit a cigarette and pondered the situation.

Should I open the parcel? If I did, would there be anything to show I'd done so? It was contained in a self-seal envelope. I might be able to steam it open — but probably not without leaving some evidence of having tampered with it.

Or should I take it in to the office? Would that blow my cover with George? Was it worth the risk?

George had said he'd arrange for the package to be collected by a courier that afternoon. There really wasn't time for me to take it to the office in any case.

I decided I would take some photographs of the package but not to attempt to open it. I would phone Brian later at home and update him on the latest developments.

Chapter 44. George — September 1998

As I sat back in my business class seat and savoured the glass of champagne the stewardess had handed me, I reflected on the last week or so. I'd tied up several new vineyards for next year's Wine Club promotions — that side of the business would continue to launder the proceeds from the drug importation. That took my thoughts to Carol. I still hadn't cracked that one. When she'd first expressed interest in working for me, I'd wondered about her. Her cousin John always seemed so straight. Even when I'd suggested some sweeteners for the computer orders he turned me down flat.

I didn't think there was anything to worry about though. She didn't have any problem with taking that package back to UK with her. In fact, she seemed to be quite prepared to take a few risks if the money was right.

The sound of the warning tone attracting our attention to the seat belt sign interrupted my thoughts about what else I'd like to do with Carol. I put away the magazine I'd been scanning and prepared for the landing.

An hour and a half later I was home. I checked the answer machine for messages. There was just the one — but it was enough. "Contact me immediately you return." I didn't need to ask who it was from.

I sent him a text.

"What's the problem?" I asked

"Driver unavailable, stupid cunt pulled yesterday. Need to discuss," came back the reply.

"Shit! " I thought.

"On my way. Be with you in 2 hours," I answered.

"Fine," was Frank's closing response.

I made good time along the M27. Frank was finishing a call as I was shown into his office.

"Drink? " he offered.

"Just a coffee please," I told him. "I'm driving and don't want to be done for being over the limit."

"Pity someone else didn't think about that," he said. "that stupid wanker, Evans, got pissed last weekend and was involved in an accident. The passenger in the other car was killed and they're throwing the book at him. What the fuck he thought he was up to I have no idea. I'll have his bloody balls for it believe me!"

Evans was the driver we'd organised for the demonstration tour. With the tour planned to start the following week, we could be in trouble. Almost as much trouble as Evans would be once Frank's lads got hold of him.

Well, there was no doubt Evans was in the shit — but maybe we weren't.

"There is an alternative Frank. Remember I mentioned Carol — the girl I'm planning to use as an interpreter for the trip? "

"You mean the bird you're shafting? " Frank was not renowned for his subtlety! Mind you, maybe I had given him the impression all I had to do was smile and any girl dropped her knickers for me.

"Yeah — well," I replied with a sheepish grin, "she says she can drive the coach. She also brought that package through customs without asking any stupid questions." It had been Frank's idea to test her. In fact, the package had been totally innocent – it was just some yacht fittings — but she wasn't to know that.

"Check her out. Make sure she can handle driving the coach. In the meantime, I'll try and find someone else."

Chapter 45. Nigel — September 1998

'd hoped business would pick up again after the summer but, if anything, it was tailing off even more. Some clients were even experimenting with campaigns on social media. I'd had to let a couple of the studio staff go and a third left to join another agency.

Nicky was smug over the fact I'd persuaded her to split the business. Her work had held up very well — even growing while mine stagnated. When I started to suggest merging the two again, she asked if I thought she was stupid.

"You have to be joking, Nigel. You split the company because it looked like your side would make a lot more than mine to cut me out of the profits."

"Absolutely not," I'd insisted. "I did it to give you the flexibility to develop the business in your own way." It sounded plausible even if it was a lie.

"Don't take me for a fool, Nigel. I may have just been your PA before, but running the PR business has shown me what I'm capable of. The last year has also revealed how badly you treat other people. This latest move has made up my mind. I want you out of my life and my flat so please arrange to remove your things by the end of the week. I'll find another office to work from." With that she turned on her heel and left my office.

"Piss off then, you cow. See if I care," I yelled after her.

But it did leave me even further in the mire. I was now homeless. As usual my bank account was overdrawn —so finding alternative accommodation and putting down a deposit wasn't going to be easy. I couldn't even tap into the business account — the wages were due next week and there was barely enough in that account to cover them.

I told Bill and Jerry to come to my office and explained Nicky was moving out.

Jerry looked at Bill who gave the slightest of nods.

"So are we," said Jerry. "Bill and I are setting up on our own."

Fuck. Another couple of Judases.

"Bugger off then, the pair of you. You've obviously been planning this for a while and must have talked to the clients — so you're fired for professional misconduct. You can whistle for your salaries."

Bill shrugged his shoulders.

With that, they walked out.

Bastards.

I slumped in my chair. Pulled out a bottle from the bottom drawer of my desk and poured a very large scotch. As the spirit hit my throat, I considered my options. There was one possibility: George.

It was his fucking fault I was in this position. He was the one who'd cut back on the advertising leaving me high and dry. He owed me. Not just for causing the latest problems but for all the cash I'd slipped him when he was with SeaCon — and the girls. Mustn't forget the girls. Oh yes. George owed me. Big Time.

I looked at the bottle and thought about pouring another glassful. Shit, this was no time to feel sorry for myself.

I phoned George and invited him for a drink that evening at the casino I knew he used.

I was in the bar when George arrived.

"What'll you have?" I asked.

"Usual, please." The barman obviously knew what that was and served him.

"So, Nigel, what was so urgent?"

"I had to fire Bill and Jerry today and Nicky's left."

"So, no more nooky for you, eh?"

"It's no bloody joke, George. You cancelling the advertising has left me in a hole. I reckon you owe me for all the chips I slipped you and for the girls and other hospitality."

"You don't think the work I've pushed your way over the last year paid for that? Not to mention letting you get away with overcharging SeaCon."

"To some extent," I had to concede.

"So, seems to me, Nigel, that we're even."

"OK — but how much is it worth for me to keep quiet about other things?"

He furled his eyebrows, picked up his drink, took a sip, then said:

"I don't know what you're talking about."

"Like the coke you provided that time with the girls. You and I both know where it came from."

"And?" he asked.

I really didn't want to lay it out but I'd come so far and couldn't back out now.

"I know you're involved in the importation and I know the wine and perfume offers are cover for it. I'm right, aren't I?"

He took another drink.

"Look," I added, "I don't give a toss what you're up to. I did wonder how you got the money to finance the advertising but it wasn't my concern. All I'm asking for is a small cut to help me keep my head above water at the moment. It's in neither of our interests for me to go under."

George finished his drink and smiled.

"I'll think about what you've suggested Nigel. Not that I'm admitting anything. In the meantime, I suggest you go home and not do anything precipitous."

He shook my hand as he indicated the way out.

As I drove back to Chandlers Ford, I was a lot happier than I'd been on the way up. I was sure George would see sense. I'd bet a couple of grand a month would be peanuts compared with the turnover from the import business.

Chapter 46. George — September 1998

For Christ's sake George — what do you have between your ears? Cotton wool? Or is your brain really between your legs?"

I'd known Frank would be pissed off that Nigel was trying to blackmail me — but I'd had to tell him. Nigel really had no idea what he was taking on, threatening to go to the police with what he'd guessed.

"Sorry, Frank. You know how it is. I'd had a few drinks and we were just relaxing with a couple of girls and it just slipped out." The truth was that after years of being the underdog in the relationship between Nigel and me, I'd become the more successful partner and I'd wanted to rub it in.

Frank shook his head in despair. "You're a complete prick, aren't you?"

I bowed my head and agreed with him.

"So, where do we go from here? There's no question of putting him on the payroll. Can he be discouraged? Or do we need a permanent solution?" Frank asked as though discussing sorting out an unreliable car.

Could he be threatened? Maybe. Broken limbs were a serious disincentive to grassing. But would it be enough? I really wasn't convinced.

"Hall is in a mess. He's about to lose everything that's important to him. His company will go down the pan if we don't help, his mistress has dumped him and he'll probably have to sell his yacht. He's drinking heavily and probably using more and more coke. No. I don't think he can just be discouraged."

Christ, was I really signing the death warrant of someone I used to regard as a mate? Then I remembered how he'd treated me when Mary Sanchez had fired me. There'd been no friendship then — now it was him or me.

"OK, you prat. I don't suppose you've got the stomach to do the job have you?"

The answer was probably obvious in my face. Shit, I wouldn't know where to start.

"No, I thought not," Frank said, contemptuously. "Leave it with me."

"Thanks, Frank, and I'm really sorry to drop this on you."

"Thank your luck stars that the businesses you run for us are performing and that we're too far along on the tour plan to change — or you might have been joining Hall. Any more cockups like this and you won't be as fortunate."

I didn't need telling that I'd been walking a tightrope.

"Right Frank. You can rely on me."

"Piss off out of here. I don't want to see your sad face until I send for you."

I left, very relieved to be in one piece.

A few days later, I saw on the local news that a yacht had exploded at a mooring in Chichester harbour. I poured myself a large scotch and stared at the television as the newscaster announced that there had been one casualty. There was an interview with the owner's former girlfriend.

"Nigel had been having business problems recently and had been drinking heavily. We'd split up and he was living on board. He was usually so careful about turning off the gas supply on the boat but it seems he must have forgotten."

The reporter turned to the camera. "Well, there you have it. The police say that they are not looking for anyone else in connection with the incident. Now back to the studio."

Shit. Maybe Nicky was right. Maybe Nigel had just forgotten to turn off the gas and it had built up in the bilges. It was a perpetual problem on boats. Maybe he'd just been too drunk to check. Maybe he'd gone below and lit one of his cigars. Maybe.

Chapter 47. Carol October 1998

'd finally persuaded Brian to let me drive the coach. "Just be very careful and don't take unnecessary risks" were his final instructions.

Monday morning, I finished packing my bags and caught the train to Southampton. As the taxi from the station dropped me off, I could see the exhibition unit in the car park; Raven's had done a superb job on the exterior — the graphics were certainly eye-catching. There was no possibility of the coach blending into the background. The overall scheme was a stylised outline map of

Europe with the NavStar logo superimposed. The display unit looked like a giant rally car.

George was standing outside talking to a guy I didn't recognise. He put his hands on my arms and kissed me on both cheeks.

"Carol, this is Jeff – he's here to make sure you're up to speed on the NavStar system."

Hmm, you normally expect computer techies to look geekish but Jeff certainly didn't fit that description. He was about five-eleven and smartly dressed. Instead of jeans and a T shirt with an anti-establishment logo, his suit looked made to measure, not off the peg, and his shirt and tie and polished shoes rather than sandals were very smart. His sparkling blue eyes and welcoming smile warmed an otherwise chilly day.

Did I just say 'sparkling blue eyes'?

He held out his hand and I took it; he squeezed gently and I held it a fraction longer than I'd planned to. Oh, come on Carol, this is no time to fancy someone – just as you're going to be away for a month.

"Shall we?" he gestured at the steps into the vehicle.

I climbed into the coach and sat at one of the demonstration positions; Jeff next to me. I could smell his sharp aftershave; I couldn't identify it but it certainly wasn't Brut or Old Spice.

"OK, what do you know about the system?"

"I know it uses satellites to work out our position, plots it on the map on the screen and works out how to get to where we want to go and provides directions on screen and verbally."

"Spot on. So, the first thing we need to do is switch on and load the map for the region you're in – typically one country though some do cover more than one. This takes a minute or two."

"I gather you're doing quite a tour," he remarked as he pressed the 'on' button.

"Yes, down through France – then over to Italy and back up through Germany and the Netherlands."

Chapter 47 – Carol October 1998

"Sounds like an incredible trip. OK – so the system has booted up now we load the first map for the UK. The maps also include significant locations outside the country for through route planning."

His fingers played across the keyboard as he entered the details.

"You normally need to enter the latitude and longitude of the waypoints – that's the places you want to pass through or get to. We're working on using postcodes and equivalents abroad — but they're not ready yet."

"Yes, George mentioned that; he's provided a list of the locations I needed to visit."

"Well, I've actually loaded the list you're using for the tour onto the system — you just need to select the name from a list. We're planning to include this feature in future releases of the software but it's not quite ready so you'll be testing it for us."

"Let's hope it works, I've been concerned about making a slip entering the lat and longitude and ending up hundreds of miles from where I want to be."

An hour or so later, Jeff had finished my training and I'd loaded the first stage on the coach's own system. He handed me a wallet containing several CDs.

"You've got one for France; another for Italy — which also covers Switzerland and Austria, one for Germany and finally one covering Belgium, Netherlands and Luxembourg and, of course, one for the UK. OK?"

"Fine."

"Well, I guess we'd better go and join George for the press reception."

The fact I was to be driving the coach had, apparently, been seized on by the PR company. They'd phoned those magazines and local TV and radio media which had previously declined or not responded to invitations and pointed out the additional interest an attractive woman driver would generate! So much for trying to keep a low profile — and for chauvinism! Mind you, I had been using my feminine wiles to get the job in the first place so I suppose I shouldn't complain.

I'd told George I'd had experience of driving coaches before while working as a tour courier. That had been untrue.

I did, however, have an HGV licence as a result of an argument with a male colleague some years previously. His attitude to women drivers had been they should stick to taking the kids to school and shopping in something like a Metro. Anything larger and they couldn't handle the size. He'd claimed it was something to do with spacial awareness. He had to eat his words when I turned up at the office with a licence to drive HGVs after a concentrated course! The coach shouldn't prove any problem.

The journalists seemed as interested in the fact that I'd be driving the vehicle and my accommodation on board as in the NavStar system.

"Are you totally tied to the vehicle all the time? What happens if you want to get away for an evening, maybe go for a meal?" one asked.

"Or go shopping? It's not exactly going to be convenient in a supermarket car park, is it?" added another.

"You're quite right," I replied. "Fortunately, we did think about that and we've used a luggage compartment in the back for a motor scooter as well as a portable generator."

"Can you really handle such a big vehicle?" asked the obese reporter from the South Coast Globe, removing the cigarette dangling from his mouth long enough to take a sip of the scotch we'd provided.

"She can handle my big rig any time," I heard another whisper to his colleague. He was answered with a guffaw.

Christ. Let's get on the road. I thought.

I was due to take an overnight ferry to Ouistreham that evening which would only leave me a half hour drive to the first demonstration the next day. As the last of the press left, George came over to me.

"Everything clear?"

"Yes George."

"There's been a slight change to the itinerary. The demonstration in Milan has been cancelled so we're taking the opportunity to have the vehicle serviced there as well as change the panels. You'll have a few days in a hotel while it's in the workshop. Or you could do a bit of sightseeing."

"Oh. Right — I'll probably be glad of a break by then."

"OK, well, I'm off — I have a meeting in town later. Have a good trip and I'll see you in a few weeks." He leant across and kissed me on the cheek.

Jeff looked quizzically at me.

"What's up?" I asked.

"Nothing." He paused, looked as though he was about to say something then just repeated "No, nothing."

"Nothing?"

"It's none of my business — but, well, are you and George… "

"What! Are George and I what? Seeing each other? Is that what you think?"

"Sorry. It really is none of my business."

Was he jealous? Interesting.

"You are right, it isn't. But to answer your question. No, George and I aren't an item. Oh, he'd like us to be but I don't fancy him. I just wanted this job so I played along with him a bit."

"I'm glad. I'm not sure I trust him. There's something about his business that doesn't feel right."

"If you feel that way, why do you work for him?"

"I don't work for him; he's the distributor for the NavStar system that we developed for sailing and are now adapting for vehicles. It's taken a very large investment particularly digitising the maps. I'm probably talking utter bollocks — he's probably just an entrepreneur with access to the funds we need."

I was relieved to hear that Jeff wasn't involved in George's seedier ventures but I didn't dare tell him the truth about my mission.

"I guess few successful businessmen are totally straightforward — they always seem to take short cuts or run close to the wind somewhere along the way. Doesn't mean they're total rogues."

"I guess not. Look, I don't suppose you'd be interested in dinner, would you?"

I had plenty of time before I needed to get to Portsmouth.

"I'd love to."

The next morning, as I waited to drive the coach off the ferry, I thought back to the previous evening. Jeff had been wonderful company and a great kisser. I really hoped I'd see more of him when I got back after this trip.

If I got back.

The queue started to move and I followed the other vehicles to the customs check point.

I knew John thought I was taking too big a risk. Equally, he would probably not have been as worried if I hadn't been female.

Why did guys think I wasn't capable of looking after myself and suggesting I shouldn't do what would be just part of my job if I'd been born a man? It pissed me off.

I put the thoughts behind me as I took back my papers from the French douanier.

"Merci. Au revoir," I said and returned to the coach. I swung out of the bay where I'd been stopped and left the terminal. My route would take me south and west – then back across France and down the eastern side before heading into Italy. I had more than 5,000 kilometres ahead of me before I reached Milan where the display panels would be replaced and where I anticipated the drugs would be concealed aboard. Then it would be up through Germany then into the Netherlands before catching the shuttle back to the UK.

Chapter 48. Carol — 20th October 1998

Two weeks and eleven stops to demonstrate the equipment later, I pulled up outside an industrial unit. I was surprised to find George waiting for me.

"Good morning, darling. How has the tour been so far?" He held my shoulders and kissed my cheeks. I pulled back from him.

"Excellent. There's been a huge amount of interest."

"That's great — looks like you've been doing a fabulous job for us. We've already had some orders through. Well done. So, what are your plans while the unit is serviced?"

"I'm heading for the slopes near Mont Blanc —I'm meeting John. I don't know if there'll be enough snow for skiing but it'll be good to get some mountain air and stretch my legs after sitting driving most of the last month. Avis should be delivering a car for me."

"It's already here. They dropped it off an hour ago. It's the Renault Clio Sport over there." He pointed to a bright yellow car across the car park.

I transferred my case from the coach to the Clio then drove out of the yard, relishing the responsiveness of the little Renault compared with the brute of a vehicle I'd been hauling round France and Italy.

Eventually, I pulled into the car park of a small hotel on the edge of Courmayeur. I soon registered and headed for my room and dropped my case on the bed before picking up the phone. It rang twice before being answered.

"Hi John, just arrived, I'm in room 106," I announced.

"Great, I'm in 112, how was your drive?"

"Fabulous. What incredible scenery. Anyway, I'm going to have a bath — what time shall we meet for dinner?"

"Eight? You're on my way to the stairs so I'll knock on your door."

"Fine, see you then, love."

I turned on the bath taps and added a generous dose of bath oil then stripped off. As I slipped into the water with a glass of wine in my hand, the stress of the day drifted away. I realised the operation was entering its most dangerous phase but it would soon be over and Frank and his cohorts would, with luck, be under lock and key and off the streets.

John knocked on my door just as I slipped on my shoes. We hugged then walked arm in arm downstairs.

"Drink first or straight into dinner?" he asked.

I was certain he'd have another go at me over the job I was doing if we had a drink in the bar and hoped he'd be less inclined to make a scene in the restaurant.

"I'm hungry, I didn't stop for lunch so let's eat now," I lied.

"OK. But don't think I'm not going to nag you later in any case."

I stopped and faced him.

Chapter 48 – Carol October 1998

"John, listen. I'm doing my job. It's important. In fact, I believe it's absolutely crucial. I know you're worried about me and I love you for your concern. But you are not going to stop me so please drop the subject."

He looked at me in shock.

"You're right," he admitted, "but I can't bear the thought of losing you too."

"I do appreciate that but I don't intend letting anything happen to me," I assured him. "We won't be making a move against the gang until we are in the UK. Then I'll be protected by the team. It's possible, in any case, that this is just a dry run."

"You don't think it is though, do you?"

"No, I don't. I doubt if George would have turned up in Milan if it had been. Now, subject closed or do we fall out?"

John held up his hands in surrender and we went into dinner.

The following morning, we decided to have a walk up the mountain as there wasn't enough snow for skiing. We sat on the top of a ridge, having a picnic lunch we'd taken with us, while I briefed John on the trip so far. I'd already given him a floppy disk containing my report for my boss and three rolls of 35mm film I'd shot of details of the coach.

Strolling back to the hotel, I felt totally invigorated — stretching my legs and breathing in the clean air had done me the world of good. That evening, there was a local folk group in the hotel bar and we sat around a roaring fire, drinking wine and joining in any of the songs we recognised.

"What do you fancy doing tomorrow?" asked John as we reached our rooms.

"How do you fancy taking the cable car up Mont Blanc?" I suggested. So, next morning after breakfast, we drove through the tunnel to Chamonix. The view from the top of the cable car was breath-taking. We had to try the glass bottomed 'step into the void' — with, apparently, nothing under your feet for a thousand metres.

On our last day, we had another hike up the mountains. And that's when disaster struck.

On the way back down, I tried to jump across a stream, misjudged it and fell awkwardly on the other side. My ankle gave way as soon as I tried to stand on it.

Chapter 48 – Carol October 1998

"Shit, shit, shit," I said, realising that it was serious. "How could I be so stupid?"

John checked the ankle and looked at me with concern. "I think you may have broken it."

"I can't have done. It'll just be a sprain," I replied; more in hope than confidence.

Using John as a crutch, I made it down to civilisation and a telephone where we were able to call a taxi. Back at the hotel. I just wanted to go to my room but John insisted that I get the ankle checked out. Unfortunately, the nearest hospital was twenty miles away so John drove the hire Clio.

The hospital confirmed John's diagnosis; I'd broken a bone. Fortunately, it didn't need pinning but it still needed to be set in a cast. What an idiot I'd been. The whole operation was now jeopardised as there was no way I could drive the coach.

John was silent as we walked out of the hospital and got in the car.

As he pulled onto the autostrada, he turned to me. "There's only one way to save your operation, Carol. I'm going to have to take your place."

"You can't. It's not your job, it's mine."

"Well, you certainly can't do it with your foot in a cast can you? And no one else from customs can take your place, can they?"

"It's too dangerous for you."

"But not for you?"

"It's my job and I need to see it through." I was protesting but I knew he was right. I couldn't do it.

"Carol, we both want this gang stopped. You can't do it. Customs can't replace you but I can. We did it often enough at Greenbreaks. What other option is there?"

Damn! John was right. There was no other choice if we weren't to let the gang get away Scot free. On the other hand, was it really worth risking John's life for? I tried one last appeal.

"It's not worth risking your life for John."

Chapter 48 – Carol October 1998

"Carol, two nights ago you were saying how important this job was. How it was vital to break this gang before they did any more harm. 'it's absolutely crucial' were your own words."

"Yes, but . . ."

"But what?

I looked him in the face. His concern was obvious. I bit my lower lip before conceding.

"OK. I really don't like it, but you're right. There is no option. Pull off the autostrada when you can. And find somewhere secluded to pull up."

As John stopped, I took off my jacket and removed my bra from under my T-shirt and passed it to him. The road was quiet so he was able to put on the bra and stuff it with spare socks. With my jacket over his T-shirt, we knew there'd be no way anyone would realise we'd switched.

Entering the hotel, 'Carol' picked up the backpacks and handed me the crutches the hospital had provided.

'She' went to the reception desk for our keys.

"Goodness," the receptionist remarked, "what happened to Mr Ives?"

"He tried to jump across a stream and broke a bone in his ankle," 'Carol' explained.

"Typical men, always trying to show off." She shook her head in despair as she handed over the room keys.

Once in John's bedroom, we raided the mini-bar and I went over the details of the trip — especially the remaining leg and briefed 'Carol' as much as I could remember about conversations with George and Frank to try to ensure 'she' wouldn't be caught out.

It wasn't just my injured ankle that kept me awake that night. I tossed and turned as my mind churned through the thousand-and-one scenarios that could lead to disaster. The gang had killed before so wouldn't hesitate to do so again if they realised that John wasn't me or if they suspected that we worked for Customs. How would John as Carol handle George's advances. Shit, what a mess this was.

"Don't say a word," John declared when I opened the door to him. "We've already discussed whether I should take your place and there is no option."

I stared into his eyes and he held my glaze with a determined look that brooked no argument. I stepped back and looked him up and down — I could have been looking in a mirror. I knew he'd cross-dressed frequently before Ann and Samantha were killed but, even so, I was amazed how convincing he was. The make-up and hair were flawless and 'she' was wearing one of my miniskirts, exposing legs that would draw the attention of any red-blooded male.

"Ok, I accept that you look convincing and I doubt if anyone will notice the switch but I do have one suggestion. If you have your hair cut any change in your appearance will be put down to the new style. What do you think?"

"Makes sense to me. There's a hairdressers next door — I'll pop round there and see if they can fit me in while you order breakfast for us."

'She' came back just as the waiter was serving coffee. "They can do me in in 30 minutes"

Just before noon, we set off back down to Milan taking the opportunity of the drive for me to quiz 'Carol' on the mission and the 'relationship', such as it was, between George and me or rather 'her'.

Chapter 49. John as Carol — 21ˢᵗ October 1998

I'd taken Carol's place in the Panto but I'd been playing her playing Cinders not trying to convince everyone I was Carol. Even at Greenbreaks, my impersonation had been quite superficial. But could I really convince George and the other gang members that I was Carol? I was going to have to spend a lot of time with George and, as Carol had warned me, he would probably come on to me. How would I handle that? Maybe he wouldn't be around.

Well, that optimistic thought was dashed as soon as I pulled up next to the coach. George was just getting out of the vehicle with another guy. George ambled over to me while the other person scurried back into the workshop.

"How was your break, darling? Have a good time with John? Love the hair by the way." He held my shoulders and kissed my cheeks.

"It was fine thanks — except that my idiot of a cousin broke his ankle jumping across a stream."

Chapter 49 – John as Carol October 1998

I gave him the details as I opened the boot, took out my bag.

"Is everything ready then?" I asked, "any problems with the changeover or the service?"

"No, none. Everything is ready to go. The schedule is the same. We've got all day tomorrow to get to Munich ready for Monday."

"We?"

"Yes, I've decided to come with you for the rest of the trip."

BUGGER! That's all I needed.

"Don't you trust me to do a good job promoting the kit?"

"Nothing like that Carol. You've done a fabulous job. It'll give us a chance to get to know each other better as well as giving me a break from the office with my own personal coach tour."

"I see. Are you planning to sleep on board too?"

"No, don't worry, I like my comforts too much — the bunk on board looks far too cramped, I'll use hotels at each stop."

The journey to Munich was breath-taking at times and numbingly boring at others. I lost count of the number of tunnels we passed through. Having driven our own exhibition vehicles plenty of times, handling the coach was no problem at all.

Eventually, we pulled up at George's hotel not far from the factory where we'd be demonstrating in the morning.

"See you tomorrow," he said as he got out.

I watched him go into the reception and breathed a sigh of relief. I thought he might have suggested having dinner together. If he had, I'd been ready with the excuse of being shattered after nearly seven hours driving but it hadn't been necessary. Long drives after full days' demonstrations would give me excuses for most of next week but I anticipated problems once we got into the Netherlands with much shorter legs. Oh well, I'd deal with that when I got there.

Our last demonstration would be near Eindhoven before catching the Eurotunnel back to the UK. The schedule was for us to finish the demonstration on the Friday then drive down to Eindhoven and stay there until the Monday.

Chapter 49 – John as Carol October 1998

George had arranged parking for the coach for the weekend at the factory we were presenting to on Monday.

"I thought we could have an evening out tomorrow, there's a casino in town. We could get a meal and have a bit of fun playing the tables," he said as we parked up outside his hotel.

I knew George liked a flutter and it was probably safer to keep him occupied like that than risking closer contact. I'd overlooked other attractions offered in casinos.

"Sounds good. I'm getting a bit tired of take-aways and microwaved meals in the coach."

"The trip starting to drag, is it?"

I shook my head from side to side. "Not at all, I've enjoyed it and happy to do other trips — but a bit of civilisation would be good."

"Well, look, I've got a bit of business to take care of in Amsterdam tomorrow — I've got a hire car being delivered first thing; but I'll be back late afternoon so I'll pick you up here at, what, seven thirty?"

"Seven thirty will be fine," I confirmed.

There was an Indonesian restaurant just across the road from the coach so I picked up a novel I was reading and walked over. I'd heard that Holland had inherited its rich heritage of Indonesian cuisine from the days of the Dutch East Indies. I wasn't disappointed. I started with Aneka Laut Lilit – King crab and shrimp on lemongrass skewer followed by Gulai Domba, a braised lamb curry with coconut and cinnamon and rice. It really did make a change from microwaved pasta!

I spent the next morning at a laundrette and supermarket, both within sight of the display unit, topping up my supplies. The vehicle attracted the attention of employees going to and from the factory and I had to explain several times why we were there.

When George pulled up in his hire car at 7.30, I was ready for him. I'd dressed in the Little Black Dress that Carol had packed 'just in case' and strappy three-inch heels. The dress was shorter than I'd usually wear — it came to just above my knees. I'd kept my make-up fairly low key; I didn't want to give George any

232

encouragement. I'd spritzed myself with Carol's Dune perfume — that was one taste that she and I didn't share; I preferred Rive Gauche.

After locking the coach, I slid into the passenger seat next to him. He patted my leg as I fastened the seat belt. Oh hell. Maybe I should have declined his invitation. This could go so badly wrong. The trouble was that if I'd turned him down, it might have made him suspicious.

Our dinner reservation was for eight. There was a band playing and, while we waited for our starters, George insisted on a dance. I was surprised to find that he was experienced at Salsa. Anne and I had loved Latin-American and had often been applauded for our performances at the dances we'd attended. My problem was that I was used to taking the lead and I now had to let George lead me. Fortunately, the music was reasonably quick so he had no excuse to get me into a clinch. If we could keep this up, it would be fine.

"You've done this a lot before, haven't you?" he asked as we returned to our table. "But you've got to stop trying to lead me." So, I hadn't got away with it.

"The trouble is," I said, "there are always too few men at club nights so I often had to take the lead when dancing with other women."

George nodded his head "I know what you mean — it was the same where I went. Women outnumbering the men; mind you that suited me," he smiled.

The waiter arrived with the wine and showed George the label. George nodded his approval then sipped the sample the waiter poured.

"Yes, that's fine," he confirmed.

Between courses, we returned to the dance floor. I was enjoying myself — especially the swirl of my dress around my legs. Our moves got more and more adventurous with George swinging me around him, me sliding between his legs, leaning back so far that my head almost touched the floor. At the end of the dance, my right knee was on his hip, his left hand was on my thigh and his right behind my back as I leant backwards — my left hand on his shoulder. Our eyes were locked together as he pulled me upright. I felt his erection pressing against me. I could see what was coming next as he held me close. His lips brushed mine. My body wanted to respond — but my brain told me that would be suicidal. Fortunately, my brain won.

"That was fabulous, I haven't danced like that for a couple of years," I told him as I slipped from his arms and applauded the band. I then realised that other dancers near us had stopped their own dance to watch us and the applause wasn't just for the band but for our own performance.

We returned to our table as our main courses arrived. I was in a dilemma. George's intentions were obvious but, even if I'd been prepared to go along with them, that was impossible. And, that raised another question. Just how far would I be prepared to go with a guy? Dancing with George had been wonderful and when he'd leant forward to kiss my lips, it had taken all my willpower to pull away from him. I'd also been aware over the last few days that it felt completely natural to get up each morning and dress as Carol and I'd started to wonder how it would be reverting to being John when the trip was over.

So, how was I going to handle George? He was going to want to go to bed with me. How could I avoid his advances without arousing any suspicions? Think girl, think. Girl? Shit, where did that come from? Obviously, I didn't have the equipment to have intercourse with George even if I'd been prepared to. I'd read some erotic trans stories where 'traps' would allow their partners to have anal sex while hiding their own genitalia but that had never seemed realistic and I didn't fancy it anyway. There were other options. I'd heard of some of the girls at the groups I used to attend giving men hand jobs or oral which had satisfied them. Would I be prepared to go that far if there was no other alternative? If it was that or abandon the mission? Would I be prepared to do the equivalent of 'Lie back and think of England'?

I felt George's hand rest on mine. "Penny for them."

"What? Oh, sorry I was miles away."

His fingers were stroking the back of my wrist.

"This looks great," I said, taking my hand from under his and picking up my knife and fork and cutting into the Sea Bass the waiter had just served.

I was certain George was involved in drugs — and I hated that trade with a passion; but he was also an amusing companion and I enjoyed his attention and flirting over dinner.

Chapter 49 – John as Carol October 1998

After we'd eaten and George smoked a cigar over coffee while I had a cigarette. I excused myself to powder my nose. As I returned to the table, George stood up.

"Fancy the tables?" he asked. As I acquiesced, he slipped his arm around my waist and we walked through to the main casino area. We played the tables for a while — but George seemed pre-occupied and lost interest in the roulette after less than an hour.

"I used to enjoy gambling but, I don't know, it just doesn't appeal as much anymore. Come on, let's dance instead," he said.

The music was lively so we were soon back in the rhythm and I was following his lead as we swung around. Eventually, the band switched to a much slower number and George pulled me to him. I rested my hands on his shoulders as his arms circled my waist — one hand resting on my bottom. I could smell the intensely masculine aroma of the cigar he'd smoked earlier. It felt totally natural being in his arms and when his lips found mine, I responded. I knew it was reckless but, in that instant, I just didn't care.

He pulled me closer still and slid his tongue into my mouth to entwine with mine. I wished I was a woman and he wasn't the target of a custom's investigation and we could take this further. I wanted so much to make love; to have a man make love to me as a female.

But I couldn't and I came to my senses.

I swivelled out of his arms, took his hand in mine and said "I need a drink."

The only available table had banquette seating; I shuffled in and George slid in next to me; his arm along the backrest behind me and his hand on my shoulder. I somehow needed to extract myself from the corner I'd got myself into. But I didn't know how.

Damn, I'd done exactly what I knew I shouldn't have done. I realised too, that my problems weren't just escaping George's advances without screwing up the entire investigation. It was what to do with the rest of my life. Before this trip, my cross dressing had usually been limited to a few hours here and there — and the very occasional weekend away. I'd now been 'Carol' for two weeks and it just felt 'right' somehow.

The latter issue could wait. The priority was to deal with George. Could I plead a headache? Could I get him too drunk to do anything? Whatever I did, I had to avoid him getting suspicious.

The waiter brought a bottle of champagne and we clinked glasses.

"Don't get too drunk, darling," whispered George. "I have plans for later."

It was obvious he wasn't going to have too much to drink either.

Headache then? Bit of a cliché. Or pleading time of the month? But that had been Carol's excuse just a few weeks ago. Would George be aware of dates? Probably, knowing his ability with numbers.

I was running out of options.

I put my glass down. The band had started a slow number.

"Come on, they're playing our tune." George needed no more encouragement.

When the music switched to a faster number, I threw myself into the moves then after he'd swung me around his back, I slipped from George's hold and collapsed onto the floor.

"Shit, bugger, ow, that hurts. Help me up, darling."

"I'm so sorry Carol. That was my fault, letting you go. Are you OK?"

"It's my bloody ankle. I've twisted it. I can't put my weight on it. OW!"

George supported me back to the table — concern showing in his eyes.

A waiter came across to help and sent for the manager. He took me into his office while they called a cab.

"Your family seem accident prone especially your ankles," commented George.

I smiled wryly at him. "We do, don't we."

"I'm really sorry, darling. It's my fault."

"It's no-one's fault, just one of those things. But why tonight of all nights?"

When a taxi arrived, I hobbled to it and cuddled up to George as it took us back to the coach.

"Are you sure you'll be OK?" he asked.

"I'll be fine."

"I could stay and look after you."

"It would be too much temptation, darling. Then I'll make it worse."

God, I really was laying it on.

He hadn't mentioned whether I'd be able to drive the coach back to the UK but I knew he'd be thinking about it.

"Look love, much as I want you to stay, we still have to get the coach home. If I rest it, I'm sure it'll be OK by the time we're due to leave on Monday. It's my left ankle anyway and the coach is automatic so I don't need to use it while driving — so don't worry about that. And there will be plenty of time for us later."

He nodded his head. "You're right sweetheart. I'll come over in the morning to see how you are."

With that, he phoned for a cab, the one we'd taken from the casino having long gone.

He sat next to me on the couch and pulled my head to him for a kiss. Maintaining my role of frustrated lover, I responded.

Then we heard the noise of a taxi outside.

One final kiss and George stood up. "Sleep well, darling."

"You too, love."

I kept up the pretence of the sprained ankle with George on the Sunday; hobbling around while he took me across the road to the Indonesian restaurant for a meal. On the Monday, I showed a significant improvement but stayed in my cabin while he presented the kit to the potential customers.

It was just before nine when we drove off the shuttle. The customs inspection had been fairly cursory; we'd been asked to open the luggage compartments, ostensibly to check for illegal immigrants and I knew that was when they had hidden a tracking device. We pulled out of the terminal and headed for George's industrial unit.

George turned to me. "Change of plan, Carol. We're dropping the vehicle in Croydon not Shoreham."

"What? Why? How do I get home from there?" I demanded.

"Don't worry, we'll organise a car for you."

The traffic initially thinned as we drove up the M20 towards London then built up again as we approached the capital.

"Take the next exit," George instructed.

I flicked on the indicators and took the slip road.

Chapter 50. George - November 1998

Pull over into that lay-by. Ok stop and switch off the engine. Get out and look as though you're checking the tyres for a puncture," I told Carol.

While she checked the tyres, I watched for any other vehicles that might have followed us off the motorway. None came past so I was pretty confident we weren't being followed — unless customs had a large enough team to pass us from one to another. As far as I could tell everything had been totally routine coming off the shuttle but you couldn't be too careful.

I'd be very glad when we'd off-loaded the consignment. Not that I'd be safe even then if there was an investigation at any time. Bringing in the drugs under the cover of the chandlery and wine club had been fairly small time. If I'd been caught, I probably faced a couple of years inside. I'd then come out and have the money I'd transferred into an off-shore account. It'd be the equivalent of £40K per year. Not a bad deal.

This trip took it to an entirely new level though.

I stood to make two million. Two fucking million. But. And it was a big BUT, if we got caught, we'd probably get fourteen years. I'd be 55 by then. Not exactly in my dotage but even so. Maybe I shouldn't push my luck. Get out after this trip.

My thoughts were broken by Carol climbing back on board.

"OK, darling?"

"Of course. There wasn't anything wrong in any case was there. I assume you were just checking for a tail — though why you'd be concerned I've no idea." She winked at me and went to sit back into the driver's seat.

She really was gorgeous. Would she be waiting for me if I did get put away? Not likely, was it? Mind you, if I went down would anyone believe that she was innocent? She could be spending time in Holloway while I was in Brixton.

Maybe I should tell Frank I'd had enough. Take Carol, find a tropical island somewhere and spend our time making love in the sun. Strange, I hadn't yet gone to bed with her — but she was different to any of the girls I'd had over the past few years and I found myself prepared to wait. She was fun to be with, happy to bend the rules, intelligent, a fabulous dancer and had a terrific figure and beautiful face. Jesus, what was happening to me?

I knew that Frank wouldn't let me quit but I had to get Carol out whether she liked it or not.

"Where now?" she asked.

I told her to drive round the roundabout, then re-join the motorway."

The heavens burst as we took the M26 link to the M25 and Carol activated the wipers to clear the downpour. Lightning flashed and peals of thunder drowned out the road and traffic noise. Brake and hazard warning lights ahead indicated problems and Carol slowed the vehicle. Eighty kilometres per hour became sixty, forty then twenty; then we stopped with a hiss of the brakes. The jam extended as far as we could see; which, in these conditions wasn't that far. Inch by inch we crept forward. We could now see flashing blue lights amongst the orange and red ahead.

A traffic officer was directing drivers to merge into the outside lane to pass the obstruction. God, I wouldn't want his job on a night like this. Then we could see the accident. An HGV had squashed a small family car into the rear of another trailer. It wasn't possible to tell what sort of car it had been but I didn't give much for the chances of anyone who'd been in it.

Carol's face was a mask of grim determination. Her lips squeezed tightly together. Her eyes focussed on the road ahead. We picked up speed again but she held it to ninety. Signs for the M23 appeared ahead.

"Take the exit and follow signs for London," I told her.

"Fine. Wouldn't it have been easier to programme the NavStar?"

"It would; if I'd had the coordinates for our destination." The real reason was that I didn't want to leave any trace on the system of the drop off point.

"Ok, turn left here onto First Avenue then second right into Churchill Road. Now pull up in front of those shutters."

I got out and was about to ring a bell when door opened and Frank stepped out.

"Good trip? He asked. "I expected you half an hour ago."

"Fine, there was an accident on the M25 which delayed us."

Frank had signalled one of his men and the shutter door was rattling open.

I signalled to Carol to pull the vehicle inside.

"That's the bird you've been shafting, is it?"

I didn't deny Frank's comment — well, I guess I had given the impression that things had gone further than they had.

Chapter 51. John as Carol

hear you've done a great job for us," Frank told me as I got down off the coach. "Here's a bonus for you."

I looked inside the envelope.

"Thanks very much. Not sure what I've done to earn this but, well, thanks again. And let me know if you need me another time."

"Don't worry. We will. I can see you know how to do what you're told and not ask questions. I'm sure you know how to keep your mouth shut too. Don't you?"

"Keep it shut about what? All I've done is drive a display vehicle around Europe and demonstrate some equipment. Nothing to keep shtum about is there?"

"Absolutely right. Good girl. Right, George, my boys can deal with things here. Denny can drive you and Carol home."

Chapter 51 – John as Carol November 1998

George put our bags into the back of Frank's Mercedes. Denny started the car and pulled off the forecourt onto Churchill Road and had just turned onto First Avenue when a police car pulled across in front of us and two other vehicles with flashing blue lights went past us and turned into Churchill Road. Yet another pulled up behind us.

Denny started to reach inside his jacket when the door windscreen shattered and a pistol appeared next to his head.

"Armed police, put your hands on the steering wheel," I heard. Denny did as instructed.

My door was opened and I was pulled clear before being forced to the ground. I made no attempt to resist or protest my innocence. I knew it would be sorted out later.

George had been forced onto the pavement about five feet from me. An officer was pulling his arms behind him and putting handcuffs on his wrists.

"She knows nothing about what's been going on, she's just been driving the vehicle," he said gesturing at me with his head.

I looked at him. Jesus. It seems he really had fallen for Carol — or had he fallen for me pretending to be her?

"You can let this one up." I heard a familiar voice say. "She's with us."

The officer who'd been holding me down extended his hand and helped me up. As I got to my feet, I saw it was Carol's boss. "Are you OK?" he asked.

"I'm fine, thanks, Brian."

George twisted his head to look at us. "What the fuck? If you're ..." He closed his eyes in resignation and just lay there.

Brian took me to one side while we let the police deal with the rest of the gang. I was grabbed from behind and spun round. To my relief, it was Carol hobbling on her cast-bound foot. We hugged each other.

Carol indicated a bag by her feet. "I've got some of John's clothes here. Do you want to change?"

I thought for a moment. "No, I'm fine like this, thanks."

A smile appeared on her lips. "OK, Angela."

241

We caught up with Brian as he was standing by the coach talking to another of his team as we approached.

"Not good news so far," he said. "We've looked behind some of the panels and can't find any contraband."

"I was sure that's where they planned to hide it," I said. "Maybe this was just a trial run."

"We'll take the vehicle to our own works and strip it down in the morning. I suggest you two go and get some rest. We'll debrief tomorrow."

Carol and I were back at her flat about forty minutes later.

She opened a bottle of Cava and handed me a glass.

"So, come on. Give. You've changed. This isn't just about dressing any more, is it?"

"I don't know. I really don't. I've felt totally comfortable being you. Even when George started to come on to me, it felt quite normal to respond and, at that point I really wished I was fully female."

"So just how far did you and George go? Do I still have any reputation?"

"Not as far as I was tempted if you must know. But I did manage to avoid blowing the mission. We danced and we kissed but nothing else. Mind you it looks like the mission is blown anyway if it was just a trial run. I just can't believe they'd go to those lengths though."

"I agree. If they were doing a test trip, surely they'd have just done a handful of venues then come back. Doesn't make sense to spend four weeks. No, there's got to be something there. Anyway, nothing we can do about that now. But come on, dish the dirt I want more details about how you felt with George."

We finished the wine and I picked up the overnight bag I'd been using on the coach. Carol noticed.

"There is a pair of your pyjamas in the spare room if you prefer."

I knew I had to resolve the matter sooner or later. Taking them out of the drawers, I pulled them on. It felt strange but I decided to wear them.

The next morning, I woke to the smell of freshly brewed coffee. I grabbed a cup then showered. So, decision time. Is it John or Angela today? I needed to know for myself. Of course, the fact that I was wondering probably gave me the answer. If I really was John, there'd be no question. I'd just be him without thinking.

Nevertheless, it was Carol and John who left her flat and drove to the unit where the coach was being examined. The display panels were stacked against the wall already but there was no sign of any drugs. Engineers were examining other parts of the vehicle but each time they completed an area, there was a shake of the head.

Finally, Brian Halliday turned to Carol.

"Damn. It's a bust. I was convinced you were onto something," he said.

Carol looked disheartened. We'd relied on finding a haul to justify my having taken her place. Now there were no mitigating circumstances and she could be in serious trouble.

"Very strange," I said. "When the police arrived, George made a point of saying that Carol knew nothing about what was going on. Why would he do that if there hadn't been anything to hide?"

"Maybe he didn't know that the drugs weren't on board this trip. Maybe Fielding was testing him too. Who knows? But we haven't found anything. OK lads, put the panels back on the coach."

I watched as two burly customs officers picked up one of the panels. Why would it need two men to handle the panels? They were lightweight foam on frames. They shouldn't weigh more than a few kilograms each.

"Stop!" I called.

Instead of hiding the drugs behind the panels, the gang had put them inside the panels so each weighed ten times as much as the ones we used in our vehicles. The total haul was more than nine hundred kilos

Our decision for me to take Carol's place was vindicated. She not only avoided a disciplinary hearing; she received a commendation.

My own boss was delighted when my involvement was rewarded with an opportunity to bid for a Customs and Excise IT contract. He offered me a directorship but I'd decided to work with Jeff to develop and market the NavStar range. Jeff was one of the few individuals who knew the whole story about my involvement — he and Carol were going out together.

Chapter 52. John – December 1998

Tony and I were having a coffee while his team put the finishing touches to our stand at the Design Systems exhibition at G-Mex in Manchester. I was still working out my notice with Desktech – this show would be my final job for them.

"You still OK for dinner this evening?"

"Yes, looking forward to it."

"You remember last year you put me right about thinking I'd seen you cross-dressed and that I'd mistaken your cousin Carol for you."

"Yes, I'd lent her my car, if I remember correctly."

"You said you were giving her the jewellery I gave you as a Christmas gift. To go with the dress and shoes I thought I'd seen you wearing."

"That's right."

"Well, while she was working with me this year on George's coach, I said I hoped she like the jewellery. She didn't seem to know anything about it nor about a blue dress. Funny that. Anyway, better get on with snagging the exhibition stand for you. I'll catch up with you later."

The stand sorted, we returned to our hotel just a short walk away. We'd ended up with adjacent rooms – not by design, mine had been booked by my secretary and Tony's by his own company.

I had a leisurely bath – then dressed. I was just finishing when Tony knocked on my door. I opened it and Tony, with a look of disbelief, blurted out "Carol, lovely to see you, I didn't know you were joining us, this is a delightful surprise" as he leant forward and kissed me on the cheek.

"Carol isn't joining us, Tony. Can you just fasten this for me?"

I passed him the necklace he'd given me the previous Christmas.

Printed in Great Britain
by Amazon